Praise for

FIVE EQUALS ONE, Vol. 1,

2019 recipient

of

NATIONAL INDIE

EXCELLENCE AWARD (NIEA)

e-book version

Fresh moments, surprises, endearing characters, thought provoking, convincing and timely.

> —*Cindy Ruby, M.Ed, Kirkland, WA*

A most enjoyable read that humorously confronts us with an unconscious ideology of racism without lecturing or judging.

> —*Janice M. DeLange, Ph.D., psychotherapist/Social Work professor [UW, WMU and GVSU], Grand Rapids, MI*

An engaging story about a woman, her husband and a cast of characters that would make Dickens proud.

FIVE

EQUALS

ONE

~◇~

VOLUME

1

Mary Korte

BY THE SAME AUTHOR

FICTION

Five Equals One, Volume 2

Five Equals One, Volume 3

NONFICTION

Only a Shoebox to His Name

COMING IN 2018

NONFICTION

Formatting Your Fantastic Book

RHYMING PARODIES
(fiction based on actual events)

Bully Jake and Grace's Fate

Hats Off to Mr. Boar

My Mind Is Totally Mine

FIVE EQUALS ONE

VOLUME

1

~ <> ~

MARY KORTE

HAVET PRESS
www.havetpress.com

FIVE EQUALS ONE, *Volume 1*

Editing consultant: Claudia Sherrill, MBA, MSIM

Cover graphic design © 2017 by Matt Hinrichs.
www.matthinrichs.com

Havet Press
www.havetpress.com

ISBN: 978-0-9864148-7-9

Printed in the United States of America

FOR HUMAMITY

It makes no difference

where you fit on the rainbow spectrum.

You are, and always will be,

a gift to be treasured.

—*Mary Korte*

ACKNOWLEDGMENT
and
DEDICATION

CLAUDIA SHERRILL, when we first spoke on the phone, you stated you wanted to randomly select and read three pages of my manuscript before committing your time. We met. You made your selection and began reading. I waited. When you lifted your eyes from the third page, my throat tightened. Upon hearing, "Okay, I'll do it," I managed to say, "Thank you."

Six weeks later, we met again. Besides giving me constructive criticism, you said, "I read five books at a time and I read all genre. Of all the books I've ever read, I've never read one like this. It's very different. Your characters are well developed, and the story line is unique, but you have some work to do."

Thus, began our working relationship.

Thank you, Claudia, for all your editing, writing tips and encouraging words. I feel fortunate to have received your services before cancer robbed you of life. In appreciation for your guidance and inspiration, I dedicate *Five Equals One* to you.

TRIBUTE

On a cross-country trip, my husband Lowell (driving) and I (reading aloud a draft of *Five Equals One*) are deep into Montana cattle country when I ask, "Where are we?"

"I don't know. I've been looking for the turnoff sign."

The upcoming sign says, *Helena 5 miles ahead*. Helena? Where's Helena? I pull out a road map, do the math. Shocked at the distance we've traveled, I say, "Sweetheart, you drove ninety-five miles past our turnoff. You even went through Missoula. Didn't you see the exit signs?"

"No. I didn't see any exits. A semi must've been blocking the turnoff sign when I drove past it."

He uses the next off ramp to reverse our direction. I calculate *his* blunder—two hours out of the way, two hours to backtrack, four hours wasted. I cross my arms, look straight ahead, nurse my anger.

Fifteen minutes later an ah-ha thought pricks my dark cloud of injustice. My anger dissipates. Now humbled, I say, "I just figured out why you missed the turnoff. You were so taken by my story, you blocked out everything but my voice and the road ahead, didn't you?"

His eyes emit surprise. He nods.

"Thanks. You couldn't have given me a better tribute."

His shoulders relax. Our eyes connect. We both smile.

◇•◇•◇

Contents

SANTA'S ETHNIC NICKNAMES

SOWETO when BLACK

FREDDIE when WHITE

PIPESTONE when RED

HUM-BOW when YELLOW

OTOÑO when BROWN

◇•◇•◇

CHAPTER 1

What if someone told?

"Shelly. Oh, that girl. She's so brazen. What if she were to blab his secret? Fiddlin' nutcrackers. If she did, all that stuff his poppa drummed into his little-boy head would likely come true. What if . . ."

Hey, girl, what's with you thinking such rubbish?

Mitzi's alter ego, which she long ago dubbed as her *nattering Tomacita*, often challenged her thinking. Especially when she was drowning in worrisome head chatter.

"Those *What ifs* are back, pestering me. And my screaming, 'Go away! Leave me alone!' doesn't help? And neither does your butting in." Angrily fluffing her pillow, then pulling its sides to her ears, she muttered, "Yeah. As if this old bag of feather could drown them out."

Tick-tock, tick-tock . . . Eyeing her bedside clock ratcheting its big hand minute by minute toward dawn, she moaned, "O-o-oh, it's not even 4:00 a.m. and those annoying *What ifs* are . . . are driving me crazy.

Duh! Of course, they are, girl. It's Christmas Season Blessing Day.

"Every year, it's *What if* this, *What if* that. Oh, why do I put up with his nonsense? If only he'd reveal that stupid secret of his. The stubborn moose. Yeah. I used to beg him

1

to tell, but would he listen to me? No. Two years I hounded him. Then I did what any sane person would do. I threw in the towel. One day I just said, 'That's enough.' And ever since, on Christmas Season Blessing Day, my anxiety flies off the charts . . . like through the ceiling. Ugh. What a headache."

Face it, girl. His refusal to share his secret isn't all that worries you. Admit it. You're also afraid for him.

"Yeah. I am. But must you remind me of that! And him? He has no idea how much I worry. Mark my word. Today, if I were to say something, he'd dismiss it with a flick of his hand. He'd say, 'Stop worrying, hon. Come on. There's no way anyone's gonna figure it out.'

"Sooty bricks. It's bad enough ninety percent of the world refuses to believe he's real. But if someone outside our so-called *safety zone* were to find out that eighty percent of the time, he's not what he makes himself out to be . . . Oh, God help us if that ever happened."

As she gazed at window-silhouetted moonlight showcasing Santa's stomach pitching to and fro in cadence with his snoring, Mitzi said with less intensity. "Oh, sweetheart, I'd love to cuddle with you. But if I do, you'll sense my distress and pressure me to get it out. No. No way am I going to open up that can of worms again. Once was enough." She shuddered. Not from the chill in the room but from recalling past arguments. Then she said with conviction, "No. I'm not starting another fight over your ridiculous secret. And I certainly don't want to worry you about my worries. Still, I don't want someone outside this Region figuring out your secret and then hurling cruel words, maybe even ice bricks at you. Oh, sweetheart, why, why, every year do you put yourself at risk. If only you wouldn't jet off every Christmas Season to some God-only-knows place to pretend you're . . . you're you."

Girl, you know he loves pretending to be a Santa Claus helper. Face it. It's in his blood. He's got to do it.

"Yeah. I know. He says, 'No one will ever know it's me.' If only he wouldn't do that. Fat chance he'd ever give it up though. He loves kids too much. Not to mention the hype of it all. But watch. Sooner or later, someone's gonna figure out he's not always White. And when that happens, he'll be ducking reporters coming in from everywhere. Yep. Just like his poppa feared, they'll twist the facts. They'll make him out to be a freak. Shimmering icicles. That kind of publicity will likely ruin him."

While her fingertips massaged her throbbing temples, Mitzi fought her anxiety by reciting the mantra she'd devised thirty-eight years ago, two years after she and Santa married. "I love him as Soweto. I love him as Freddie," she doggedly rattled it off in her head. "I love him as Pipestone. I love him as Hum-Bow. I love him as . . ." Much to her dismay, her mantra failed to slow her negative thoughts one iota. Conversely, like oceanic waves gaining momentum, they flooded her mind with scenes of Santa, confronted by reporters, falling to pieces.

"Same old, same old," she groused, knowing the *what*

ifs weren't about to up. Not one let to readily admit defeat, she persisted. "I love him as Soweto. I love him as Freddie. I love him as . . . Oh, what if Shelly were to mouth off his secret to some world-renowned reporter? Mustn't think that. I love him as Pipestone. I . . . Yeah. What if some country, like the USA or Russia, were to figure out his secret? Why, the media would have . . ."

Knock it off, girl. Stay focused on your mantra.

"Okay, okay. I love him as Hum-Bow. I love him as Otoño. I love him as . . . What if some crazy kooks, like his poppa feared, whisked him off to some secret research laboratory? Holy walrus turds. I'd never see him again."

Stop it! For taffy tarnation, girl, stop thinking such rubbish. Concentrate on your mantra.

"Yeah. Right. Okay. I love him as Freddie. I love him as Pipestone. I love him as . . . but Shimmering icicles, someone could . . ."

Girl, stop your fretting. Stay focused.

"Okay. I love him as Hum . . . Yeah but, with his one-of-a-kind genes, he'd be worth a mint on the black market. Some crazy scientist, out to make a bundle, might . . ."

STOP! STOP! STOP!

Her mind in a twitter and realizing not another wink of sleep lay in her cards, Mitzi bolted upright. "This is not working. I'm wide awake." She checked the time. "Fritterin' fiddlesticks. It's only four-thirty." Shifting her eyes to Santa's splayed-out form, she grumbled, "Why is it sleep never eludes you? You're out the minute your head hits the pillow and you always sleep through the night. Oh, how I wish I could do that."

Minutes later, flip-flopping her slippers over the hallway carpet, she lamented, "Why? Why do you have to be such a fraidy-cat? If only you'd reveal that stupid secret of yours, I wouldn't have this worry every Christmas Season. Yeah. I'd probably still be sleeping."

Reaching her corner of the living room, settling into her recliner, she opened her laptop. *ZIP.* A stream of incoming e-mails flashed before her eyes. Clicking on one from her friend Shooting Star, she gasped. "What! You've got to be kidding. A temp rise like that! That's never happened here before."

An hour later, still not the least bit sleepy, she shut down her laptop and headed for the kitchen, muttering, "Think I'll whip up a German pancake, top it with some sliced apples. Yeah. Like his momma used to make. And since I know the recipe by heart, it should be a no brainer. Don't have to think. And today, that's a good thing."

Standing PJ clad at a kitchen counter, mindlessly cracking eggs, Mitzi again relied on her mantra to fight her head's *what if* chatter. "I love him as Soweto. I love him as Freddie. I love him as Pipestone. I love him as Hum-Bow. I love him as . . ." On and on she chanted. Still, the nattering persisted, annoying her to no end.

Cradling her bowl in the crook of her arm, mindlessly stirring her pancake batter, she swept her eyes over the room. They, heavy with anxiety and unsettled as much as her mind, darted from her jasper canister set from India, to her framed collection of world-wide silver teaspoons, to the antique milk can and butter churn salvaged years ago from cousin Martha's reindeer farm. Most mornings she found the coziness of her kitchen, and all her decorative mementos, comforting. But not today.

For a moment, her African violets, lining the kitchen's east windowsill, garnered her attention. Sometimes she doted over them for hours. "They're a testament to your green thumb," Santa often said. Their sapphire-blue florets surrounded by verdant green foliage usually brought a smile to her lips. Today, working a familiar question off the tip of her tongue, her teary eyes merely blended their colors into blurry blobs. "Why? Why does he have to be such a stubborn moose?" Setting her mixing bowl on the counter, staring at nothing in particular, she answered her own question. "Because he just is. Because he's a carbon copy of his poppa; stubborn and dead set in his ways."

Heeding her late mother-in-law's directive for making a delicious German pancake, *First, my dear, preheat the cast-iron pan,* she slipped the weighty hand-me-down into the oven and set the timer. "Should be hot enough to sizzle butter in fifteen minutes."

Leaning into the nearest counter, she stared down at her daisy-print apron and chanted, "I love him as Soweto. I love him as . . ." Her mind, heading for la-la land, slid a yesteryear ditty onto her tongue. Absentmindedly, she recited it. "Does she love me? Yes! She loves me. Does she love me? Yes! She loves me. Does she . . ." Her words opened the door for old memories to pour in.

Mitzi, slipping back in time, saw herself, a child of six, standing in a field of weeds on her family's century-old farm near Harlan, Kentucky. Spotting a sun-yellow daisy at her feet, she stooped to pluck it then glimpsed the house. No hate-filled face was glaring at her from any window. Eyes back on her flower, she interpreted it's slight nod as, "Go. Run before the Red Head sees what you did." Desperate for some alone time, she, clothed only in ragged underwear, slithered like a garter snake through the weedy field, slowing only once to look back at the farmhouse, a farmhouse so hewn in by nature's reclamation, newcomers had difficulty finding it.

If satellite surveillance had existed back in the 1940s, it would've shown an unkempt apple orchard beyond a dilapidated fence to the east of the farmhouse and an entanglement of underbrush shoring up a thicket of gnarly old trees to the west. This *thicket* lined and nearly obliterated the quarter-mile lane leading up to the house.

To the north, the satellite's powerful lens would've captured an old barn, but not the hay hidden beneath its sagging roof. Sadly, until time reduced it to nothingness, the rotting fodder would serve only to incubate baby mice and other little creatures for hungry snakes lying in wait.

To the south, the satellite's lens would've captured a mammoth, weed-choked field which, sadly, hadn't seen the till of a plow in more than twenty years.

The rundown old farm, a good eight miles from town, proved to be a child abuser's paradise. With no electrical wires connecting it to the power poles that ran parallel to the country road, the few travelers who sped by at fifteen-to-twenty miles per hour were oblivious to its existence. Mitzi's stepmother hated the inconvenience of *no* electricity, but she loved that *not a soul* could hear her young victim's screams.

Seeking reprieve from her stepmother's wrath, and the sweltering heat, Mitzi glanced back to see if her stepsister Karen and half-sister Janice were following. Relieved they weren't, she settled into a slow trot.

Not long after the man called Daddy jerked her away from loving relatives and plopped her down into the chaos of his blended family, she learned the folly of trusting either sister. Both got away with blaming her for *their* misdeeds. Little protégés of their mother, they often taunted her with hateful ditties. Ditties meant to demoralize her. Many evenings, when her father worked the four-to-twelve shift, they, at the urging of their mother, would prance around, nose thumbing her while singing a string of belittling putdowns. *You're a stupid idiot, a scumbag and a bowie-hunky, too. You're a nincompoop, a sneaky kraut, . . .* These, and many other degrading remarks, not only solidified her scapegoat role in the family, they reduced her to tears.

Along the narrow path, weedy barbs, snagging Mitzi's bare skin, drew blood. She didn't care. Her secret hideout lay just ahead, between a tinder-dry coal shed and a dilapidated fence. Her secret space was hidden well by an entanglement of overgrown briers and a canopy of low-hanging hickory-tree branches. In her hideout she had all she needed. A rock to crack hickory nuts and a sprung bobby pin to dig out the nutmeat.

Finding safety in woodland her stepmother never treaded, she'd close her eyes and will herself into the arms of her birth mother. Her vivid imagination introduced her to her mother's tender touch. Tears accompanied her begging plea. "Please, mommy, please come get me and take me away from this place. Please."

Each hideout reprieve lasted until an insidious scream pierced her ears. *Bohunk, where the hell are you?* It was her cue to run like lightning, to plant her feet in front of her stepmother, to stand submissively and await her fate.

Mitzi, yielding to her long-ago memory, recalled how desperate, yet hopeful, she felt while sitting against that old shed, plucking petals off daisies and chanting wistfully, "Does she love me? Yes. She loves me. Does she love me? Yes. She loves me."

"How many times did I sing that ditty when alone in my hideout? Always, I said *Yes. She loves me* because I couldn't bear the thought of my mother not loving me. Oh, how I clung to the belief that someday she'd come and whisk me away from my hellish predicament. But she never came. I didn't want to believe she was dead. Nobody talked about her and I didn't dare approach my dad. Why? Because the redhead never left us alone for a second. Sooty bricks. I didn't even know her name."

As if on automatic pilot, Mitzi started mouthing her chant. She hoped it would stop her head's *what if* chatter much like her daisy-ditty chanting had soothed her emotional pain at age six—when alone in her hideout, imagining the warmth of her birth mother's arms.

While stirring her pancake batter, she rhythmically spun the words from her lips. "I love him as Soweto. I love him as Freddie. I love him as . . ." Rather than helping, they left her with an unspoken sense of despair—and more *what if* chatter. "*What if* people taunt him? *What if* they make him out to be a freak? *What if* . . ."

Her frustration seemed to be urging her to smack the counter with her wooden spoon; but knowing the ensuing racket would likely wake Santa, and also spatter batter everywhere, she merely tightened her grip on it. "Dancin' Prancer. His secret makes him so vulnerable, and there's not a thing I can do to protect him."

As she poured the pancake batter into her pre-heated pan, hot tears flowed down her cheeks. Hurriedly, she set the empty bowl in the sink, then slid the sloshing pan into the oven. "That's done," she said, staring at a trembling hand—one that seemed detached from her body—lifting a corner of her apron to sop up her weepy tears.

Year after year, Mitzi fought both the chatter in her head and her ensuing anxiety. Fear of someone revealing Santa's racial secret consumed her every Christmas Season. She hated this worry. But not until her husband completed both his Santa Claus helper stint and his Christmas Eve run did it lessen.

Most days, she kept her *what if* chatter at bay by focusing on her work as production coordinator. But always, the morning of Christmas Season Blessing Day, she couldn't shake the blitz. She hated this worry, but much to her dismay, the holiday always gifted her with it. Luckily, she found some release through a good cry long before Santa woke. Her dear, dear husband didn't know she worried about him nor did she want him to know.

"All these years of marriage and never a Christmas Season without worry. Why? I wish, oh, how I wish I didn't know the answer to that question, but I do."

She set the oven timer for forty-five minutes, then plunged her fists deep into her apron pockets. Stiffening her arms, twisting her neck back and forth, she hoped the tension residing there would ease up. The act, rather than relaxing her, triggered a long-ago scene, one in which she was anchoring her nerves to the seams of her apron pockets—like she was now—while pleading with Santa to reveal his racial secret. Recalling the scene, she spoke as though he were standing right in front of her.

"Whenever I suggested you make your secret known to the world, you'd turn into a riled bear. Never would you listen to reason or even consider the merits of getting it out. Taffy tarnation. What's it been? Forty years of marriage and still the futility of it haunts me. Every time I pleaded, 'Please, dear, please tell your secret,' you'd throw your head back and yell, 'No! No! No! I'll never, ever tell.' And then, seeing your face reddening up, I knew better than to press the issue. Oh, why do you have to be so stubborn? Why? Why are you so hell bent on keeping your racial changes secret from the whole world?"

Girl, why are you working yourself into such a dither?

Mitzi, nostrils flaring wide, drew in air to re-fuel her wrath. "Listen, you *nattering Tomacita.* Yes. I *need* to tone down my anger. So, am I going to? Sure. When I'm good and ready. And listen. I wouldn't be so steamed up if those *What ifs* hadn't robbed me of a good night's sleep. And you and I both know they wouldn't be hounding me if it weren't for you-know-who's dumb secret. Sooty bricks. Who knows why he insists on keeping that stupid secret a secret! Fritterin' fiddlesticks. I certainly don't."

Contemplating her last remark, she slumped her shoulders. "Hmm. That's not true. I do know." Her self-truth triggered a faraway look, one forging the way to step into the past. "Yeah. I do know why. You made that stupid promise to your poppa. You promised to never, ever tell. Lord knows, every time I tried to get you to break *your little secret,* you fought me tooth and nail. All my urgings ever did was turn you into a riled bear. And then, what did I do? The only thing I could do. I let it go. I finally realized I was wasting my time. Prancing Dancer. No matter what I said, you wouldn't budge. So, I clammed up. 'Subject closed,' I

12

said, vowing to never mention it again."

Much like her commitment to the secret-keeping law, it was a vow she intended to keep. Forever. Yet, in keeping it, she unwittingly created a breeding ground for those nattering *what ifs*. Every November first, like hordes of insects descending in a breeding frenzy, they invaded her mind with a vengeance. *What if this . . . What if that . . .*

She checked the minutes left on the oven timer. "Fiddlin' nutcrackers. The world would go crazy if anyone blabbed about my husband's yearly racial changes. Yeah. If he revealed it now, a stream of reporters would hound us relentlessly. Oh, what a mess that would be. Even so, sweetheart, I've always thought it would be better if you told rather than taking the risk of someone exposing you. Especially someone outside this Region.

"Sweetie, you don't know it, but sometimes I get so frustrated. To be honest, there are times I find myself wishing someone would *out* you. I know I shouldn't think such things, but, you stubborn old moose, you have no idea what I go through every Christmas Season. I worry and worry about you. I spill a lot of tears, too. Mark my word, Mr. Hum-Bow Claus. Someday, someone is going to let it slip. I just know it. Yeah. You think that secret-keeping law your poppa had the Senate pass when you were a little elfin will protect you forever. Well, I've got news for you. People don't always keep secrets. Oh, they intend to, but the best of intentions can, and do, go by the wayside. Just watch. Someday, someone here will *out* you. Or, some outsider will figure it out. And then what? Oh, God, help us if that ever happens."

A glimpse of the wall clock fast ticking toward Santa's wake-up time triggered Mitzi's panic button. Noting the hour, she pulled a tissue from a box on the counter and dabbed at her eyes. Hurriedly, she gathered up her gummy baking utensils. "I've got to get this place cleaned up and myself calmed down before he wakes up."

A self-pressured sense of urgency—only because she was a bit neurotic about keeping things tidy—set her to work stuffing her baking utensils into the dishwasher. Once that was done, she cupped her hands under the faucet and doused her eyes several times. As the near-freezing water eased their puffiness, she wished it would also ease her worries.

Resolutely she mumbled, "I need to . . . No. I want to look cheery before he gets up. Like I'd never been crying." Grabbing a towel, patting her face dry, she said, "Now to do some pushups, stretches and lift some weights. Got to get rid of this headache."

As if on automatic pilot, she hung her apron on its peg behind the pantry door. Stretching out on her exercise mat, she pulled her knees to her chest. First one, then the other, and then both together, again and again. No chanting. Just slow, yoga-like breathing.

Twenty minutes later, a little less distraught, she poured herself a cup of hot cranberry tea. Sitting at the kitchen table—one side of which butted against the windowsill lined with her African violets—she squinted to read the thermometer tacked to the outer window frame. "Holy walrus turds. Does that thing really say twenty-three degrees? I can't believe it's gone that high already."

Mitzi rarely gave a rat's tail as to where that mercury line stood. Seldom did she check it. Today, as she stared at it, Shooting Star's e-mail popped into her head.

Caught the late-night news. They said the temperature will rise from forty-two below to fifteen above by 6:00 a.m. and it's supposed to climb even higher. Possibly go up to forty-something by this afternoon. Can you believe that?

"No, I can't believe that, Shooting Star. And I didn't believe it when I read your e-mail either. But now, . . ." Hesitating, lifting her mug to her lips, she blew ripples across its steamy surface. After whiffing its fruity aroma, she took a sip, then said, "What a fluke. Never has this happened before. If this keeps up, we'll be saying, *dripping icicles* instead of *shimmering icicles*."

Hoping to get an update on the weather, she reached behind and turned on the radio. Twisting back around, glimpsing the wall clock, she mumbled, "Sooty bricks. It's almost seven-thirty. I've so much to do before I . . ."

STOP! From somewhere inside her head she heard her *nattering Tomacita* yelling *STOP! STOP!* And for once, she heeded her directive.

With the onset of a smile, she felt her face softening. Cognizant of the rich, cinnamon scent permeating the whole cottage, she relaxed her shoulders against the back of her chair. Closing her eyes, she pictured Santa lying in bed, mouth wide open, snoring loudly. Playfully she spoke her next thought. "Ah, sweetheart, I bet the aroma of my German pancake is sending your Hum-Bow nose into a twitching frenzy." Sighing, grateful the worst of the Season's *What if* assault was behind her, she lifted her mug to her lips and savored another sip of tea.

Whiffs of Mitzi's German pancake were luring Santa toward wakefulness. Actually, his mouth was starting to salivate for the breakfast treat. Sliding his tongue over his dry lips, he willed his eyelids to rise to half-mast. "Yum, yum, German pancake. My favorite. Guess that ruins my plan to catch some extra winks." Revisiting what he just said, he popped his eyes open and said sarcastically, "Yeah. Right. As if I could actually get in a few extra winks on *this* day."

As his nighttime grogginess dissipated, his thoughts turned to Mitzi. "Guess I'm lucky because she sure sticks by me no matter what. And I've never doubted her faithfulness. No. Wait. There was that one time. Let's see. When was it? Eight years ago, I think. No matter. We got it all ironed out. Anyway, I guess, just like any other couple, we've had our ups and downs. Much as I hate to admit it though, she sure taught me . . ." Stopping mid-thought, he patted his tummy and grinned. "Yes, Mitzi, I remember when you let me know, in no uncertain terms, that you'd no longer tolerate me taking you for granted. Back then, I was clueless. Actually, all during our first thirty-two years of marriage I had no idea I was taking you for granted. Sooty bricks. It never hit me until you went berserk on me. Yeah. Not until you ran away eight years ago, did I realize how good I had it. And yes, what you put me through back then was hell. But today? Hey, it sure makes for good daydreaming."

To acclimate his body to the idea of getting up, Santa stretched his limbs toward the four corners of the mattress. But the comfort of the bed, willing him to stay, was too much. Curling up on Mitzi's side, he muttered, "I'd sure love to squeeze in some extra winks or maybe do a little daydreaming." Fighting the urge to succumb to either, especially the latter, he scolded himself. "Listen, you lazy old bloke. Now's not the time to get caught up in a daydream. Especially the one about Mitzi's charade." Still, the pull to go there was strong, but he battled it with determination. "Not today, mister. That one will have to wait for a stroll through the ice sculpture park because, as you well know, it takes at least two to three hours to run through it. Now, stop stalling. Get your butt out of bed. Get out there in the kitchen and enjoy Mitzi's German pancake while it's still warm. And you'd better show her some appreciation for getting up early to make it too."

Off flew the covers. Rolling onto his back, dangling his feet over the side, Santa pit-patted the floor for his slippers. Finding one, then the other, he wiggled his toes into them.

Still reluctant to get up, he linked his hands over his well-endowed tummy and started singing. *Oh, it's Christmas Season Blessing Day, time to put our play away . . .* Midstream, he switched to a childish tantrum. "But I don't want to get up. I don't want to get up."

Five minutes later, he sauntered into the kitchen. Setting his eyes on Mitzi's German pancake, he said, "Ah. So, there's the culprit that woke me."

"My treat," she said, topping her smile off with a wink.

Santa, playfully sidling up to the love of his life, planted a kiss on her lips. "Smells scrumptious, my love. And thank you. It was so sweet of you to get up early to make it."

"You're welcome, sweetie."

As she spoke, Santa leaned back and studied her eyes. He didn't know, and he couldn't tell, that she had been crying. Still, he sensed, like he had every November first for the past three decades or so, that something was troubling her. For years, he said nothing. Nor would he today. He used to. But always, he heard the same thing. "Sweetheart, nothing's bothering me. Really. I'm fine." Even though his heart was heavy with concern, he decided not to press the issue. Still, it bothered him. "I wish she wouldn't be so tightlipped. Knowing her though, I'll never be privy to whatever is troubling her. Oh why, after all these years, why does she still hold back on me? Trust issues, I guess."

"Hold your plate out, sweetie," Mitzi said, poking the puffy pancake with a knife, "And I'll cut you a piece. Fixings are on the table, next to your morning paper."

18

Santa, hovering, but not wanting hot steam in his face, pulled back. Seconds later, a loaded plate in hand, he marched to the table, cooing, "Oh, what a treat." Once settled in a chair, he slathered the fluffy pancake with gobs of butter. Next came drizzles of maple syrup, a sprinkle of blueberries and a mountain of whipped cream. As the first mouthful of the delicacy tantalized his taste buds, a glow of ecstasy bloomed on his face. Swallowing, winking at Mitzi, he said with gusto, "Mm, mm. It's perfecto, my love. Perfect-to."

"Just like your momma's?"

"Yep. U-u-uh, no. It's better."

In keeping with his morning ritual, Santa flipped open the *North Pole Gazette* and propped it so its back page, the comics, faced him.

Mitzi, her plate full, sat down opposite him. Narrowing her eyes, she stared at the front-page headline. Annoyed about it being the same as last year's—and every year before that—she read it aloud with a hint of sarcasm. "Hmm. Feasting and Merrymaking to Follow Santa's Blessing." Glancing at Santa, she waited for his reaction. When none came, she said in a taunting twang. "Whacky walruses. Why do they always have to print what everyone already knows?"

Santa, lowering his paper, met her defiant stare with one of his own. "Ah, she's picking a fight. I know it. Something is going on in that little head of hers. Something she's not willing to share." Pithily, and loudly, he

19

responded to her question with a question. "Taffy tarnation, hon, why do you always have to bring that up?" Angrily flipping his paper open to its full spread, he spouted, "Hon, you know just as well as I do. They print that because it's tradition. Our tradition."

"Tradition!" she yelled, upping her voice to match his. "If you ask me, it's nothing but a waste of ink and paper."

Santa flinched. Arching his brows, he peered over his paper and enunciated each of his next words with forced calmness. "My dear, a little ink and paper ain't worth worrying about. Besides, it can't cost that much."

"Who's worrying? I just think it's a waste and, . . . and stupid. Come on. Man up. Admit that it's really stupid to print what everybody already knows."

Santa rolled his eyes. "Hmm. Wonder who's gonna win this little tit-tat? For sure, it ain't gonna be me." Clamping his lips together, he retreated behind his paper. But rather than picking up where he left off, he just stared at it. "Nope. I'm not giving in. I'm going to make my point." He lowered his paper, cleared his throat and said decisively, "Like I said, love. It's tradition. So, face it. Some things stay the same around here, like the . . ."

"Like the weather," she spouted smartly. "Betcha an hour or so from now, it'll be so warm outside we won't be able to see our breath." Chalking one up to her credit, she crossed her legs and batted her eyelashes at him.

Ignoring her flirtatious tease, Santa yelled, "Whadaya mean? Our breath is always frosty when we're outside."

Then, turning to check the outside thermometer, his eyes popped. "What!" He hated to admit it, but the high mercury line proved her right. "Well, blow me down an iceberg slide. It says thirty-one degrees. Don't tell me a falling icicle crashed into that thing and knock it off kilter."

"You haven't been outside yet, have you?"

"No. But if that thing's right, something has to be wrong. Maybe . . . Uh, do you think some war-crazed country messed up our atmosphere with a nuclear bomb?"

"No, sweetie. Nothing like that happened."

"Are you sure?"

Mitzi smiled reassuringly. "Yes, sweetheart, I'm sure." Reaching across the table, gently tapping the tip of his *Asian* nose, she added, "Got an e-mail from Shooting Star this a.m. That girl went on and on about this temperature spike. But neither she, nor the news I listened to since, said anything about a war or bombing. So, stop fretting. Here. Have some more tea to wash down that pancake."

Tipping the teapot, she flicked her eyes back and forth from the stream of steamy tea filling his cup to the shocked look on his face. "Come on, Hum-Bow. Stop worrying. Just chalk it up to Mother Nature. She's probably pulling an old trick. Or, perhaps, a new one."

"You think so?" Turning back around, he moved his eyes from the teapot she was setting back on its trivet to her face. "Wonder what's going on in that little head of hers. Guess it's best to leave well enough alone." Anxious to read his favorite comic, he picked up the paper.

Mitzi, not about to let it lie, said testily, "Yes, it's got to be her doing. But why'd she have to pick this day of all days to lay a heat wave on us?"

Deep lines creased Santa's brow. Lowering his paper, he shot back, "What's with you? First you tell me not to worry. Then you complain about the nicest day we've ever had. Of all things. You, a sun lover, upset over a little warm weather. Why, I'd think you'd be jumping with joy." To further make his point, he set his steely eyes on hers, challenging her to a stare down.

Ignoring his invite, she turned away, saying, "Hey, don't expect me to buy that argument."

He smiled weakly. "Look, hon, I think this is great weather for our Blessing Day holiday."

She exploded. "Great weather! Don't give me that bog wash. Hiking up that mountain in those fur-lined suits . . . Why, we'll roast like, . . . like pigs in a Hawaiian luau pit."

"Hmm. It never occurred to me how hot those suits might get. I have to admit they are bulky. But hey, if we start early and take it slow, it shouldn't be that bad."

"Dear, look out there. That thermometer has climbed a few more degrees since we last looked at it. And don't you think two miles, over half of it up Jingle-Jangle Mountain, is a long way to hike in a heat wave? And tell me this. Why in taffy tarnation did you have *that* speech-giving platform built on top of *that* mountain anyway?"

"Oh, love, I don't know. I guess I thought it would be rather novel."

"Novel! It'll be exhausting. That's a long way to hike."

"Come on, dear. It won't be that bad."

"Yeah, well, I don't understand why you built it way out there in the boonies. On top of a mountain no less."

"Hey, wait a minute. I didn't build it. The college kids did with a little help from some high school gofers."

"Yeah. Right. Blame the kids. But hey, you're the one who picked that site."

Santa, exasperated at this point, slowly exhaled through lips rounded in the shape of a button. Heaving a sigh, he laid his paper aside and said through a quirky smile, "Okay, love. I confess. I'm guilty. Go ahead. Lock me up. Throw away the key, but . . ."

"But what?"

"But first, may I please have another piece of your delicious German pancake? Hmm? Please? Please?"

Mitzi, in a huff, turned to leave. "Help yourself. I've got lots to do before your speech-giving hour."

Santa, savoring his second piece of German pancake, fixed his eyes on an icicle hanging outside the kitchen window. Its thaw, dripping to the sill—an unusual sight in the North Pole Region—held his attention. Minutes later, after swallowing his last bite and realizing his over-loaded stomach had no desire to move, he leaned back, locked his fingers behind his head and let his thoughts run wild.

"Hmm. With this temp rise, I suspect we'll have us a

nice crowd today. Can't wait to set foot on that new platform. And to think, some folks thought I was nuts picking that site. Of course, building it way up there on Saucer Plateau was risky, but I knew those architect students would figure out a way to do it. Yes! Finally, I get to do what I've wanted to do for years. Today, I'm gonna strut around Saucer Plateau. Way, way up high, on the very tiptop of Jingle-Jangle Mountain.

"Oh, and did those students ever show those *stuck-in-the-snowdrift* old codgers a thing or two. Got to hand it to them. They didn't let those old farts unnerve them one bit. It was pretty sad though. Those fellows were sure bent on making those kids believe all that hole drilling would crumble the mountain. Of course, it didn't. Yeah. And later, seeing those fat posts cemented firmly in deep wells of fast-drying cement, rising high into the sky . . . Well, after that, all those old codgers went around swearing to everyone they met. They said, 'Hey. Those posts. They'll stand tall for more than a thousand years.' Now, how funny is that? And, of course, they had to make a big ta-do about the high cost of it all. 'Hey,' I told them, 'so, what if it cost a bundle to ship those Douglas fir poles up here from Canada.' Pugh! Who cares about the cost? Yeah. It cost a lot to get them here, but they were needed to make that platform sturdy, and also safe. Especially since it rises twenty-five feet up from the ground. Not to mention, that chimney top rises another five feet from its center. Ho, ho, ho. Today, I get to wiggle my fat tummy through a thirty-foot-high chimney.

Wow. Never before have I climbed through a chimney that tall.

"And the whole Region gets represented. Let's see. Who suggested we carve the suburban names, one on each of the four outer posts, and North Pole Village on the center one? Wasn't it Pietro? Yeah. It was him.

"Ho, ho, ho. I, Santa Claus, get to strut around a platform that sits right dab on top of the northern most tip of the world. Yep. I'll be able to look east to Sleigh Valley, south to Krisville, west toward the Rudolphtown Mountain Range and north to the sprawling plains of Kringleland, all while strutting around that platform. Yahoo. What a day this is gonna be."

Santa eyed the wall clock. The late hour spurred him to break from his thoughts, to scold himself.

"Hey, you old bloke. Enough dillydallying. It's almost time to leave and look at you. You still need to get dressed and you should check your speech one more time. After all, it's got to be good enough to foster cooperation and dampen ornery attitudes for the entire Christmas Season. Ho, ho, ho. What a day this is gonna be."

CHAPTER 2

Why is she baiting me?

It wasn't like Hunter Swift Bear, a junior at Sleigh Valley High, to volunteer for a task he considered more suited for girls. Yet, he did so for one reason: to get time alone with a girl, Shelly Jasselton, a North Pole High sophomore. When she volunteered to decorate the new platform with crepe paper streamers, he zeroed in on her voice. As she spoke, her striking beauty held his attention. When she finished, he frantically waved an arm and yelled, "Santa, Santa, I'll, I'll help do that."

"Good," Santa shot back. "Two should be enough for that task."

Now, climbing Jingle-Jangle Mountain at the same pace the sun was rising behind it, his mind drifted back to the night he and hundreds of other students had entered Dasher Hall to attend a platform-planning meeting. Shortly after it had gotten under way, his best friend Pietro piped up. "Santa, what if we carved the suburban names, one on each of the four outer posts, and the words *North Pole Village* on the center one? If we did that, the whole Region would be represented, and it'd look kinda cool."

After Pietro's suggestion received a unanimous vote of approval, Hunter heard a sweet voice coming from his far left.

"And, Santa, I think it'd look even cooler if we tied streamers to those posts. Long ones. In different colors."

After glimpsing the owner of that voice—an attractive blonde—Hunter turned to Santa and volunteered for the same task. Again, his obsidian eyes, strikingly infused with longing, sought the girl. Drawn to her beauty, he didn't realize he was staring until she cut her eyes his way, registering his presence.

Embarrassed at being flushed out, he scanned the crowd as if searching for someone. A few seconds later, setting his eyes on Santa, anyone looking his way would've assumed he was taking in all the suggestions and rebuttals being voiced around him. Not so. His ears, cordoned off by his awakened emotions, heard not a word. Turning to glimpse the girl again, his eyes—colliding with hers—flared brighter than a young deer suddenly dazed by an on-coming snowmobile's headlight.

Panic drove Hunter into a duck-down slump. He might've run had he not been wedged in on all sides. Barreling his back, jamming his long legs into the space beneath the two chairs ahead of him, he felt confident he was out of the girl's sight. Twisting sideways, he motioned to his friend to lean in close.

Pietro, having witnessed the whole *peek-a-boo, I-see-you* interaction, tilted his head to get the skinny.

"That chick over there, that blonde," Hunter whispered, motioning with an upward thrust of his head. "Wow. I'd sure like to be her snow gander."

"What! Her? The Candy Man's daughter?"

"Yeah, man. She's a knockout."

Pietro, grimacing, warned, "Don't go there, bozo. She ain't nothin' but trouble. Big trouble."

"You know her, huh?"

"Yeah. I know her."

"So, what's her name?"

"Shelly. Shelly Jasselton."

"She's cute."

"Cute! *Estás loco?*"

Hunter, aware they were fast becoming a spectacle, quickly shot back, "Shh! Keep your voice down."

Pietro, rolling his eyes, said, "*Dios Mío!* Haven't you heard what they say about that chick at my dad's restaurant?"

"Nope."

"Hey, every guy who catches her eye ends up a basket case." Fearful for his friend, he pleaded, "Come on, man. Ya gotta steer clear of her. I'm tellin' ya. She's a heart breaker. And worse yet, she's got a reputation as a nine-some b— Uh, I ain't gonna say that word cuz I know you don't like it. But I'm tellin' ya. She's trouble. Big trouble."

"Hey, why ya saying that, man?"

"Taffy tarnation, bozo. Where've ya been? That chick treats guys like crap. Man, what she does to her little bro . .

. Hey, I'll admit. Sometimes I stick it to my little bro. But her? She goes way beyond what's called for. Guess you've never seen her in action, huh? Well, have ya?"

Hunter, his face telling all, voiced nothing.

"You're helpless, man. And *loco en la cabeza*. And me? I ain't sayin' no more. No more ever."

Keeping silent on anything, especially something that grated him, was not Pietro's strong point. Hunter, knowing this, always waited him out. Thirty seconds later, biting his tongue, Pietro said, "Look, bozo. It ain't just me sayin' this stuff. I hear it from lots of studs who hang out at our restaurant. She's trouble. Now take her little bro. He ain't got no weight. He doesn't stand a chance. So, my advice. Steer clear of that b—. I mean her."

Hunter, amused by Pietro's rhetoric, retorted coolly, "Yeah, well, lots of chicks don't get along with their brothers. So, if I get the chance . . ."

"Chance! Fat chance. Listen. It ain't gonna happen."

"Come on. I betcha I can score with her."

"Hey, dream boy, it's high time you did a reality check. Take a good look at that mug of yours in the mirror. And ya better do it soon, too, cuz you're not *lily White* ya know. And believe me, that chick is picky, and gettin' pickier. Won't give a guy a second glance unless he's more than twenty-one. And right now, let me tell ya. I hear tell she's been layin' them baby-blue eyes of hers on Mark."

"On who?"

"On Mark. Mark Barthlin. Mitzi's office manager. Hey,

bozo, where've ya been? Doncha know? That chick started playin' him as soon as she set foot in Mitzi's office last month. You know, as a volunteer. And believe me, she's got him pantin' after her like a male husky chasing a bitch in heat. So, why even try? Man, you ain't got no chance."

Hunter, now on the defense, retorted, "Wanna bet. The way I figure it, . . ." Sighting Pietro rolling his eyes, he stopped mid-sentence and tugged at his coat sleeve. Pietro responded with a tilt of his head. Hunter, knowing he had his attention, thrust his head toward Shelly and said, "Hey, man, what's wrong with your eyes?"

Pietro, pissed, yanked his arm away from Hunter's grip and let him have it. "My eyes! Hey, bozo, it's you who's blind. I see all them chicks at yer football games. I see 'em checkin' ya out. You goin' out to the field. You runnin' them touchdowns. You comin' off and headin' for the locker room. Them chicks. They got their eyes all over ya. They been wantin' to kick ass with ya, man. And what do you do? Nothin'. You pay 'em no mind. What a jerk. Ya could've had any one of 'em, easy like. Could've had a steady snow goose by now. A hot one for at least a year or more. Taffy tarnation. If only I was so lucky. Wish I had chicks pantin' over me like that. Can't figure it. Why ya pay 'em no mind. Not a one of 'em. Hey, they were all pretty nice. Hot lookin', too. Know what I'm sayin'?"

Hunter bore his eyes deep into Pietro's.

Pietro, matching his stare, yelled in a high whisper, "Hey, doncha go lookin' at me like that." One heavy sigh

later, he said with less intensity, "Hey, man, I'm just tryin'
to be on the up 'n up with ya. I know you're gonna do what
you're gonna do. But ya can't say I didn't warn ya. Just
remember. I'm warnin' ya this. You're gonna get into a heap
of trouble if ya hook up with that chick. Ya ask me, you'd
be better off turnin' them hormones of yours off. Or, at least,
directin' them to some other señorita. One that's been
runnin' after ya. One that'll show ya some respect."

Disgusted, Pietro kicked the rung of the folding chair
ahead of him. The kid sitting in it turned around and glared
at him. "Oops. Sorry." Pulling his leg back, he cocked it over
his knee. Still steamed and frustrated, he, giving Hunter a
caustic look, spat out, "You're helpless, man. Helpless."

Hunter, aware he'd upset his buddy, reached over and
tugged at his coat sleeve. Pietro, reluctantly giving in to his
beck and call, tilted his head sideways. "Stop your fretting,
man. I'll be okay. You know I like a challenge. That I, uh,
like checking things out for myself. Anyway, I can take care
of myself. Always have, ya know."

Pietro shook his head and laughed derisively. "You've
just been ignorin' me, huh? I've been wastin' my breath.
Okay. Go ahead. Ask her out. But I'm tellin' ya, bozo. Fat
chance she'll accept. Amigo, it ain't gonna happen."

"Betcha five it will."

"Easiest five I'll ever make," Pietro said, sticking his
hand out to Hunter. The sound of their hands connecting,
sealing the deal, cracked in the air.

"And hey, bozo, I expect you to ante up with a date.

One that's soon. Not like sometime next year. Cuz I ain't gonna let ya drag this thing out forever. So, pick a date. Tell me right now. When ya gonna make this happen?"

"Christmas Season Blessing Day."

"Yeah?" Pietro's face bore a look of startled surprise. "Wow. That soon, huh?"

"Yeah. I think I'll ask her to the festivities."

"Like I said, bozo. Fat chance." Pietro, his eyes full of skepticism, folded his arms and rested them on top of his rounded abdomen.

Hunter, mocking his posture, oriented his eyes forward. He had acted macho with his best friend, but doubt was churning his insides. Still, despite knowing Pietro had the skivvy on lots of kids, he couldn't imagine the pretty blonde, who set his heart palpitating every time he glanced her way, being anything but a sweetheart.

He didn't want to believe Pietro—him saying Shelly was stuck up, a heap of trouble and wouldn't date anyone under twenty-one—but cynicism tore at him. "Maybe she'll snub me. Yeah. She'll probably stick her nose in the air at this half-breed and just walk away. Like I don't exist. That would be humiliating. No. That would be racist."

In a meeting hall lively with debate, Hunter withdrew into a cocoon of hushed silence. While luxuriating in thoughts of planting kisses on the pretty blonde's sensuous lips and soft neck, he absentmindedly pulled his long braid forward and brushed its thick, bundled end back and forth under his chin. A glimpse of its beaded sheath—a reminder of his Indian heritage—triggered thoughts that intermingled with his longing for her.

"I'm not one hundred percent Indian, but I look it and I'm not ashamed of it like my dad is. Hmm. Will she hold that against me? Will she snub me? Sooty bricks. Dad was so afraid of that, but I'm not. Take my hair." Grimacing, he said, "Grandpa, dad used to make me get those ridiculous haircuts. But after you passed, I stood up to him. I flat out refused to step inside a barbershop. And oh, as my hair got scragglier and scragglier, you wouldn't believe the killer looks he gave me. But when it was finally long enough to braid, I twisted it into a short nub. Then, I stared into the mirror and said, 'Now, bozo, you look just like Grandpa.' And dad got over it."

From that day forth, Hunter proudly displaying his Indian heritage by braiding his hair. Still, knowing his grandpa had broken tribal tradition by marrying a freckled, redheaded immigrant from England, he had to accept his blood was tainted with White man's genes. He also knew his English grandma, who died when he was an infant, had had a reputation for being quite outspoken. Their firstborn child, Samuel—Hunter's father—had inherited his mother's red hair, fair skin and freckles, plus a yen for White man's ways, but not her feisty attitude. Now, reflecting on it, Hunter was glad his genes had flipped back a generation. Yes. He could only lay claim to a fourth even though many said he looked full Indian.

On his trek up the mountainside, Hunter kept revisiting

the events of that first planning meeting where he, after catching sight of Shelly, sat mesmerized by her fetching smile and flirty blue eyes. Enamored by everything about her, he hardly heard another word being said around him.

The meeting dragged on and on, giving him ample time to sneak-peek glimpses of her. Taking in her beauty, especially her milky-white skin and long blond tresses, he wondered if he had made a poor choice about his hair. Following that thought, words drilled into him by his late Grandpa Swift Bear—from the time he started walking and talking—popped into his head.

Hunter, always be proud of your Indian heritage and don't forget to respect everyone else's.

"Sooty bricks, Grandpa, I am proud, but look. Over there sits a girl I want to hook up with. A girl who probably doesn't even know I exist. And maybe, just maybe, my Indian heritage and this braid are in the way."

That night, submerged in a sea of platform planners, Hunter reflected on how hurt his grandpa would've been had he voiced such cultural negativity directly to his face. As he considered the consequences of such an act, he squirmed. Attempting to hide the heat of shame creeping up his neck, he lifted his coat collar, closed his eyes and willed all thoughts of his grandpa to go away. But his grandpa's spirit was strong, and even though he didn't want his nearness, or his wisdom, he could feel his vibes and almost see his look of all knowing. Slouching down in his chair, he toyed with the end of his braid until Pietro's backhand swat, stinging his thigh, startled him.

"So, when ya gonna ask her out, bozo?"

"Huh? Oh, I don't know. Probably soon."

"Yeah. Right."

Now, approaching Saucer Plateau, when and how to ask Shelly to the festivities consumed him. "Will I get up the courage to ask her before time slips away? I sure hope so. But what should I say? Everything I've rehearsed seems quirky. If only I had something down pat, but I don't. Guess I'll just have to wing it."

Winging it did not fall within the parameters of Hunter's comfort zone. "Sooty bricks. She's up there already. Okay, bozo, it's either now or never."

Spotting Hunter popping through the opening beside the chimney, Shelly, her eyes glinting serious intent to play him, rose from her squat-down position. Teetering on her heels, she said, "Hey, where've you been?"

Hunter, breathless not only from his long trek up the mountainside, but also from the sudden onslaught of her beauty, sucked in a ragged breath before answering her question with a question. "I'm not late, am I?"

"No. I just wanted to get an early start."

The tartness in her voice brought a grimace to his face. "She's a showoff all right. And a stuck-up snow goose, too. Maybe I should forget about asking her to the festivities. Sooty bricks. I've certainly got enough information to do so without losing face."

Chewing his lower lip, fighting the urge to bolt, he thought back to when he had asked around about her. The words of his North Pole High football rivals still rang in his ears. "Shelly Jasselton? Yeah. I know her. She's hot, but snooty as hell. Hey, man, watch out. That chick can be downright cruel. She'll play ya and then, she'll drop ya. And her brother, Jordan? She treats him like crap."

Everyone's description of her as cruel and mean troubled Hunter. Each kid he talked to clearly felt sorry for her younger brother. "What kind of monster is she? Shimmering Icicles. I'd like to get to know her, but . . ."

Day and night, since the first platform-planning meeting, Hunter wrestled with his yo-yo feelings. Despite Pietro, all his friends, even some teen elves he hardly knew, warning him to steer clear of her, he longed to get to know her. Still, other times he felt like bailing out.

"Why'd I have to put money on the line with Pietro? Prancing Dancer. If I hadn't, I wouldn't be in this mess. Now my honor is at stake. And a bet's a bet. Okay. I can do this. All I have to do is get one date. Just one date. Then, if she proves to be like everyone says, that'll be it. I'll drop her. Yeah. Good plan."

Turning his attention to the task at hand, Hunter compared Shelly's dwindled-down pile to his untouched heap. "Fiddlin' nutcrackers. She snuck up here early and divided it in half. Like she decided to stick it to me that she's in charge. So, what's she gonna do after she finishes hers?

Stand around and make me feel nervous?"

Realizing he already felt nervous, but not wanting Shelly to pick up on it, he tried keeping his voice calm as he made another go-round at drawing her in. "Can you believe this crazy rise in temp? I mean, it's never been warm like this before. Bet this day is gonna make history, huh?"

"Yeah, and this place too." Shelly, popping up unexpectedly, twirled a streamer above her head. Savoring the look on Hunter's face, she flitted across the platform. Deliberately she added a few sensuous moves to her routine. Three spins later she stopped in front of him.

Hunter, his eyes drawn to the softness of her lips, realized he was staring. Embarrassed, he looked away.

"Hey, did you ever wonder why Santa never picked this spot before?"

"No," he answered, avoiding her eyes.

Shelly, catching his every nuance, stifled a giggle. "Hmm. He's itching to get close but afraid to show it. Maybe if I tease him a little more." A spin of her toe set her cavorting effortlessly across the platform. Pairing her sexy gyrations with flirtatious glances, she easily drew him in. Slowing her pace, accenting her moves with eye-popping sexy twists, she asked, "Well, doncha think this is a cool place for Santa to give his speech?"

Hunter, not wanting her to know how much she was turning him on, welcomed a stirring breeze, a breeze that seemed to come out of nowhere. One deep sigh later, feeling a little less sweaty, he mumbled, "Yeah. It's a cool spot."

Eyeing her strutting by, he lowered his voice to a whisper. "And you're cool, too." As her fluid movements held his stare, he mulled over the negativity he'd heard about her. "She can't be as bad as everyone makes her out to be. She can't. Yeah. She comes across as snippy, but there's something about her. For sure, she's a challenge, but she's also smart and really, really gorgeous."

Reluctantly turning away from her one-woman show, he stared down at his pile of streamers and winced. "Whacky walruses. This sure sucks. I'd rather be out there cavorting with her than tying these stupid streamers to these posts." He felt like kicking them. Instead, he bent down and selected one.

Hunter's intent was to stay focused. He couldn't. Frequently he sought Shelly's presence. Each stolen glimpse shifted his heartbeat up a notch. It also warned him time was running out. Anxiety over when and how to ask her to the festivities slowed his progress. He couldn't seem to concentrate on the job at hand.

Shelly, aware of his sneak-peeking, could hardly hold back a snicker. With a disinterested air about her, she asked, "Do you think maybe this place could've been sacred Indian ground that just got deregulated?"

Hunter felt his stomach knotting. The possibility of Saucer Plateau, or even the whole Mountain being sacred Indian ground had never occurred to him. "Deregulated? I have no idea. I suppose it's possible. I mean, maybe it was."

His curiosity piqued, he closed his eyes and searched

inwardly for something his grandpa might've shared. One incident came to mind: himself, hiking up Jingle-Jangle Mountain, working his short legs doubly hard to keep up with his grandpa's long strides. As a little tyke, he had only half listened to his stories, the remnants of which were now vague. What the mountain had meant to him, or even to his tribe, Hunter didn't know. Neither did he know if it had been registered. However, he did know his gut was screaming, "Yes, bozo. The mountain is sacred."

Bozo. Hunter often referred to himself as bozo when stumped by something. He had fallen into this habit after Pietro anointed him with the clownish name in first grade.

Knowing his grandpa would've frowned on such self-denigration, he looked around as if checking to make sure he hadn't heard him thinking that thought. Ironically, he started communing with his spirit. "Oh, Grandpa, right now I don't feel good about this platform being up here. It bothers me. I sure hope we haven't desecrated anything sacred to you or your tribe."

"Hey, with Santa speaking from up here this afternoon, it'll probably be easy for everyone, anywhere around this mountain, to see him. Doncha think?"

Reacting to Shelly's intrusive voice, Hunter jumped. Recovering quickly, he said, "Yeah, I guess so." Bent on reconnecting with his grandpa's spirit, he leaned against the railing and stared at nothing in particular.

"Grandpa, you said this mountain had rumble once, shortly before your lifetime. And the first you learned about that *time* was when you were about five or six, when you were going to climb to its top. By yourself. But you didn't go because some tribal elder filled your heart with fear. Remember? You said that he said when he was a young warrior, the mountain scared him half out of his wits. That he was up there, ready to set foot on Saucer Plateau when the whole mountain shook. And it spooked him so, he ran lickety-split all the way down it with a mess of boulders chasing his backside. And you said ever since then your tribe has revered this mountain."

After focusing on that bit of folklore, Hunter closed his eyes and visualized his late Grandpa Swift Bear saying quite seriously, "Son, many moons ago our tribe camped around this mountain, but never on it. And that young warrior almost getting killed? Well, that taught me to respect it. Many times, I climbed that mountain, but never did I set foot on Saucer Plateau."

Blinking away that scene, another with his grandpa, when he, himself, was about ten, came into sharp focus.

The hike up the mountain had been exhausting, but the slip-sliding down had been exhilarating. They had laughed till their sides hurt. Reaching the bottom, Hunter had watched and listened carefully as his grandpa lifted his eyes to the mountain and said reverently, "Hunter, our tribe always called this mountain by its Indian name, *Mount Koyukon*. And we respected it. But I guess those days are gone forever." His grandpa's contemplative look, plus the mountain's original name, stayed with Hunter.

"Grandpa, I wonder if this mountain resents having fat posts crammed inside its belly. And who changed its name from *Mount Koyukon* to Jingle-Jangle Mountain? What a blow that must've been to you and your tribe. I can't imagine . . ."

Bright sunlight, pushing its way through a bank of clouds, distracted Hunter. He squinted. Hand shading his eyes, he looked down at the Victory Trees. "Grandpa, something puzzles me. How did Santa know these trees would grow here? Did he somehow know the mountain would protect them? Sooty bricks. I never realized . . . Wow. Look at them. From up here, they look like an arrowhead pointing straight toward Krisville. Know what, Grandpa? Even though it's fun looking down on them, I don't think Santa should've had this platform built up here. But to be honest, it probably wouldn't be bothering me if Shelly hadn't brought up that sacred Indian stuff. That got me to wondering. Hmm. Maybe I'll go down to the courthouse after the holidays and look up some old records."

Deep in thought, Hunter not only sensed his Grandpa's presence, but him speaking as well. "Hunter, listen to your feelings. They run true like our great northern waters. And, son, don't be chicken. Act on them if you think it's the right thing to do."

"Why are you telling me this, Grandpa?"

"Hey, what's up?" Shelly asked, unaware she was intruding into his reverie for a second time.

Startled, Hunter jerked his head slightly. "I don't know.

I just have a funny feeling."

"Like what?"

"Like something's not right. Especially with it being almost forty degrees and all."

"Hey, with this gorgeous weather, what could possibly go wrong?"

"I don't know. Something could, you know."

"Like what?"

Hunter, reluctant to say more, but knowing she was expecting an answer, said with hesitancy, "Like, . . . like, uh, . . . uh, maybe those college students goofed at putting in these posts. Or something like that."

Shelly bristled. "Elf Hunter Swift Bear, what's with you? How can you even say that? Or, . . . or even think it? Hey. All those guys worked their sled-running buns off and, . . . and dancin' Prancer, they want a flag up from Santa just as much as we do. Besides, Santa had the Region's best engineers overseeing it."

"Yes, but something tells me . . ." Hunter, sighting Shelly trucking toward him, her eyes ablaze with anger, stopped mid-sentence. As she rooted her feet in front of him, his eyes, flaring wide, advertised his shock.

"Hey, what's with you? You know nothing's ever gone wrong before and nothing will this year either."

Startled, leaning backward over the railing, fitful words tumble off his tongue. "Yeah, but, . . . but you know, there, . . . uh, there could always be a first time. Something could go wrong. Like, uh, like disaster could strike. Or uh, this mountain could blow. Or, or uh, . . ."

Shelly, hell bent on curtailing his doomsday thinking, stiffened her arms out behind her and thrust her head forward. In this stance, she strained to meet him eye to eye, but she couldn't. Even standing on tiptoe, she was too short to make it happen. But what she lacked in stature she made up in lung power. Headstrong, bent on getting her point across, she let it rip. "What do you mean, 'There could always be a first time'? What are you anyway? Some kind of doomsday jerk out to jinx our most revered holiday? Listen. Talk like that is stupid and crazy and, and . . ." Thrusting a balled fist under his nose, she finished in a clipped voice, "See this?"

Hunter jerked his head back and stared at her menacing fist. Assessing it as too close for comfort, he backed away. But she, like an angry tsunami with issues, kept shoving it into his face. "Hey, buster, stop this doomsday stuff, or I'll give you some of this, and don't think I won't do it either. I'm warning you, . . . you, you, doomsday jerk. You better think twice before pushing your luck with me."

Too rattled to muster an immediate response, Hunter just stared down at her ruffled peacock stance. Fortunately for him, what had earlier rendered him speechless now bought him time to conjure up a plausible comeback.

"Ah, Grandpa, I remember what you taught me to do whenever I didn't know what to do. You said, 'When faced with a bad situation, take time to analyze it, try to see it for what it really is, and if that doesn't work, look for the humor in it.' Humor. Yeah. Gotta look for the humor."

As the freshness of a deep breath seeped through Hunter's veins, relaxing him some, his confidence rose. "Ah, yes. This little mite's blustering is sort of funny. But can't she see? With my football-trained body, I can easily block her first blow." Holding back a grin, he stared down at the mighty, but cape-less Shelly.

"So, Grandpa, you want me to find the humor in this? Well, I see it and it's just too funny for words."

As he recalled his grandpa's wisdom—coupled with reframing Shelly's verbal assault as humorous, especially her threat to attack him—Hunter tilted the corners of his mouth into a cryptic smile. Laughter, like a tidal wave pounding a beach, welled up inside him. He tried squelching it, but its force was beyond his control. Turning his back to her, he slumped over like a depleted hot-air balloon and burst into rollicking laughter.

Shelly, riled by his mocking laughter, felt hot blood surging through her veins. Like a sparked stick of dynamite, she exploded. "You think I'm kidding, huh? Well, let me tell you. Nobody laughs at Shelly Jasselton and gets away with it. Do you hear me? Nobody."

To Hunter, her threat felt like a blast of heat from a roaring coal furnace. "Wow. Pietro said she could go off like a firecracker when you least expected it, but I sure didn't expect this. Sooty bricks. This girl doesn't let up."

Posturing defensively—spreading his feet slightly, extending his palms forward—he eyed her guardedly.

Slowly, he slid his feet backward. She, like a haunting shadow, matched each of his steps. As they moved in sync, the sound of her clenched fist ramrodding the palm of her other hand seemed to overpower his heavy breathing, and hers, too.

"Is this little mite insecure or what?" As soon as Hunter thought this, more advice from his grandpa popped into his head. "Hunter, when you find yourself in a sticky situation, take a little time to analyze what's going on before you act. And remember. Things aren't always what they seem to be."

"Good advice, Grandpa. Yeah. It seems to me, Shelly's deliberately stretching it. And sooty bricks, I think she's trying to control me, too. But why?"

Hunter had no idea that Shelly's hostility *mirrored* nothing more than her habitual ploys to keep her younger brother Jordan in check, to unnerve him, to remind him she was top wolf in their family's pecking order. Nor could he have known that his backing off, but not backing down, had thrown her for a loop. And he certainly didn't know that his reaction to her behavior was having a profound effect on her.

Shelly couldn't figure out what went wrong. Always, guys bowed to her rule, like Jordan always did. Like all guys did, except her father. She prided herself at being a master at making guys squirm. Seeing them jump to her command delighted her to no end. It also heightened her sense of power. But today, her blustery tactic didn't work with Hunter. He turned the tables on her. He crushed her intent with laughter. As he did, a feeling new to her—humiliation—almost took her to her knees. It also made her think. "Is this how my brother feels every time I put the screws to him? Every time I lord over him?"

Hunter, holding his ground, yet casting an uneasy glance Shelly's way, kept trying to figure out what had gotten into her. "There's got to be a reason for her meanness. Why is she acting so bitchy and unreasonable? One thing I know. A physical altercation with this girl is the last thing I want." Anxious to distance himself from her, he stepped backward. As he did, he shifted his eyes from her white-knuckled fists to her quivering jaw. He sensed she didn't know what to do next, and neither did he.

Still trying to make sense of her explosive hissy snit, Hunter thought about how his father had often reacted to his mom's anger. Not until this moment with he, himself, the target of a female's wrath, did he understand why his father sometimes, but not always, withered under his mother's rage. "Yeah, dad. How many times did I see you walking away without saying a word? I couldn't figure it out until one day, by chance, I caught you, head tilted toward the ceiling, muttering, 'God help me. It must be that time of the month again.' Hey. Maybe it's Shelly's time of the month. Yeah. She's probably having her period, and if so, I guess me laughing at her was just too much." Concluding that, he began apologizing, using the same words his father used with his mom.

"Hey, I'm sorry. Okay? So, just cool it. Okay?"

"Yeah, well, I wasn't going to hit you. Really, I wasn't. I was just playing you."

As Shelly's hands dropped limply to her sides, Hunter tried to get a read on her eyes. He couldn't. She had tilted her head down. But he did notice reddish blotches creeping up her neck, coloring her cheeks. "Hmm. Looks like her blotchy skin is telling on her. She's embarrassed. No. I'd wager she's more than embarrassed. She's probably mortified."

Warily, he eyed Shelly slinking away. "Whew. I'm sure glad that's over. Bet she needs time to cool down and I need time to get this job done."

Hunter, knowing he needed to get and stay focused on his task, bent down and grabbed a handful of streamers. His intention was good, but his mind, unwilling to let it go, kept reeling. "What if it wasn't her monthly? What if she has hissy snits like this all the time? Yelping walrus pups. What guy wants to put up with that!"

Making his way around the chimney, heading for the Kringleland post, he thought about the bet he had made with Pietro at the year's first platform-planning meeting. "Yeah, man, you're on. I'll bet ya five bucks. And watch. I'll score with her. You'll see."

For weeks, he had sweated not only about whether it was worth his time—given everything he had learned about Shelly's snooty reputation—but also about when to ask her, how to ask her and, above all, how to win that bet.

Still, at the moment, after what had just transpired, he toyed with the idea of bailing out.

Seconds later, rising from measuring and cutting streamers, he felt a chill shrouding his shoulders. Not a weather chill, but a chilling sense that someone was standing beside him, trying to hug him. Paying attention to it, he suspected it was his grandpa. "Okay, Grandpa. I know you're vying for my attention again. So, what are you trying to tell me now, huh?"

Closing his eyes, clearing his mind, he waited. Slowly, a vision of himself at age twelve, sitting by his grandpa's bedside filtered into his head. It was as if the scene was appearing from behind a hazy fog, one that was slowly rising and dissipating. Trusting his grandpa's spirit, he let himself meld into the vision.

By age twelve, Hunter had seen many animals die. But his Grandpa? Ill-prepared for the inevitable, he shifted uncomfortably. When his old mentor tried to speak, he leaned forward to hear what the dying man was about to say. "Hunter, even though I'll be, . . . be going away soon, to, . . . to my happy hunting ground, I'll come whenever you, . . . you need me. All you need, all you have, . . . have to do is, . . . is be quiet, close your eyes and, . . . and think of me and I, . . . I'll come. And sometimes, if, . . . if I think I need to, I, . . . I'll come without you, . . . you even seeking me. You hear?"

"I know, Grandpa. You're reminding me you'll always be there for me. I get it. But right now, Grandpa, it's this girl. I'm not sure I want to get involved with her. She's so scrappy. So explosive. So spunky. So feisty. Feisty!" The word triggered the last serious, on-the-trail chat he'd had with his beloved mentor before death claimed his spirit. "Yeah. That fateful talk happened about four months before I turned twelve, huh, Grandpa? And I didn't want to listen. I remember you started it with, 'Son, I think it's time you get some learning about girls.'"

Learning about girls! Those words flooded Hunter's mind—actually his whole being—with anger. Even so, he knew better than to contradict his grandpa. Openly he could not say anything disrespectful to him. If he did, he'd have to live with the shame of doing so for the rest of his life. Inwardly, he exploded. "What! You want me to learn about girls? Sooty bricks. Don't tell me I've got to sit through another *birds-and-the-bees* sex talk. No! No! No! First my teacher. Then my mom. Then my dad. And now you! Why? All that stuff about a guy's wiggly sperms fighting to get to a girl's squishy egg to make a baby is yucky. And girls bleeding every month? Yuck! That's disgusting. If girls do that, I don't ever want anything to do with them. Not ever, ever, ever."

At eleven, going on twelve, all Hunter cared to know about sex—that is, what made sense to him—was he had a penis and masturbation felt good. At his young age, he didn't even know the act had a name and he didn't care. He and his buddies just called it *jacking off*.

Thinking about it now brought color to his face. He

hadn't always felt good about doing it. Although, it always felt good. Time after time, he'd try to keep himself in check, but his raging hormones always won out. Afterward, he'd berate himself, even question his sanity. This back and forth reasoning (*It's okay. No. It's not okay.*) went on until his dad barged into his bedroom one day and *caught him in the act.* Tying a streamer to the post in front of him, thinking about it, Hunter smiled. "Yeah. I'll never forget that day."

He saw himself, one minute in ecstasy and the next, the moment his dad popped into his private sanctuary . . . Well, he felt like he was sitting in purgatory about to be judged by an angry God. Bolting upright, his eyes bulged with panic. And his head? It suddenly went dizzy with dread. And fear? It, dripping through his veins like battery acid, made him shake and also paralyzed him. Shame moved in, too. It turned his face crimson red, while embarrassment dropped his head to bowed penitence.

In this stance, lifting his brow just enough to catch his dad's eyes seeking his, his breath froze halfway up his windpipe. He expected the shaming, the berating to begin. It didn't. An uncomfortable silence followed. His dad cleared his throat. Intent on catching his dad's barely audible words, he cocked an ear.

"Oops, sorry, son."

Hunter, slouching over, breathing normally again, couldn't believe he wasn't in trouble. His dad, having said his piece, moved one foot out into the hallway. Hesitating, still gripping the doorknob, he suddenly swung his head back around the doorjamb.

"Now what?" Hunter, holding his breath, settled his eyes on his dad's curly, red whiskers, which lately were graying. His dad, feeling uncomfortable, directed his gaze toward the football banners tacked above Hunter's chest-of-drawers. Eyeing his Dad's face, Hunter could tell his lips—half buried in a forest of whiskers—were struggling to draw thoughts from his mind. Ironically, if he had been one of his dad's patients, his dad would've had no trouble addressing the issue.

"Son," he finally said, staring at the floor, "I don't want you to feel badly or even guilty about what you're doing. All guys masturbate. And girls do it, too. It's normal. Quite normal. And there's nothing wrong with doing it as long as you do it privately. And, son, I'm really sorry for barging in on you. I should've knocked."

Hunter watched his dad pulling the bedroom door shut behind him. Dumbfounded, he sat, listening to his dad's footsteps receded down the hall. As they got fainter and fainter, he mumbled the new word over and over. "Masturbate. Masturbate. Masturbate. So, that's what it's called." Pride welled up inside him. At first, he didn't know why. Giving it some thought, he figured it out. All his life he had spent far more time with his Grandpa Swift Bear than he ever had with his dad. His dad worked long hours and his grandpa had conveniently been there to pick up the slack. He had grown up viewing his grandpa as a pal. His love and respect for him had evolved naturally. Yes. He went to his dad for major decisions. Like, to get permission to do things and to show him his report card. But nothing as weird as this had ever happened.

After their little surprise encounter, Hunter realized he could probably ask his dad anything. Why? What was different? Lying on his bed, mulling it over, it came to him. His dad had talked *to* him like a young man, not *at* him like a misbehaving little elfin. He had shown him respect. Falling back on his pillow, basking in his freshly germinated, special connection with his dad, he grinned from ear to ear. He had a new-found veneration for him, but little did he realize the importance of it. In less than a year, death would pull his Grandpa Swift Bear's soul beyond Father Sky, to the spiritual realm of his tribe's happy hunting ground. It would be a pivotal point in Hunter's life. Without his grandpa, he'd have to turn to his dad for guidance into manhood.

"Come, Hunter," his grandpa said on their last hike up Jingle-Jangle Mountain. Moving off the trail at a snail's pace, he motioned with a shaky hand for Hunter to follow. "Let's sit over here next to this ice boulder, out of the wind. It looks like a good place to do a little powwowing."

Dutifully following his beloved grandpa's directive, Hunter slid his backside down the icy boulder and balanced his weight on his haunches. Even though he could hardly bear hearing the sex talk again, he steeled himself to listen with respect. But his grandfather surprised him. His lesson for the day turned out to be nothing about sex. Girls, yes.

But no sex talk.

"Son, I know you're not much interested in girls yet, but someday you'll settle down with a woman. I'm sure of it. All I hope is, you'll find yourself a woman who is kind and loving and also a bit *feisty*. One who says whatever she thinks, just like your grandma used to do with me. See, women like that, they make the best wives because they're really sure of themselves. Take it from me, son. It's that kind of woman who keeps a guy in line. Never allows him or anyone else to walk all over her.

"And son, I hope whoever you hitch up with has an independent streak. Pick someone who's not wishy-washy or sneaky like. What I mean is, pick a woman who will put you in your place, but won't stab you in the back. Now, if you do hitch up with a woman like that, one with a feisty streak, believe me, she'll not only be a lot of fun, she'll bring fire to your life just like your grandma did to mine. Now your grandma, she was one fine woman. Feisty, but also tender and caring and very wise."

As his grandfather paused, Hunter sought his eyes. His far-away look told him he was recalling a past moment. "I'll tell you this, son. Your grandma, she was a hot-tempered, feisty woman if ever there was one. Yeah. She sure kept me on my toes. And fun . . . Oh, I sure do miss that woman." Turning, placing his gnarled index finger in the middle of Hunter's sternum, he finished with, "Now, son, you just tuck all that away in there. In your heart. Okay?"

54

"Yeah, Grandpa. I tucked your advice away in my heart all right. So deep, I forgot all about it. That is, until now." Feeling a chuckle rising, he said, "Grandpa, you're something else. And I think it's ironic that Shelly is proving to be the type of young lady you encouraged me to find. Feisty and outspoken. Okay. You win. I won't give up. I'll step back into the fire. Watch me."

CHAPTER 3

Did I blow it again?

After their little tiff, Shelly, convinced Hunter viewed her as the wackiest girl ever, fought back tears. Head hung low, too embarrassed to look his way, she leaned against the Rudolphtown post, trying to muffle her sobs. The truth was hard to face. Her mean streak, which she had nurtured and honed to perfection over the years, had reared its ugly head and ruined her plans to hook up with this terrific-looking guy. On top of that, guilt, triggering one awful memory after another, was forcing her to revisit many of her parents' chastising remarks.

"Shelly, why do you have to be so smug, curt, bossy, arrogant, demanding, and downright mean to your brother?" Over the years, she and her parents frequently locked horns over her meanness toward Jordan. To her, it was a game. Again, and again she heard, and always ignored, "Shelly, stop being so cruel to your brother." – "Shelly, can't you once, just once in your life say a nice word to your brother?" – "Shelly, give your brother back his ball." – "Shelly, Jordan is not your slave. Understand?" – "Why, Shelly, why? Why do you have to be so spiteful to Jordan?"

Every day, since *the cute little intruder* had arrived on the scene thirteen years ago, remarks like these had bombarded her ears and she had ignored them all.

Despite Jordan learning at an early age to avoid her, she continually went out of her way to make his life miserable. She loved the game. Harassing him. Setting him up. Manipulating him. Cornering him. Making him squirm. Year after year, she chalked up point after point in her little book of nasty endeavors. However, never in her wildest dreams did she anticipate that she would fall victim to her own vindictiveness.

"Whacky walruses. Am I destined to turn off every cute guy that comes along by hissing at him like I have at my brother all his life? Is this a wakeup call? And Jordan? Mom and dad keep harping about how fast he's growing lately. Even rubbing it in that he'll soon pass me up. That he'll soon be taller, and a lot stronger than me. Stronger!" Visualizing the muscle mass that had popped out on her brother's arms and chest lately, she shuddered. "Shimmering icicles. He could turn on me. He could start lording over me. Wow. Would that ever be scary. No. No way will I ever let that happen. Got to stop it. But how?"

As if by telepathy, she heard her mother's voice. "Shelly, you'd better start changing, and soon."

"Me change? Hmm. Me be nice, not be mean to Jordan? And start growing up like dad's been harping at me to do for years? Okay, you guys. Just watch. I'm gonna do a three-sixty. I'm gonna *kill* Jordan with kindness. I'm gonna love him with all my heart. You'll see, Dad. Just like you've wanted. I'm gonna stop treating little Jordan like he's nothing but a dirty rug under my feet. Guess you won't be throwing that into my face anymore, huh, Dad?"

Realizing her excitement had pushed her voice up a notch, Shelly turned to check on Hunter's whereabouts. Spotting him down on his knees, cutting streamers, she let out a sigh of relief. "Whew. Glad he didn't hear me." As she continued to drool over his handsome physic, a mixture of longing and sadness wilted her body into a ragdoll slump. Turning away from him, she resolved, "I will do this. Yes, little brother. from now on I'm gonna be kind instead of cruel to you. And that'll be okay since it's me who's doing the deciding.

Whew! What a wakeup call. I've probably lost my chance with Hunter, but I'll be different with the next guy. I will get this meanness out of my system. Starting today, Daddy dearest, I'm gonna love my little brother just as much as I've hated him. No. No. I'm gonna do better than that. I'm gonna be the best sister ever. Holy walrus turds. Have I really hated him forever!"

Shelly's strong self-talk dredged up horrific scenes, which, in turn, triggered guilt; guilt she did not want to face. "I need something to do." Scanning the platform, sighting a flutter of streamer scraps, she dropped to her knees and started gathering them up. "Guess it's cleanup time." As the irony of those words hit home, she produced a faint smile. Crawling around like a whipped pup, stuffing streamer scraps into her pockets, she felt almost as if for penitence she was collecting the many thorns she'd inflicted on her brother over the years. Yet, it was Hunter, not Jordan, who dominated her thoughts.

"What are my chances now? I want him to notice me, but after the way I acted earlier, he'll probably never speak to me again. Maybe I should apologize. Apologize! Me? No. No way am I going to crawl on my hands and knees to any guy." Yet, without realizing it, she was doing just that.

On his rise from cutting streamers, Hunter caught sight of Shelly coming his way. The wind, catching and flipping her hair, constantly reframing her lovely face, set his heart palpitating.

"Taffy tarnation. How could such a beauty acquire such a rotten reputation? She's got good parents. So, what went wrong? Maybe if she had a grandpa like mine. Yeah. There were times when he was tough on me. Like when I came home from school one day, bragging about getting the best of a kid who had angered me. 'I showed him, Grandpa,' I said, expecting him to say something like, 'Good job, son. I'm proud of you.' Instead, he laid into me."

"Son, never spit back when someone spits at you. Instead, *Be* kind. *Be* gentle. *Be* patient. And if you keep those three *bees* buzzing around in your head, you'll make more friends than enemies."

"But, but he . . ."

"No *buts* about it! I expect better of you. Hear?"

"The three buzzing bees as you called them, Grandpa. *Be* kind. *Be* gentle. *Be* patient. Well, at eight, I couldn't understand why you expected me to be kind to someone who was so mean. Now, those three buzzing bees make sense. Believe me, I'll use them. Starting right now."

Hunter, gazing longingly at Shelly, felt a sensation in his chest only one word could describe: *yearning*. He yearned to hold her close, to stroke her hair. And more than anything, he yearned to kiss her. "Sooty bricks. What's it gonna take to get hooked up with her? And those lips. I'd love to kiss them. Kiss them! Yeah. When will that ever happen? Probably never. And that gorgeous hair. Oh my gosh, she's crawling this way. Hmm. Maybe I can touch her hair without her noticing."

Shelly, head down, deep in sorrowful thoughts, had no idea she was nearing Hunter. "I sure screwed up. He'll never look at me or even speak to me again." Bouncing up, seeing his face not more than five inches away from hers, she gasped audibly.

Caught off guard by her sudden rise, Hunter—eyes flaring wide, heart nearly jumping out of his chest—jerked his hand to his mouth and faked a cough.

"Hey. You okay?"

"Yeah. Yeah. I'm, [*cough*] I'm okay. But, [*cough*] but I uh, . . . uh, I was just thinking. Uh, why don't you start down the ladder while I tie these, [*cough, cough*] these last few streamers to the Kringleland post?"

Hunter didn't expect to hear *Okay* in a surprisingly sweet voice. But he did. Taken aback, he cocked his head and stared at Shelly flitting off toward the ladder. "Wow. What a beauty." He longed to run after her, to pull her into his arms, to kiss her. But fearing she'd rebuff him, he held back. Looking was all he dared to do. And looking he did. Longingly, he took in the sway of her wispy blond hair cascading down her back. Next, her graceful walk drew his eyes to the fullness of her hips. From there, he sized up her lithe, ballerina legs. Lastly, sighting the toe tip of her right boot reaching for the top ladder rung, "Wow!" road along the stream of his long exhalation.

Shelly, sensing his eyes upon her, felt a little giddy, and happy. "Yes. He's still interested in me." Abruptly turning to face him, she shouted with unsuppressed glee, "I'll race you down to the Victory Trees."

Shocked by the invite, yet pleased, Hunter yelled back, "You're on. Soon as I'm done here." After knotting his last few streamers, he scooted over to the ladder and peered down at her. She, with hands clasped behind her back, beamed him up a coquettish smile.

"Ah. Maybe I still have a chance. Yes. Maybe. That is, if my nerves don't get the best of me."

Grasping the ladder on the backside of the chimney, he playfully bounced his feet down the supporting post instead of using its rungs. Blessed with agility, he had no fear of falling. Yet, in a hurry, he lost his footing and dropped the last few feet to the ground.

"Glad that's done," he said, popping to his feet. Surprised at finding himself talking to thin air, he wondered what happened to Shelly. Looking around, he spotted her off to his right, stepping backward, putting distance between them. "Cool! She's inviting me to be playful. Yes! Yes!" Like a carefree rabbit, he loped through the snow, yelling, "Hey, wait for me." She, rather than waiting, kept moving further and further away. He, having just cranked his legs to their full momentum, sighted—unfortunately a little too late—a solidly packed snowball flying toward him. Caught off guard, he had no time to veer from the flying missile.

SM-M-MACK!

On impact, his neck snapped back, and his face, assaulted by the icy slush, bore a look of startled surprise.

Shelly, amazed and amused at hitting her target dead on, yelled, "Bull's eye." Rollicking with laughter, zigzagging through the snow, she nearly fell to her knees.

And Hunter? Well, he just stood statue still, staring cross-eyed at hunks of snow ski jumping over his nose and down his chin. Poor guy. He looked more forlorn than a wound-down toy soldier. Still, he couldn't hold this look very long. The sight unfolding before his eyes—Shelly, drunk with laughter, stumbling over her feet—tickled his funny bone. As she skedaddled off, glancing his way with guarded, lioness eyes, his pouty lips gave way to a smile. A quick shake of his head rid the wet residue from his face. Teasingly he yelled, "Hey, you promised not to hit me.

Remember?"

She, laughing hysterically, managed to say, "Yeah. I remember. And I didn't hit you. The snowball did."

Hunter loved seeing this side of Shelly—carefree, happy, stumbling about, succumbing to playful whims. "So, you're testing me, huh?" Rising to her alluring challenge, he bent down and scooped up a heap of snow. Packing it into a ball, he teasingly yelled, "Hey, thanks for showing me this stuff's just right for snowball making. And hey, I bet you didn't know this *ol' Indian boy* loves a good snowball fight."

"Well, this *ol' White girl* loves one, too." Stooping down, she scooped up the makings for her next missile. Packing and rounding her orb, she eyed him juggling his. "Let the games begin," she yelled. Popping to her feet, she took off running down the mountainside. Peering over her shoulder, she wondered when he would start his pursuit.

Hunter purposely stalled to give her a head start. Starting out a few seconds later, he yelled, "Just wait. I'm gonna get you good."

"Oh, I'm sure you will. But hey, I don't care, cuz I got you first. So there."

Their playful words, colliding and bouncing off Jingle-Jangle Mountain, followed them down the mountainside as each tried to outfox the other.

Shelly, the first to reach the meadow below, sought refuge near a Victory Tree. She didn't want to call a halt to their play, but she was too exhausted to continue. To let

Hunter know she was all done in, she pulled a crumpled streamer from her pocket. Waving it, she begged, "Stop. Please stop. I'm out of breath. I can't . . ."

"Giving up, huh? Well, since I zapped you at least a hundred times, I guess that's okay."

"Hey, hotshot, I got, *[gasp]* I got in my, *[gasp]* my share of hits, too." She peeked around some branches to make sure he was empty-handed. Then, stepping out into the open, locking eyes with him, she smiled coyly.

Hunter, smitten, said with tenderness, "Hey, you really are out of breath. What do you say we cool it a bit?"

"Yeah. I'm, *[gasp]* I'm all for that."

"Bet you didn't know that that's my tree you're standing by."

Shelly shot him a quizzical look. Navigating her eyes around the tree, she said smartly, "Really. Your tree, huh? If that's so, then, why isn't your name on it?"

Hunter laughed. "Hey, I'm not kidding. It's mine. I mean, kinda. See, my tribe lays partial claim to it."

"What! Are you crazy or something? All these trees belong to Santa."

"I know that. Everybody knows that."

"Then, why do you call it your tree?"

"Because my Grandpa Swift Bear planted it."

"You're kidding."

"Nope. I'm dead serious. My grandpa used to tell me the story all the time."

"What story?"

"About why Santa had these Victory Trees planted."

"Oh, Hunter, everyone knows that old story. It goes like this. Santa and Mitzi took a vacation to the States back in the seventies. And Mitzi got mad because all he wanted to do was traipse through plant nurseries. She thought he was crazy shipping eleven saplings up here from, . . . uh, from Oregon, I think. And she predicted they'd never grow in this frigid climate. But Santa insisted they would. And as soon as they got home, he picked eleven husky elves to plant them in this V formation. And, of course, he did all that to celebrate the end of World War II. Right?"

"Wrong."

"Whadaya mean, wrong? That's the way I heard it."

"Look. You got it all right except he didn't plant these trees to celebrate the end of the War."

"He did, too."

"No. He didn't. Listen. That was one of my grandpa's biggest complaints. He used to say, 'Hunter, elves come here and talk about how Santa had these trees planted to celebrate the end of the war, but that's not true and . . .'"

"Then, why'd he have them planted?"

"To represent what should be done to prevent another world war."

"I don't understand. What do you mean, 'what should be done?'"

"See that tree down there. The one at the apex of the V formation? The biggest one."

"Yeah." Shelly, standing on tiptoe, strained to get a

better look.

"My grandpa said it represents the mediator."

"Mediator? What in taffy tarnation are you talking about?"

"What these trees represent. And those trees over there. Notice they all lead down to the mediator tree."

"Yeah. So, what?"

"Well, they represent one side of the conflict and the trees over here, they represent the other side. Now do you get what the mediator tree is all about?"

"Yeah. It gets both sides talking. It's the go-between."

"Right. That's why Santa had it planted at the apex of this V formation. And all that space inside there, where it's illegal for us to step ever. Well, guess what it represents?"

"What?"

"The negotiating table. An imaginary one, of course."

"Oh, really."

Hunter felt like saying, "Yes. Didn't you know that?" Not wanting to get her riled again, he chose to enlighten her instead. "Look. The way my grandpa explained it was . . . Well, he told me Santa had these trees planted in the shape of a V to represent two warring factions. That the apex represents where they come together to work out their differences and the outer ends of both tree lines . . . Hey, see this tree we're standing by and that one over there just opposite from this one?"

Shelly, tracking his pointed finger, nodded.

"Well, these two trees, the furthest ones out, they

represent each warring country's military stuff. You know, battleships, missiles, guns, and stuff like that. And, according to my grandpa, Santa purposely had them planted far apart so they wouldn't have to battle for sunshine. Get it?"

"So, Santa wants warring countries to talk. So, do these trees represent peace is possible if countries will just sit down and talk out their differences?"

"You've got it, and ..." Hesitating, cupping a hand over his eyes, Hunter looked up at Saucer Plateau. "Know what? I bet when Santa starts his speech—because he loves these trees so much—I bet he's gonna face this way."

Shelly, knowing what he was getting at, said, "And this'll be the best spot to watch him from, right?"

"Yep. And hey, you wanna join me?"

"Sure. But we better get going. It's getting late."

"Wow! Wow! Wow!" beat rhythmically inside Hunter's head as he mulled over what just happened. "I don't believe it. I popped the question without even thinking and she accepted. Wait 'til I tell Pietro. And hey, that means I won the bet. Yes! He has to pay up."

"Thanks for setting me straight about the Victory Trees," Shelly said, distracting him from his thoughts. "I love adding stuff to my history collection."

"History collection. You collect history?"

"Sure do. Right here," she answered, pointing to her head.

"Ah, then. Do me a favor. How about tapping into that

little brain of yours to find out why we always have turkey on Christmas Season Blessing Day. Sooty bricks. You'd think they'd change up once in a while. Maybe serve ham or steak, or better still, hamburgers and French fries."

"Are you kidding?"

"No. I'm dead serious. I'd really like to know why we always have to have turkey and those yucky cranberries. I hate cranberries and turkey is *not* my favorite meat."

"Dancin' Prancer. If you feel that strongly about it, why don't you revolt?"

"Revolt!" As soon as the word flew off Hunter's lips, he felt torn. "By the way I said that, she knows I won't do any such thing. Bet she's testing me. Gosh, I want to work on a relationship with her, but . . ."

As he tried guessing Shelly's intentions, something his grandpa once said popped into his head. "Hunter, stand up for what you believe to be right. Don't be afraid to voice your own thoughts, even if they seem off kilter from what others think. Yes. It takes courage to be the odd man out, but it's important to speak your mind. And if others put you down for it, so be it. Just look at it this way. They're not, and never will be, your true friends."

As much as Hunter wanted to ignore his grandpa's advice, he couldn't. Deep down he knew he was right. Still, he feared if he held strong to his values, Shelly might bolt. He felt torn. He didn't want to come across as a sissy, but neither did he want to take a pushy, aggressive stance.

"What can I say that'll sound sensible, that won't send

her off on another hissy snit? One thing I know. Whatever I say, it has to be something that'll keep her from changing her mind about attending the festivities with me. But revolt? That, I could never do. So, how can I be *my own man*, like my grandpa said, without getting her miffed? Ah, I know. I'll do what my father suggested during our last talk. Let's see. How did he put it?"

"Hunter, you've got to learn tact. Hold back from jumping to conclusions. Take a little time to think a situation through before saying anything. Get your facts straight before you open your mouth. Your grandfather taught me that. Surely, he brought it up a time or two with you, too."

Before losing his nerve, Hunter blurted out, "Hey, uh, I don't think anyone in the North Pole Region has ever started a revolt before. Generally speaking, all disputes are negotiated. And that's a fact."

Shelly was quick to respond. "Well, if you don't like it, at least go complain to Santa about it."

"Yeah. Maybe I will," he said flippantly; but deep down, he knew he probably never would.

For the next five minutes, snow crunching under two sets of boots was the only sound that punctuated their serene surroundings. Walking on, Hunter dared to do what he had wanted to do all day. Raising his arm, he swung it around Shelly's shoulders. The move seemed so easy and natural. To his surprise, she nuzzled in close instead of pulling away. She also broke the silence.

"Don't you know why we always have turkey and cranberries at our festivities?"

"No. I've always slept through my history classes."

"Hey, if you'd defrost that icicle brain of yours, I'd tell you," she chided, slipping her arm around his waist.

As she made her move, Hunter gulped. Releasing a stream of air like one does when blowing on a hot, roasted marshmallow, his thoughts went to Pietro. "Wow! He'll never believe me when I . . ."

"It's all because of greed," Shelly announced.

"Greed. What are you talking about?"

"Why we have turkey and cranberries on Christmas Season Blessing Day."

"What's greed got to do with turkey and cranberries?"

Shelly turned and put a finger to his lips. "Shh, and I'll tell you. See. It's like this. About forty or fifty years ago, or something like that, some rich dude down in the States, he decided to get the jump on Christmas sales. So, he stocked his store early and drummed up this Thanksgiving Day parade idea to get people out shopping. And he figured he'd make lots of money if he had a star attraction. You know. To draw in a big crowd."

"And that's where Santa came in. Right?"

"Right. And that stateside dude wanted the real Santa Claus for his parade. Not a helper."

"So, what's that got to do with us having turkey and cranberries on Christmas Season Blessing Day?"

"Duh. It's like this. Santa was their guest. So, they had

to feed him. And the first time they served him cranberries, he said, 'What's this red sauce?' When they said, 'Cranberries,' he bellowed, 'Well, bless my snowy-white whiskers, I didn't know these little red pearls were fit for human consumption.'"

"Don't cranberries grow wild wherever there's a bog? All over the Northern Hemisphere?"

"Sure. But back then, only wild animals ate them."

"And Indians."

"Oh, yeah. I forgot about *the Indians*." Shelly giggled.

"So, they fed him cranberries and turkey and Santa liked them so much he said, 'Fiddlin' nutcrackers, we've got to have us a yearly turkey feast like this at home.' And then, he flipped on his thinking cap and came up with this bright idea to serve turkey and cranberries on Christmas Season Blessing Day."

"Hey, you tricked me. You already knew."

"Oh no. Did I blow it again?" Hunter, unsure, scanned Shelly's eyes, hoping to guess her thoughts. "Is she upset or disappointed or what?" Unable to read anything there, he answered as honestly as he could. "Listen. I wasn't trying to trick you. Honest. I was just putting two and two together as you were telling it. After all, everyone knows how Santa likes to eat."

"Yeah. I hear tell he puts away more than a quart of that sauce every holiday. That can't be true. Can it?"

Hunter shrugged. "Who knows? Maybe he does."

"You think?"

"Listen. With Santa's ethnicity changing every year, anything's possible. And say, isn't his so-called *metamorphic change* about to happen soon?"

"Yep. A couple weeks from now. On his birthday. At the stroke of midnight. Or, a minute or so after midnight."

"So, he'll change from Asian, or from symbolic Yellow, as he likes to put it, to what?"

"I don't know. I can't keep track. It's either Black or White. Or, uh, maybe it's Brown. I don't remember."

"You, little Miss History Collector, can't remember?"

"Hey, I'm not perfect. Besides, who cares? Santa's just Santa no matter what he looks like."

"Yeah. I guess you're right."

Hunter, saying no more, found himself mentally communicating with his grandpa again. "Grandpa, you could always read me like a book. And if you were here right now, well, you'd know I'd like to kiss Shelly, but I'm a little nervous about trying it just yet."

"Hunter, uh . . ."

"What?" Hunter, immediately attentive, wondered if Shelly had guessed his thoughts. He waited anxiously for her response.

"Hunter," she repeated, her voice soft but pensive, "what do you think would happen if someone were to break the secret-keeping law? Like, uh, . . . like maybe saying something *accidently* to a person outside our Region about Santa changing in appearance every year."

Hunter, struggling to digest what he didn't like

hearing, stopped dead in his tracks. Had he not bit his tongue, he would've yelled, "What, reveal Santa's secret? Are you crazy? I know you have a reputation for being bold and sometimes too candid, but I can't believe you'd do such a thing. How could you even think about breaking the law drilled into us since birth? The law folks migrating to this Region have to pledge allegiance to. The law meant to keep Santa's racial changes secret from the outside world forever."

Hunter, deciding to take a tactful approach—as his father had urged him to do in other situations—said prudently, "Hey, you're not thinking about doing that, are you? Or, uh, you haven't already done it. Have you?"

Shelly, kicking the snow buildup beside their path to smithereens, answered cuttingly, "No I didn't and I'm not going to either."

"Then, why'd you bring it up?"

"Because I think it's stupid to keep secrets all the time, and even more stupid for Santa to hide his racial changes from the whole world. Especially since being different is no longer a big deal."

"But that's the way it is. It's, . . . it's part of our culture. Besides Santa promised his poppa he'd never, ever reveal it to anyone outside this Region. And you know everyone who lives here has to keep that promise. So, that's just the way it is and always will be."

"Okay, I accept it. Okay. So, drop it. Okay!"

Her huffy response told Hunter he hadn't said what she

wanted to hear. Still, he tried reasoning. "Listen. Everyone here has always respected . . ."

"I don't want to talk about it anymore. So, drop it. Please! Anyway, here's my lane."

As the two stopped and faced each other, Hunter's thoughts went into a whirl. "Fiddlin' nutcrackers. Why does she have to get so riled? And what if she leaks Santa's secret. Sooty bricks. I kinda like her, but if she were to blab his most guarded secret and at the same time tell everyone I'm her boyfriend. Oh no. Folks would think . . ."

Shelly, quite astute, sensed her opinion—which didn't seem shocking to her at all, just the right thing to do—had slid a wedge between her and Hunter. "I never should've confided in him. At least, not yet." Hoping their date was still on, she said with hesitancy, "Meet you at the Victory Trees at eleven forty-five. Okay?"

Hunter, saying no more, fished for his pocket watch. As he manipulated it in his hand, he recalled that it had been one of his grandpa's most prized possessions. Now it was his and he cherished it. Staring down at its gold casing, he thought back to the day his father handed it to him, saying, "Here, son, I think you're grown up enough to take care of this. Your grandpa wanted you to have it."

Neither said a word as the watch transferred from the hands of one generation to the next. Still, what Hunter remembered most was not *the joy of receiving it*. Yes, he was surprised and thrilled that his dad was entrusting him with it, but what stuck in his mind as it was placed in his hand was the slight tremor that had passed from his father's fingers to the palm of his own hand.

Keenly observant, as his grandpa had taught him to be, he could see his dad was struggling to hold back tears. Upon hearing, "Son, I think your Grandpa was much closer to you than he ever was to me," he threw his arms around his dad and held him close. In the moments that followed, he sensed his dad—sobbing quietly in his arms—was not only grieving the loss of his father, but also regretting what he hadn't said to him before he died.

Hunter, a little emotional after recalling that scene, avoided Shelly's eyes. "There's always been a schism between those two. But why? Was it because grandpa didn't like dad passing himself off as one hundred percent White? Wow. That sure grated on grandpa's nerves. One thing about dad. Once he made his mind up about something, that was it. And grandpa? He sure clung to his old Indian ways. Yeah. Neither one could see that the other's choices were okay. And me? I was always caught in the middle. Fiddlin' nutcrackers! I like being Indian. Actually, I've no qualms about being part Indian and part White."

"Where'd you get that?" Shelly asked, curiosity widening her eyes.

"Ain't it a beauty? It was my Grandpa's."

"Your Grandpa Swift Bear had a watch like that?"

"Yep. Want to hear the story behind it?"

"I'd love to, but it's getting late."

"Oh. Okay," Hunter said, squelching his letdown feelings with a forced a smile. The story of his grandpa rescuing a lost hunter who had somehow gotten separated from his party, and then, receiving the watch a month later in the mail, was a favorite. "Will she want to hear it another time? Hopefully." He pressed the side notch. The lid flipped up, exposing an ivory face embossed with golden Roman numerals.

Shelly, used to digital clocks, stared at the position of the hands for a moment before blurting out, "Well, bless my snowy-white britches. It's already past ten-thirty."

"And you're gonna to meet me at the Victory Trees at eleven forty-five?"

"Yes. I'll make it."

"Well, . . ." Hunter, not wanting to mess up their first date, hesitated.

"Well, yourself. I'll be there before you." Smiling smugly, sending him a teasing look, she thrust her chin into the air. Then, fishing a streamer scrap from her pocket, she looped it left to right in sync with some fancy footwork. Flitting her way up the lane, she never broke eye contact with him until . . . Turning at the halfway mark, she made a beeline for her front porch, sprinting up the steps, two at a time.

Hunter, mesmerized by her performance, didn't twitch a muscle until the slamming of her cottage door rang in his ears. As it dawned on him what he didn't do, he thrust his hands deep into his jeans pockets and kicked the snow.

"Yelping walrus pups. I missed my chance to kiss her."

◇•◇•◇

CHAPTER 4

Get out of my face, and . . .

An hour later, standing near the Victory Trees, Hunter, eyeing the big hand of his watch inching toward the nine, said, "Where is she? Where is she?" Shading his eyes, he scanned the crowds. "Where is she?" Snap! As he tucked his inherited treasure away, he lifted his eyes. The array of colors in the nearest Victory Trees not only held his attention but struck him as odd. "Crepe paper. Who did this? Hmm. Santa must've sent in a crew after Shelly and I left. Looks kinda pretty. But wow. They sure had to work fast to get this done in what? An hour or less."

Stretching to see over heads, furtively glancing every which way, he—like a broken record—kept mumbling, "What's taking her so long? What's taking her so long?" Like always, when anxiety threatened to trip him up, he pulled his long braid forward and brushed its banded ends back and forth under his chin.

"Taffy tarnation. Who strung up all these streamers?"

"Oh my gosh, that's Shelly's voice." He felt his nerves fraying; but keeping his wit, he pulled himself up on tiptoe and set his eyes to scanning the crowd. Spotting her rounding the Mediator Tree, his eyes popped wide and the bottled-up air that his lungs had been hoarding spewed forth in a low whistle, making way for him to say, "Gosh, she looks prettier than any model I've ever seen on TV."

That, she did. Her black leather boots blended so well with her tights, it was impossible to tell where one stopped and the other began. Her beige, bulky-knit sweater, hiding all but the collar and cuffs of her crinkled white blouse—so easy on his eyes—brought a smile to his lips. Next, her silver earrings, catching the glint of the sun and complimenting her turquoise pendant, drew his attention. "Indian made? Hmm. Maybe. And those bracelets on her wrists, they're cool, but not as cool as her hands. Oh, how I'd like to hold and caress them."

As he took in her classy look, a warm flush crept up his neck, exposing his embarrassment. He hadn't fancied up. He never fancied up. Store-stock blue jeans, tee shirts and quilted plaid shirts were all he ever wore. "Hey, bozo, why didn't you accept mom's offer to buy you some cool duds when she took you shopping last month? At least, those designer jeans. Now, look there. The reason you should've just planted her boots in front of you."

Awkwardness had his tongue tied in knots, making it difficult to speak. And his hands? Other than rubbing them down the front of his jeans, he didn't know what to do with them. "Should I go, or should I stay?" The more he stared at the beauty before him, the more he felt mismatched which in turn played into his itch to run.

"Where's Pietro? Bet he's out there in the crowd somewhere, watching to see what I'm gonna do next.

"Hey, amigo, you'd love it if I bailed, wouldn't ya? Yeah. You'd never let me hear the end of it. Well, amigo, that ain't gonna happen. I'm staying put. And that five-spot? It's gonna be mine. But what do I do now? Grab her? Kiss her? Sweep her off her feet like lovers do in the movies?" Hunter didn't know what to do. Merely saying *Hi* never occurred to him.

Shelly, oblivious to Hunter's antsy behavior, turned to face him, saying, "Hey, what's going on around here?"

Her question, like an unexpected jolt, loosened his tongue. "What? What do you mean?"

"I mean, who wrapped up the Victory Trees with all these streamers?"

"Beats me. Maybe it was a last-minute order from Santa because it's so warm."

"Warm? That doesn't make sense?"

"Yes, it does. Look around. There's a lot of little elfins here today. And if some of them wander in there while Santa's giving his speech . . . Well, I'll wager he'd get flustered. Remember, that's sacred ground to him. As sacred as burial grounds are to us Indians. So, he must've ordered the area barricaded to keep them out."

"Yeah. You're probably right." Paying him no further ado, she rose on tiptoe, shaded her eyes and scanned the area beyond their standing point. "Hey," she yelled, startling him, "look up there."

Directing his line of sight to where she was pointing, Hunter squinted.

"See. See there. There's Mitzi and Santa. Isn't this exciting? They're heading up to our new platform in the sky. Wow. Are they ever gonna be surprised."

Spotting two red-suited figures trudging up the mountainside, Hunter said flatly, "Yeah. I see them. So, who's gonna be up there with them?"

"Nobody. Just them."

"Just them? But who's gonna run all the sound equipment?"

"Mitzi."

"Really. How do you know that?"

"I found out when I volunteered at her office last month. Mark told me. You know, Mark Barthlin, her office manager."

"Mark, huh?"

"Yeah, Mark."

"You like him?"

"A little."

"Did you ever, uh, you know. Did you ever hang with him?"

"Yeah. Kinda."

"What do you mean, 'Kinda'?"

"Well," Shelly said, evasively dipping her eyes to the ground. "We talked on the phone some but couldn't get together because of all my volunteer work and dance classes."

The dramatic drop in Shelly's voice, and her turning away as she finished speaking, told Hunter he had overstepped his bounds. Eyeing her standing with her back to him, he decided to honor her need for private thoughts. Saying no more, he began scanning the crowds for Pietro. Little did he know his questions about Mark had triggered a replay in Shelly's mind of a recent tiff she had had with her father concerning Mark's interest in her, and her interest in him.

"Get out of my face and stop telling me what I can and can't do. You're always treating me like a baby and I'm sick of it."

"Shelly, Mark is twenty-six and —"

"And I'm only fifteen. Right? That's what you were going to say. Right?"

"Shelly, for fiddlin' nutcrackers, I don't mind you dating. Just pick someone your own age."

"Get with it, Dad. This is the Twenty-first Century. Girls date older guys all the time."

"I didn't say you couldn't go out with older guys, but eleven years older is not acceptable to me."

"Eleven years older is not acceptable to me. Eleven years older is not acceptable to me. Eleven years older is not acceptable to me," Shelly taunted, pushing the envelope to the nth degree.

"That's enough, young lady!"

Determined to castrate her father's parental authority, she dug in her heels and fired her next missile. "I don't care if Mark is twenty-six and I'm only fifteen. I'm going out with him and you can't stop me!"

To her surprise, her father's usual mulish challenge, "Oh, yeah. Try me," never left his lips. Instead, he hit her with an ultimatum that sucked the wind out of her sails.

"Okay, Missy. Go ahead. Go out with him. And every time you do, it'll be another three months before I'll sign for your driver's permit. Oh yeah, and if you plan to test me, you can kiss that cell phone of yours goodbye, too."

"What! That's, . . . why that's so unfair. You, you . . ." Bristling with indignation, she stomped off to her bedroom hissy-fitting back at him. "You're cruel and mean and, . . . and I hate you! I hate you! I hate you!"

Shelly never gave in to her father's firmness or admitted he was right. She just retreated — dramatically — with a screaming encore, usually to her room where she could privately wind down her fury with a torrent of tears.

BAM! The slamming of her bedroom door set her window rattling, which she was too angry to notice or even care. Plopping across her bed, she pounded her pillow and screamed, "I hate him! I hate him! I hate him! He's so mean and, . . . and unfair. Well, I'll show him. If he won't let me date Mark, I won't date anyone else for the rest of my life. Or, . . . or, at least, not until I turn eighteen."

Slowly her anger gave way to sobbing resolutions. "I'll show you, Daddy dearest. I'll get my driver's license. And there's no way in Elk Hill that I'm giving up my cell phone. And, *[sniff]* and if you won't let me date Mark, I won't date anyone until I'm eighteen. Then, *Daddy dearest*, I'll be of legal age and there won't be a thing you can do to stop me. Oh, Mark, I, *[sniff]* I . . ."

It was a resolution she intended to keep and did keep, for a whole week until . . . It happened unexpectedly. She, sitting with her girlfriends at a platform-planning meeting, spotted a cute guy popping up from his seat, checking her out. Certain he was eyeing her, she pretended not to notice. But she did notice. Especially his awesome black braid. Like magic, her double-barreled charm kicked in, erasing all thoughts of her no-dating resolution.

An expert at whetting a guy's interest, she squirmed about, repositioning herself into one flirtatious pose after another. A forward thrust of her head sent a veil of hair cascading over her eyes. Jerking her head up, her tresses flew back, exposing her full face. Another forward thrust and her hair fell into a peek-a-boo curtain. Realizing she had a veiled-vantage point, her heart palpitated. As she took in the handsome dude's features, all she could think about was getting time alone with him. Wow. Never did she expect *the how of that* to happen so fast. Moments later, when he volunteered to tie streamers to the new platform posts right after she had, her heart nearly leaped to her throat. And when Santa, dear Santa said, "Two should be enough for that task," she exploded with, "Yes! Yes! Yes!"

Now, dealing with the emotional turmoil stirred up by

Hunter grilling her about Mark, Shelly pulled her foot back and angrily jabbed the toe of her boot into the nearest snow clump. Watching the ensuing spray landing on his ski boots, putting two and two together, her eyes throbbed with fury. "Ski boots! He skied over here. That sneaky little weasel. He knows skiing to holiday events was outlawed a couple years ago when a skier collided with old Jim Kuntz. Poor man nearly died. So, why'd he do it? He, who's so community minded. I can't believe he'd do such a thing. But he did. And where'd he stash his skis?" Intuitively she sought what he claimed to be *his* tree. Sure enough. A lone pair of skis, propped against its trunk, cinched her suspicion.

"You, you cheated," she yelled, stepping back.

"Cheated! What do you mean, I cheated?" Shocked by her sudden accusation, Hunter couldn't imagine what he'd done to merit such an accusation, especially since he wasn't her snow gander. At least, not yet.

"Moose malarkey," she retorted, motioning with an upward thrust of her chin toward his skis. "It took me nearly thirty minutes to hike over here. But you? It probably didn't take you more than five minutes on those speed demons."

"So. What's wrong with that?"

"I'll tell you what's wrong with that. You broke Santa's rule. 'When there's going to be some walkers, everybody walks so nobody gets hurt or killed.' Apparently, you *conveniently* forget that."

Hunter, his bowed head professing guilt, brought the flat of his hands together. Lifting them, resting his chin on his thumbs, he extended his fingers steeple-like. In this pose, he looked like he was about to plead for forgiveness. He didn't. Instead, he justified. "Yes, but I came in on a trail where there weren't many walkers."

"Bog wash! You probably took longer to get ready than me. Then, you raced over here on skis to beat me. So, that means you cheated."

Hunter was quick to protest. "No, I didn't. Listen." Reaching out, he caught hold of her forearms and sought her eyes. "Listen. I decided to bring my skis . . . Well, I decided to bring them just in case something went wrong."

"Oh, please. Not that doomsday stuff again." Miffed, blasting him with an icy stare, she yanked herself free from his grip and turned away.

Hunter, caught at breaking a safety rule—something he wouldn't normally do—struggled with his feelings. Whatever his options, he felt damned if he did and damned if he didn't and terribly indecisive about whether to run or to stay put. His guilt showed in his posture—head hung low, hands jammed deep into his jean pockets, torso swaying to and fro.

As always, when at a low point, even though he couldn't physically be with his Grandpa, he'd turn to him in thought. "Grandpa, I know I was going against Santa's rule, but you're the one who told me to listen to my feelings. So, I did and now look at the mess I'm in."

Silence passed into minutes as stubbornness ricocheted between the two. Hunter, glimpsing the crowds, noticed some of his classmates were slyly watching their drama. "Holy walrus turds. Strangers staring at me is bad enough. But my friends?" The mere thought of them seeing him in a pickle stew upped his embarrassment tenfold. "Too bad there's no bear den around here. I'd sure like to hide in one. Yeah. I know, Grandpa. Running solves nothing." He flicked his eyes to Shelly. "Hmm. Giving me the silent treatment, huh? Fine! Be a snob. See if I care. And, Grandpa, I've had it. This girl's more than I want to deal with right now. I'm out of here."

Turning to leave, the earth beneath Hunter's feet seemed to rise up, delivering a hard slap to his face. He reeled back on his heels as the emotional impact of that imaginary slap jarred loose one of his grandpa's wisest teachings—*In order to win, son, sometimes a person has to be willing to lose.*

"Grandpa, what are you trying to do? Knock some sense into me? Yeah. I know. You're trying to tell me the manly thing to do is to admit guilt, to offer an apology. Oh, all right. I'll do it." Turning to Shelly, he blurted out, "Hey. You're right. I cheated and I'm sorry. Okay?"

Shelly—back to him, arms looped tightly across her bosom—held true to her impish nature. A nose-in-the-air gesture and a flutter of her eyelashes signaled her intent to watch him squirm.

"Fritterin' fiddlesticks! Is she gonna stay mad at me

forever? Sooty bricks. What else can I do? Well, I know one thing. I'm tired of trying to please her. I'm just gonna be me. That's it. And if she leaves, fine. Hey, Grandpa, what do you think of that decision, huh?"

After mentally blowing off steam, Hunter didn't know if it was his grandpa's doing or what, but for reasons beyond him, he started seeing the humor in the whole situation which, in turn, relaxed him some. Deciding to try another tactic—to lighten up like his friends often encouraged him to do—he pulled a white streamer from his coat pocket and playfully dangled it over Shelly's head. She, in turn, swung at it, play-taunting him while trying hard to keep a straight face. She couldn't. Head tilted back, lips breaking into a telling smile, she drilled her eyes into his and said with a tantalizing smirk, "So, the defeated toy soldier waves his white flag and surrenders, huh?"

Hunter, acting as though her words had mortally wounded him, doubled over. Grimacing, tugging at the front of his jacket, he gyrated his head sideways and locked his sad-clown eyes with hers. His facial expression was enough to melt anyone's heart. Even hers.

"Wow! It worked. She's capitulating. And she's having trouble holding back a grin." Eyes locked on hers, he opened his arms and beckoned her to come forth.

"I'm sorry," she said, falling into his arms. "But you see, my dad says I have a bad temper, just like my mom."

"You do?" he stated, faking surprise. At that moment, holding her close, feeling nothing but passion in his heart, he could care less about her temper. What intrigued him, what held his attention, were her sensuous lips, which were now parting to speak.

"Yes. And, of course, my mom blames my grandma. She says I inherited it from her."

"It's okay, my little snow goose. You don't have to explain."

Hunter's heart beat wildly. He could wait no longer. Tenderly cupping Shelly's chin in his hand, he drew her in close. As his quivering lips found the softness of hers, he felt transported to a place he could only liken to a Heaven lit up by a fabulous display of fireworks. Seconds later, with reluctance, he pulled away. "Wow. What a way to make up."

BONG . . . The Green Holly Bell, majestically swinging in the heart of North Pole Village, began its high noon peal. BONG, BONG . . . Its bonging, signaling the beginning of the holiday's festivities, was telling everyone, "Hush. Pay attention." By the time the last high-noon bong bounced off Jingle-Jangle Mountain, the crowds had quieted. All, eyeing the new platform, waited patiently.

On Saucer Plateau—named such because it looked like a saucer sitting atop the rocky cliffs of Jingle-Jangle Mountain—Mitzi sat twenty-five feet below Santa's *Blessing*

Day platform. Tapping her microphone, she said, "Testing, testing, testing. Santa is about to begin his climb. Shout when you see him pop through the chimney top." Turning from the mike, she blew him a kiss. He, about to stick his head into the fireplace, paused, caught it, pressed it to his lips and then blew a smooch back to her. Smiling, his heart pounding with happiness, he began his ascent to the sky-high platform. Below, in the snowy meadows thousands looked on, waiting for him to pop through that chimney top.

Methodically, at a snail's pace, he climbed one soot-free brick after another. The world's fastest chimney popper, the only man alive who could ascend and descend chimneys faster than any rocket could blast off to the moon, slowly worked his way up the newly built chimney. As he did, he smelled and touched each new brick. "Oh, how I love bricks, and if there's a bad one in this stack, I'll find it."

The elves below, waited anxiously. If Santa went in, they knew he had to come out. There wasn't a chimney in the world he couldn't ascend. Anyway, that's what they thought until now. Minutes ticked by. Impatience showed in their mumblings. "What's taking him so long? Did the college students mess up? Did they make the chimney too small? Is he stuck? If he is, how will we get him out?"

After everyone endured ten minutes of worrisome goggling, a young elfin, straddling her poppa's shoulders, shouted, "There he is, Poppa. I see him. There's Santa."

All eyes converged on the rim of the chimney. Sure enough, Santa was popping through it.

The cheering—twenty million decibels of hooting, hollering, whistling and clapping—shook each niche and crevice of the mountain. A faint quiver coming through the chimney's bricks—reminiscent of a vibrating chair—delighted Santa. Chalking its cause to the sheer volume of cheering, he said, "What a treat. I'd sure love to sit here for a while. Can't though. Gotta get my eyes adjusted to this light. Gotta get moving." He blinked and blinked. Finally, able to keep his eyes open without squinting, he slid off the chimney's rim and began his first trot around the circular platform. At each post, he paused. Thrusting his arms high into the air, he turned first left then right, acknowledging the joyous ruckus below.

After his first round, the crowds, on the band conductor's cue, began singing with glee.

> *Oh, it's Christmas Season Blessing Day,*
> *Time to put away our play.*
> *Today, it's party time,*
> *All day we'll wine and dine.*
> *Tomorrow to work we'll go,*
> *Making toy production flow.*

Bright and fresh we'll face each day,
Creating what our plans convey.
Toys, toys, for boys and girls,
Dolls, dolls with pretty curls,
Bikes and skateboards greased and shined,
So, kids can stop them on a dime . . .

On Santa's second go-round, he lingered longer at each post, waving joyously to the crowds below. And what crowds. For eons, only toymakers had braved the gnawing, subzero weather for his Blessing. But today, with tantalizing forty-degree weather, nearly all the workers in the Region had come with their families. Moms, dads, aunts, uncles, grandparents, teenagers and thousands of little elfins peppered the snowy meadows.

Starting his third go-round, Santa stopped short as he contemplated, "Shimmering icicles, . . . No. Wait. Today I can't claim our icicles are shimmering. They're melting. Yeah. As I recall, one was dripping its thaw outside my kitchen window this morning. So, with this warm weather, it makes more sense to say *dripping icicles* instead of *shimmering icicles*." Carrying on, he said with a smile, "*Dripping icicles*. What a day. All the meadows down there are jam-packed. Looks like everyone in our Region has turned out for my blessing. Hmm. I wonder why. Ah, I know. It's this gorgeous forty-degree weather. Yep. That's got to be it."

Pausing, looking out toward Rudolphtown's southwest

mountain range, his eyes, filled with wonderment. "Mother Nature, you're a gem. This weather is perfect. Actually, today everything is perfect. Absolutely perfect. Oh, thank you. Thank you, my dear lady. You couldn't have blessed us with a more perfect day."

CHAPTER 5

I'm sick of doing nothing but . . .

In the North Pole Region, two things changed every year: Santa's ethnic color and the site of the Blessing Day Platform. All knew Santa woke up on his birthday with more or less melanin in his skin and always he picked a great site for the Blessing Day platform. However, this year many questioned the practicality of building it at the tiptop of Jingle-Jangle Mountain on Saucer Plateau, but doubt dwindled after the completed platform stood out like a crown of jewels on the head of royalty.

It was also common knowledge that two things never changed: Santa's hair—snowy-white since birth—and the community's beloved flagpole. It bothered nary an elf that Santa's hair never had a hue of color in it. The flagpole though became a focal point every Christmas Season. Late October, teen elves would pull it out of storage and polished it to a high shine. This year, anchored to the backside of the platform's chimney, it seemed to shout, "Look at me. I'm king of Jingle-Jangle Mountain." Still, it would have none of a king's splendor until crowned with the Blessing Day Flag, an honor bestowed upon it by Santa if, and only if, the platform passed inspection.

Strolling from post to post, eagle-eyeing joints, braces, the fitting of seams, the smoothness of rails, even the overall design of the platform, Santa marveled again and again. Like the chimney he had climbed earlier, he found not a flaw. "Wow. Those students sure did a terrific job. They deserve a double flag up."

Looking down on the hushed crowds, he said, "I know. I know. You're all waiting for my verdict. Well, since you didn't disappoint me, I won't disappoint you." Releasing the cord from its anchored pivot, he worked the colorful emblem up the flagpole. As its green and white stripes surrounding a circular map of the Region unfurled, his heart thumped with pride. "Flag, you're about to cause one fiddlin' nutcracker commotion."

His prediction rang true. Everyone, especially those who had worked on the platform, became caught up in the moment. Each, eagle-eyeing the platform, hoped to be the first to sight the Region's flag flapping in the wind.

"There it is," Hunter shouted, taking the honor.

That did it. Like popcorn kernels popping in a lidless pot, high-fives, catcalls, shrill whistles and exuberant shouts followed. "It passed inspection! Yea! Santa likes our platform. He gave us a flag up. Yea! Yea! Yea!"

Shortly after uncorking their jubilation, the excitement died down and the youth, like their elders, stood quietly, saluting their beloved flag. It proved to be a brief reprieve.

CLANG! The striking of band cymbals, echoing around

96

the mountain, was followed by a drum roll. On cue, the bandleader, dipping his baton to the drummers, announced, "Elves and elfins, our Christmas Season theme song. Please join in." Rhythmic drumming, horn tooting and joyous singing signaled the start of the festive holiday.

Santa, peering down on the crowds, voiced his heart-felt satisfaction. "How beautiful. Our whole region is singing our Christmas theme song. And those vibrations tickling my toes. Wow." Closing his eyes, swaying to and fro to the beat of the music, he added, "Ah, yes. The mountain is humming right along with everyone."

On his next go-round, the streamers Hunter and Shelly had tied to the posts—fluttering, swatting each other's tails—caught his eye and set him to imagining young elfins playing a game of tag, each in turn shouting, "I gotcha. You're *IT* now."

Gazing out beyond the streamers, he drank in the view. Visibility, clearer than a flawless diamond, beckoned him to capture the landscape's beauty for posterity. "How utterly gorgeous," he said, taking in the homes, the factories, the whole of North Pole Village. "Ah, like sunbathers on a beach, your windows and doors are soaking up the warmth of the sun." Slowly hopscotching his gaze to the suburbs, miles out from North Pole Village, he briefly spoke about each.

"Betcha there's at least a hundred reindeer farms out there in Sleigh Valley. For sure, it has the best bakery in the Region. Oh, and their cheese bread. It's to die for. And

Krisville, our software mecca— Lots of gadgetry created there, especially at Mod-Toy Electronics.

"Rudolphtown, I have no idea how many coalmines tunnel through your mountains. But oh, we'd sure be in a pickle stew if we didn't have you as our heat source.

"And you, Kringleland. Yes, you. Your sprawling plains are no more than a smudge on the horizon from here. But distance doesn't equal lesser importance."

Reflecting on his efforts to get Blitzen University and Vixen Vocational Center built in Kringleland thirty years ago, his chest swelled with pride. "Today, with the demand for complicated electronic toys, our young people need all the education they can get. Yeah. Our Urban Planning Committee was right. Kringleland has proven to be the perfect spot for our airport. Ah, this place is so beautiful; and lucky for me, all who live here are loyal to the secret-keeping law." Thinking about that law, how it came about, triggered a long-ago memory.

He slipped back in time, envisioned his four-year-old, brown-skinned self, hopping out of bed, scampering toward the kitchen to beg a drink of water. Halfway there, the sound of his poppa's angry voice startled him. Slackening his pace, he tiptoed the rest of the way. At the doorjamb—hugging the sidewall, trembling—he stole a peek. BAM! BAM! Hearing his poppa double-fist slamming the tabletop, he pulled his head back and popped his eyes wide. Then, his poppa's booming voice—so thunderous it shook the whole cottage—brought his little hands to his ears.

"No two-bit circus will ever bill my son in a freak show. No sir! Not if I have anything to say about it."

When his poppa hesitated, Santa dared another peek. Witnessing him fist pounding the kitchen table again, . . . BAM! BAM! BAM! . . . his big, brown eyes, unaccustomed to the scary scene, quivered a mile a second right along with the rest of his body. OMG! Never before had he heard his poppa yelling in rising crescendos.

"No sir. Nobody's going to put my son on exhibit in a circus. *Not* my Soweto! *Not* my Freddie! *Not* my Pipestone! *Not* my Hum-Bow! *Not* my Otoño! *Not* on my life!" His poppa's chest, rising and falling, fueling the scary, madman look in his eyes, terrified Santa.

BAM! BAM! BAM! His poppa's fist whacking the table a third time upped his heartbeat tenfold. Reflexively, he pulled back and flattened himself against the wall.

"Sh-h-h!" he heard his momma admonish.

Daring another peek, he saw her rocking back and forth, working her knitting needles faster than a machine could drop its candy canes into cellophane wrappers. The sound of his poppa's heavy boots thump, thump, thumping across the floor sent a quiver up his spine. Sighting him approaching his momma, speaking sternly as he leaned into her face, . . . Well, little Santa's breath caught in his throat.

"Listen, woman. Nobody's gonna call my son a freak. I'll make sure of it. I'll protect him from every freak-spouting scoundrel that darkens the face of this earth."

"And just how do you propose to do that?"

"How? I don't know, but I'll figure it out."

"Well, you'd better get yourself calmed down before your ranting wakes Santa, if it hasn't already."

Santa, forgetting his thirst, dashed back to bed. Under the safety of his fluffed-up feather-tick quilt, his little-boy body shook in his long-john pajamas. "*Freak*. Am I a freak?" He'd heard the word for the first time two nights ago, at the circus when, upon leaving, he and his poppa witnessed a young elfin pointing at a man—a man no taller than the lad himself—saying, "Hey, Grandma, look at that funny little man over there. He looks like a freak."

The lad's grandma, eyeing the little person, showed no hesitation in voicing her opinion. "Yes. I guess he does look like a freak and that's why he's in the circus. So, people can laugh at him. Now you just be thankful you don't look like a freak. Because if you did, somebody might stick you in the circus and laugh at you, too."

At the time, Santa thought, "Everyone in the circus must be a freak. Especially the clowns with their orange hair, fat red lips and chalk-white faces. They make people laugh. But laughing at the little man doesn't make sense. He looks like everyone else, except he's only half as tall as other guys."

Santa, in his young mind, saw the circus as a place where animals did tricks and *freakish-looking* people wore glitzy robes and funny hats. Others flew through the air, jumped from ropes and high-up swings, ate fire or did tricks with hoop rings. And the spectators? They either squealed, held their breath or said *O-o-oh* or *A-a-awe* between mouthfuls of popcorn, ice cream or cotton candy.

Thinking it'd be fun to be part of a circus—especially with such yummy goodies to eat—Santa announced upon leaving, "Poppa, when I grow up, I'm gonna be a clown."

Cuddled under his favorite feather tick, his four-year-old mind reasoned, "I must've made poppa mad when I said I wanted to be a clown. Tomorrow I'll tell him I never want to be a clown. Then, poppa won't be mad anymore."

That night, as dreamland cemented his terror into his subconscious mind, little did *little* Santa know how much his poppa's strong words would affect his future thinking and his destiny.

Two years later, sitting in his first-grade classroom, he listened intently as his teacher announced, "Elfins, today we're going to learn about a new law. A secret-keeping law that says nobody in the North Pole Region is to divulge another elf's secret. Not ever. Not unless that secret were to bring harm to someone. Now, do any of you know what the word *divulge* means?"

"That was my poppa's doing all right," Santa said, turning his attention to the elves singing in the snowy meadows below. The last line of the Season's theme song, *Each year's blessing guarantees quality toys under Christmas Trees*, rose up the mountain and faded into oblivion.

"Oh, oh. That's the end of the song. Good thing I stopped my daydreaming." Looking down at everyone cheering wildly, Santa began readying himself to bless his toymakers. This moment, he knew—with families from all over the Region standing together, united as one, waiting for him to speak—would be revered today, but nothing more than a piece of discarded time tomorrow. Presently, the moment seemed to wrap ribbons of anticipation around all those waiting for his blessing. His speech, meant to bolster a gripe-free work environment during the Christmas Season, . . . Well, he, knowing the feast would commence shortly thereafter, always kept it short.

On his next go-round, he purposely lingered at each suburban post and waved joyously to the elves below. They, in turn, cheered with gusto. To him, it seemed as though the more noise they made, the more those lovely tremors penetrated the soles of his feet. He likened them to Fourth of July sparklers, which were a delight to experience, yet quite harmless. "Hmm. Those vibrations feel so good. Surely, it wouldn't hurt to go around a few more times?"

This decision was out of character. In normal, subzero weather, Santa would stroll around the platform no more than two to three times before beginning his speech. However, today, soaking up the sun's warmth, and loving the vibrations soothing his feet, he found it easy to rationalize, "Can't say that it'd hurt to go around a few more times. Besides, look at everybody down there. They're so hyped. Sooty bricks. I bet they won't even notice. Besides, it's a perfect day for daydreaming."

Daydreaming was Santa's most enjoyable hobby.

Everyone knew he could easily get lost in one for hours. Whenever they'd spot him ambling through the ice-sculpture park on a sun-crackling day, they knew exactly what he was doing. Today, although he wasn't walking in the park, sunny, forty-degree weather was all he needed to start a daydreaming tangent.

"Let's see. I want to run through one that has some punch to it. One I can get lost in while enjoying this gorgeous day. Ah, I know. I'll do my favorite. *Mitzi's Charade*." Oblivious to time, he trucked toward the next post, rationalizing, "Hey, everyone down there is having fun. So, I'm gonna have me some fun too."

One finger tap to his Otoño nose was enough to get him started. "Hmm. Let's see. When did Mitzi pull her shenanigans on me? Wasn't it about ten years ago? No. It was eight years ago when I was Black. The last year my poppa, bless his soul, got to call me Soweto before he died. Hmm. If my memory serves me right, I'd just come home from work and I was tuckered. Yep. That's the scene."

Saying no more, Santa slipped back to that long-ago era, when it all began. Walking through the front door, dead tired after a hard day's work, he expected Mitzi to greet him with a big bear hug and a juicy kiss. Instead, she thrust her needlework under his then Soweto nose and screamed, "Do you see this sock?"

Startled, his eyes flipped back and forth from her sharp darning needle anchored between the threads of his sock to her fiery eyes. Swallowing hard, he jumped back. The possibility of his Soweto nose being slashed with that sharp needle drew beads of sweat to his brow. He couldn't believe his eyes. For years, his wife had lovingly used that needle to mend his socks. Now, she was shoving it under his Soweto nose like a lethal weapon. He had to face it. His sweet, loving wife, who rarely raised her voice, was throwing a moose-snorting conniption fit.

"Do you see this sock?" she bellowed a second time.

"Yes. Yes, Mitzi. I see it," he answered, keeping his eyes glued to her needle. Poor Santa. He, so intent on protecting his Soweto nose, could hardly think straight.

For several seconds, the two pantomimed a war dance. He stepped backward; she stepped forward. Weaving between and betwixt overstuffed chairs, the sofa, floor lamps, literally everything in his path, Santa found it almost impossible to pull his Soweto nose more than an inch or two away from her darn, darning needle.

His mind reeled with indecision. "If I grab her arm, will that stop her? Or, will she panic and run that darn needle clear up my Soweto nose? Maybe I should leave? No. Better to try talking to her." Even though exasperated, he forced himself to speak evenly, "Mitzi, why? Why in taffy tarnation is it so important for me to see that sock?"

"Because," she snapped, "it's the last sock I'm ever going to darn. I'm sick of sitting around this cottage day in and day out darning your *darn* socks. Do you hear me? I'm sick of doing nothing but *darning* your *darn* socks."

Santa, taken aback by her angry outburst, reeled. "Why? Why after all these years of blissful marriage, is she going berserk on me? Is it going to be like this from now on? Am I not going to know what to expect from her anymore? Is our marriage doomed?"

Scared and befuddled, he blurted out the first idea that popped into his head. "Dear, why don't you take a vacation. A nice, long vacation. Just you. By yourself. You could go any place you want. Do whatever you want. And you don't have to tell me where you go or what you do if you don't want to. Think about it. Maybe getting away from me for a while will do you good."

Santa, popping out of his daydream, checked on the crowds. "Still going strong, eh? Hmm. I wonder what Mitzi's doing. Knowing her, she's probably wondering when I'm going to stop all my daydreaming nonsense."

It was true. At the control panel below, Mitzi was wondering when Santa's continuous marching and the crowd's excitement would fizzle out. "Hmm. Must be this gorgeous weather." A quick peek at the near-cloudless sky confirmed her assumption. "Yep. No doubt about it. He's up there daydreaming and there's no telling how long he'll keep that up. Could be hours. And the crowds? Listen to that ruckus. Why, they're just egging him on."

For a while, Mitzi mulled over her busy schedule. With the Christmas Season beginning, she needed more help. Shelly Jasselton, who wanted to earn points toward the Moss Bay Scholarship, had come into her office two months earlier to sign up for volunteer work. Not knowing how well a fifteen-year-old would do, she only let her sign up for the month of October. On her last day, finding her to be a good worker, she asked her to stay through the Christmas Season. Sadly, Shelly declined. "Sorry," she said, "but I've already made a commitment to Sleigh Valley Medical Center for the next three months."

"What spunk that girl has. If only I was as free to say whatever I thought when I was a teenager. Yep. Loving parents can sure make a difference. And, of course, we're now living in more progressive times. Times when child abuse isn't tolerated like it was when I was a kid."

Santa's boot-clomping drew her eyes to the beams overhead. "Yes. I know, sweetheart. You're probably up there reveling in some old memory. Just daydreaming away with no sense of time. Knowing you, it'll be hours before you get on with your speech. Yep. It's a given. When that old sun comes out, you start reminiscing. Well, since I've nothing better to do, I think I'll follow your cue and settle into some daydreaming of my own."

Leaning back in her chair, closing her eyes, Mitzi drew forth her oldest memory. She saw herself, a happy toddler, sitting on a flower-patterned linoleum floor, playing with her A-B-C blocks. Her favorite teddy bear and tattered security blanket lay no more than an arm's length away. An indelible memory, etched clearly in her mind, was pulling her back to a kitchen cozy-warm with love.

A squatty, pot-metal teakettle, puffing steam like an old locomotive, sat regally on the cast-iron cookstove's front-most lid. Easily, it held a gallon of water and was kept full, and hot, all the time. Besides being readily accessible for dish washing and cleanup jobs, Gramps and Uncle Tom found it handy for softening their shaving mug soap. As for guests, it was a ready source for hot tea. Of course, if you poured it out, you were expected to fill it up again.

Kitty-corner to the cast-iron cookstove, a feed-sack curtain hung in front of a porcelain sink. Beneath it, through an ugly cast-iron drainpipe, wastewater snaked its way through the outer wall. The bacteria-rich slurry, dripping from the open pipe outside, was all Gramps needed to produce prize-winning roses on his son's rented property — property owned by Stonega Coal and Coke.

Ker-plunk. Ker-plunk. Over time, the kitchen faucet's constant mineral-rich drip, drip, drip, stained the bottom of the sink a rusty red. Mitzi knew this because her eyes were drawn to the pretty color whenever Aunt Rachel or Uncle Tom scooped her up in their arms, so she could hold her own tin cup under the open spigot.

The family's precursor to electrical refrigeration, an old icebox, hugged the outer wall across the room from the hot cookstove. Its three oak doors had latches she couldn't open. Once a week the iceman walked in weighed down with a heavy block of ice secured between the points of his jaw-spreading tongs. Mitzi loved watching him chiseling its corners and sides, sizing it to fit into its allotted space in the icebox. Not a sliver of ice was wasted. All, except the piece placed in her waiting hand, was gathered up and dropped into pitchers of iced tea or lemonade. As Mitzi sucked on her piece, much of it dribbled down her chin, soaking the front of her dress.

One lazy evening, laughter filled the kitchen as the important people of Mitzi's world sat around the table, swapping stories and downing dangerously hot coffee. From her floor vantage point, she found Aunt Rachel's and Uncle Tom's way of cooling their coffee less interesting than the way gramps did his. They just blew across the rims of their cups. Gramps habitually poured his cream-colored coffee into his Depression-glass saucer before sipping it. Fixing her awe-filled eyes on his arthritic fingers, she— holding her breath—would watch him slowly, and shakily, lifting his saucer to his puckered, paper-thin lips before gently blowing ripples across its surface. To her amazement, he never spilled a drop.

On this particular night as she watched gramps blowing ripples across his saucer to cool his coffee, a screech, a swish and a loud slam drew her eyes—and everyone else's—to the screen door. A hush fell over the room as a strange man, acting like he owned the place, sauntered into the kitchen. Staring up at him, she, unlike the others, didn't know all hell was about to break loose.

Swish! Scooped up, rising, her eyes met Aunt Rachel's. She, having lifted her niece in one swift swoop, held her protectively close. Her voice cracked as she urged, "Say 'hi' to your daddy. Say 'hi' to your daddy, sweetie."

Daddy? Her cousins called her uncle daddy. This man was not her uncle. As he approached, she hid her face in her aunt's soft bosom. Stranger shy, she resisted all coaxing. Not until the parlor's French doors closed, did she pull her face away from her aunt's bosom. Voices. Loud, angry voices of gramps and the man called Daddy's coming from behind those closed doors set her to crying, and trembling. Aunt Rachel, holding her close, covered her ears in an attempt to quiet her. It didn't help.

Mitzi didn't know the man called Daddy's intent. But Aunt Rachel did. She knew he had come to take her away, far, far away from the only home she had known since she was three weeks old, since the day her mother died.

When the arguing ended, Gramps emerged from the parlor with disgust written all over his face. Seems he, who had *no legal rights*, knew his son had come to exert *his parental rights* and he couldn't stop him.

The screen door's hinges screeched again and again as Mitzi's treasures were toted out to the car. "Going to your new home," the man called Daddy said through tobacco-stained teeth. With no more empathy than a villain, he wrenched her from her aunt's arms. Like the thief in the night that he was, he quickly carried her outside and plunked her down between an array of dolls and teddy bears piled high on the front seat of his rickety old Model-T Ford. As he did, he paid no mind to the objections and name calling singeing his ears.

Facing the inevitable, Aunt Rachel, Uncle Tom and Gramps took turns sticking their heads into the car to kiss *their* little girl goodbye. Tears streamed down Aunt Rachel's face. Uncle Tom and Gramps, both eyeing the man called Daddy with disgust, just wore sad frowns.

As they drove off, Mitzi remembered staring hard into the man called Daddy's face. Bewildered, she sat quietly, saying nothing. He didn't say anything either. Curious, straining to see over the dashboard, she fused her eyes with the headlights as they traversed unknown territory. The man called Daddy, clutching the steering wheel, drove around bends and up and down hills. Long into the night, at the high speed of twenty-five miles per hour, the jalopy's balding tires bounced over strange country roads, roads leading away from the family who had taken her in, who loved her dearly, whose hearts were now breaking.

Hours later, in the dead of night, Mitzi's sleepy eyes, met by lamp lights, squinted as the man called Daddy carried her through the front door of an unfamiliar house. Once inside, he sat her down on an ironing board in front of a strange woman with short, wavy red hair. The redhead bent over and kissed her. The first and last time ever.

Moments later she found herself kneeling on the kitchen floor, exploring the contents of a toybox while the man called Daddy and the redhead sat at a nearby table, chatting and sipping coffee.

Next, clutching the strange woman's hand, her short legs struggled to keep up as they climbed steep stairs. Upon reaching the landing, the redhead pointed to a boy sleeping on a cot in the room ahead. "That's Willard," she said matter-of-factly. "He's in first grade. You can call him Willy. And over here . . ."

Mitzi hardly had time to take in the sleeping boy's features before she was whisked away to a room across the hall. Once there, she wedged her face between two crib bars and stared into the face of a sleeping toddler, her half-sister, eight months her junior.

"That's Janice, and this is Karen over here," the redhead stated, directing her to the double bed across the room. "You'll sleep with Karen." Twelve years hence she not only slept with Karen—her stepsister who upped her in age by eight months—she mimicked her every behavior. Had to. The redhead demanded it. "You better have your plate cleaned by the time Karen finishes hers or else . . ."

From day one, the redhead indoctrinated Mitzi into her *you-better-do-as-I-say-or-else* philosophy. She soon learned if she didn't jump instantly, she could expect slaps to her face, hair yanking, shoves to the floor, kicks to her shins, violent shaking, hours of chair sitting, to bed with no dinner, etc., etc. All punishments—mostly for false accusation—the redhead peppered generously with scathing putdowns.

Mitzi, too young to have a sense of time, had no idea how long she had endured the redhead's abuse before the

111

man called Daddy dumped her near-naked, badly beaten body onto his brother's doorstep. Years later, her aunt Rachel confided, "That night, your father sped away faster than his balding tires could stir up dust, but not before I got into his face and screamed, 'That bitch of yours. If she were here right now, I'd kill her!'"

On this first of many jaunts back to relative care, Mitzi remembered standing the next morning perfectly still on the kitchen's oak tabletop as Aunt Rachel lifted new dress after new dress up to her bare front. Gramps, sipping his saucer-cooled coffee, quietly looked on.

"Too big," Aunt Rachel said, her eyes inviting input.

Gramps, a man of few words, merely stated, "Well, if ya have ta, take 'em back. Get 'er some that'll fit 'er."

"My poor Aunt Rachel. Each time I landed on their doorstep, she had to go by bus downtown, again and again, until she got the right shoe and dress sizes for me. I guess she had no other choice since I came clothed in nothing but a pair of stinking underwear. Yeah. Had she paraded my black-and-blue body before store clerks, a lot of heads would've turned, which would've embarrassed her to no end. Still, not a soul would've said anything. That's because rarely was anything ever done about *suspected* child abuse in those days.

"And dear gramps. He proved to be my best buddy. Always, I could count on him. Like, he'd sneak me a cookie whenever Aunt Rachel said no. And on sunny afternoons, we'd walk hand-in-hand to the corner drugstore where he'd treat me to candy or an ice cream cone. His small mining pension paid for everything—treats, teddy bears, dolls, dresses, shoes, even the ribbons for my hair. He outfitted me completely every time the man called Daddy dropped off my near-naked, battered body onto his brother's doorstep. Always dirty from head to toe, I smelled worse than an over-used outhouse.

"Yes. The drop-offs were a nice reprieve from the never-ending cruelty of the redhead. But then, they stopped after I turned seven. After the big auction. After the man called Daddy moved his family far, far away."

Mitzi recalled it all. Men moving furniture out into the yard. Vehicles strewn up and down the lane. Strangers hauling away whatever they won by outbidding others. All day, *Sold!* and *Stay out of the way!* fell on her ears. By late afternoon, every stick of furniture was gone.

"We spent the last night in that house hugging the hard kitchen floor, trying to sleep. Creaking noises coming from the empty rooms scared me. The whole house seemed haunted. Sooty bricks. I had no idea what was happening until three weeks later, when we landed in the cold, cold land of Rudolphtown. Seems cousin Martha, who had married a reindeer farmer in Sleigh Valley, put the bug in my father's ear. She wrote, saying the Land of Iceberg's coal mines were going full bore. Harlan's were cutting back. Thus, we pulled up stakes and headed north. What a shock. Howling winds and subzero temperatures greeted us. No trees. No grass. Just ice boulders and snow as far as the eye could see."

Back in Harlan, Mitzi remembered attending a one-room country school situated on a weedy lot. A potbelly stove kept the classroom warm and also dried mittens. A long-handled pump pulled drinking water up from the ground. Two outhouses, or *privies*, stood on the hill behind the school—one for boys, the other for girls. At recess, the younger kids played run-around games on the empty lot. The older kids played card games with the teacher.

In Rudolphtown, the teachers said *elfins* instead of *children*. The school had eight classrooms, drinking fountains, indoor bathrooms and a coal-fed furnace. At recess, elfins played with glee on swings, monkey bars, a merry-go-round and an ice slide.

On the first day of school in the new land, the redhead forbade Mitzi to play on the ice slide. "It'll wear out your snow pants," she said. But Mitzi did play on it, and got away with it because stepsister Karen, who also loved the slide, didn't tattle. Other rules though—controlling, crippling rules—challenged her to find creative ways to get her needs met.

"No, bohunk, I won't sign for you to have a library card. You're not good enough to have one." Stepsister Karen had one. But that was different. Older by eight months, and viewed as a *good girl* by the redhead, she *deserved* to have one.

The next time her classmates filed out to the mobile library, Mitzi made up a lie. "May I go? I have a library card." With a sweep of her hand, Miss Hartson motioned for her to join the others. Giddy with excitement, she ran out the door. Back she came within the allotted time, clutching the book, *Beauty and The Beast*. Not daring to take it home, she read it during free time. The next week she didn't return it to the mobile library. She did, however, sneak out another one. *The Little Lame Prince*.

A week later, sitting rigid in her seat, Mitzi watched as Miss Hartson trailed a finger along a row of books. Pulling out *Beauty and The Beast*, she asked, "Who put this library book here?" The room grew silent. Mitzi, paling, feared her teacher would march over and grill her with eyes telepathically conveying, "Fess up. I know you did it." Thankfully, she didn't. Rather, laying the book aside, she went on with her lesson. But the sack lunches in the cloakroom . . . Now, they were a different story.

Morning recess often found Mitzi edging her way to the front of the school. Beyond the doors leading into the cloakroom, lay an enticing feast—yummy sack lunches. Heisting a treat was easy. All she had to do was tiptoe in, open a bag, grab something, run outside, hide under the front steps and devour the loot.

One morning, upon opening the door, she stopped short and stared. Before her stood Miss Hartson. She expected a harsh reprimand for leaving the play area, but to her surprise, her teacher not only greeted her pleasantly, she made her feel special. Even so, she itched for her to leave so she could get on with her mission. Hearing the office phone ringing, Mitzi's eyes widened. "Yes. She's leaving to answer it." As soon as the coast was clear, Mitzi ran to the shelves and grabbed a lunch bag. Unraveling its top, thrusting her hand deep inside, feeling something smooth, round and hard, her mouth started salivating. Anxious to sink her teeth into her prize, she began lifting the biggest, shiniest, reddest apple she'd ever laid eyes on from the depth of that bag. Up, up, up to the rim she pulled it, but she never got it out. From out of nowhere, something mighty powerful gripped her arm and shook it violently, forcing her to drop it back into the sack. Looking up, her startled eyes met Miss Hartson's. Immediately, shame drew color to her face. Down went her eyes to her *shoe station*. Cringing, standing submissively still, she expected a harsh reprimand. At the least, a spanking with the wooden paddle. But when Miss Hartson opened her mouth, all she said was, "What's your phone number."

Mitzi managed to mumble, "We don't have a phone."

Dragging her feet home that afternoon, she didn't know which she dreaded most. Telling her stepmother or having her teacher contact her. Sadly, both had to happen.

Not long after attending the requested parent-teacher conference, the redhead added *you thieving bastard* to her repertoire of despicable invectives. It, and others, such as, *Shithead, you'll never amount to anything. Numbskull, get out of my sight. Stupid idiot, you can't do anything right. Bohunk, where the hell are you? You good-for-nothing nincompoop, sneaky kraut, dimwit, moron, lame brain, lying thief, low-life scumbag,* . . . All said, morning to night, with the intent to destroy Mitzi's self-esteem.

Third grade was different. The stealing stopped at school and started at home.

Thank goodness for snow pants, especially baggy-legged ones with ankle-hugging cuffs. Everything went down them. The man called Daddy's razorblade packet. The redhead's sewing kit and prized *Wonder Bread* desk calendar. Willy's pocketknife. Janice's *Little Black Sambo* book. Karen's cutout dolls. And almost on a daily basis, bread snitched from the kitchen table to appease Mitzi's hunger. To school it all went via her cuffed snow pants.

Most of her stolen treasures she crammed into her desk. The miniature desk calendar, she proudly gifted to Miss Ness, her third-grade teacher. The bread, she dug out of her snow britches and ate before getting to school.

Days when the redhead's watchful eye kept her from snitching bread off the breakfast table, she'd sneak into greenhouses on her way to school, snitch an apple or pear from a dwarf tree and run like crazy. Later, after all the fruit was harvested, she discovered back-alley trashcans held sustainable food. Burnt toast. Bruised apples. Half-squeezed oranges. Bits of scrambled eggs. Cold, greasy bacon. Whatever wasn't smothered with bitter coffee grounds went into her mouth.

"I never got caught doing that," Mitzi said, "but stealing greenhouse tomatoes on my way home from school, wow, what a daring *Peter Rabbit* adventure that was. I'd climb the fence, sneak into the greenhouse, snitch a couple ripe tomatoes, and then, I'd skedaddle out of there fast, hoping no one had spotted me. I pulled that off day after day. But like most thieves, over time, I let down my guard. Yes. I started dilly-dallying in that greenhouse, gobbling down tomatoes as soon as I picked them."

A grin spread across Mitzi's face as she recalled the day she was down on her knees, hiding between two rows of pots, mouth sucking a tomato bigger than her face.

"Pants! Sooty bricks. Here it is sixty-some years later and those *Farmer-In-The-Dell* pants are still imprinted clearly on my brain. I can still see them, rolled up a time or two, lollygagging just shy of the toe tips of two hefty boots. From out of nowhere they appeared. And they scared the hell out of me. Caught red-handed, I lifted my eyes up those pant legs. Up, up, up, past suspenders, past an open shirt collar, to the stern face of a very old man. I must've been a sight. Me, a dirty little urchin with tomato juice dribbling off my chin. I probably scared him as much as he scared me."

"'So, you like tomatoes, do ya?' the old man asked in the gruffest, meanest voice I'd ever heard. Fear constricted my throat. I said nothing. Sooty bricks. I could hardly breathe, let alone cough up an answer. Still, I kept my eyes fixed on his stern face. To my amazement, his lips broke into a wide grin. 'So, you like my tomatoes. Well, help yourself. Eat all you want.' Short and sweet. That was it. He turned and moseyed away. And me? Well, I sat there dumbfounded, staring at his pant legs waning in the distance. After that though, knowing I could have as many tomatoes as I wanted, I ambled fearlessly into that greenhouse. Each time, I'd look for that kind old man. Sadly, I never saw him again."

In fourth grade the stealing moved back to school.

Returning from her *at-home lunch* one fall day, Mitzi burst into her classroom to the chatter of two classmates seated at the reading table, finishing their lunch. Darting her eyes around the room, she caught sight of something unusual on her teacher's desk—a waded green ball. "Money!" The sight set her fingers tingling. "Could it be a dollar, a whole dollar? Candy. Wow. I could buy a lot of candy with that dollar. Then, if I shared it with kids, they'd be my friends. Yes. I have to get that dollar."

Her overwhelming desire to possess that wadded ball propelled Mitzi into fast-paced thinking. "To get that dollar, I have to trick those two elfins into believing I'm just playing." Wasting no time, she positioned her feet between two rows of desks. Arms out, hands braced on opposite desks, she swung her legs forward. Hop, hop, hop, hop, hop. Up the aisle she flew. Upon reaching her teacher's desk, she scooped up the wadded dollar, did a 360-degree turn and skipped back down the aisle with the intent to hide her booty outside, but . . .

CLANG, CLANG, CLANG . . .

"Oh, no. The bell." She hadn't expected the bell to ring. Elfins started filing into the classroom. Standing in the doorway, Miss Ness was letting elfins in, but not out. Panic set in. "What am I gonna do?" Hardly able to think, but knowing she had to find a hiding place for *her* dollar before Miss Ness called the class to order, she darted her eyes around the classroom. Where, oh where, to hide it.

After questioning Balinda about the missing money for her pictures, Miss Ness announced, "Okay, class, we're going to find that dollar if it takes all afternoon." In an army-sergeant voice, she issued one order after another. "Remove everything from your desks. Empty your pockets. Shake out every book. Take off your shoes. Yes, take off your socks, too." Up and down the aisles she marched, inspecting every book, shoe, sock and sweater pocket. Dollar searching ate up the afternoon. The wall clock said two-forty-five. Still, no dollar was found. Disappointed, Miss Ness ordered, "Put your things back into your desks. It's nearly time to go home."

"Oh, how smug I felt back then. In a few minutes, I thought I'd be walking out the backdoor with that dollar. But then, I turned in my seat and there stood Miss Ness towering over me. So many years ago. I can still see her standing there, hands on her hips, toe tapping the floor, eyeing me suspiciously. And me? I figured the best way to look innocent was to smile up at her. So, I did."

"'Come with me,' Miss Ness ordered. Grabbing my hand, she pulled me down the aisle, beyond the reading table and into her office. As she shut the door, I lowered my eyes to the chair in front of me. Upon it lay a box of greeting cards. 'Off with your jumper,' Miss Ness said, pulling it over my head.

"I remember fighting trembles, hoping for a way out. Ironically, Miss Ness gave it to me when she turned to lay my jumper aside. Moments later, relieved, I watched her pudgy fingers exploring my blouse pocket, trying to ferret out a dollar that was no longer there. Me? I thought that would be it. It wasn't. To my surprise, she undid all my blouse buttons. Off it came. Next, much to my horror, she did the unmentionable."

Mitzi felt her body tensing. The scene of Miss Ness stretching out the waistband of her underwear and peering down both her front and backside was indelibly printed on her mind. Afterward, Miss Ness, her voice sounding overly suspicion, said two words: "Get dressed."

Glad to be done reliving that scene, Mitzi slumped back in her chair. "Whew! I can't believe I chose to endure an embarrassing strip-search rather than fess up. But given how needy I was and what I was going through at home, it makes sense that I complied without making a fuss." Recalling what she did next, she smiled. Back at her seat, hand in the air, she blurted out, "Miss Ness, Miss Ness, maybe the dollar flew out the window."

At that moment, the dismissal bell rang. Almost as if it were bred into them, the entire class rose and turned to face the cloakroom doors. Dutifully, Mitzi waited for Miss Ness to dismiss her row. From where she stood, she could see the crumpled dollar under the greeting-card box on the chair in her teacher's office. Anybody could see it. It was so visible. But nobody seemed to, except her.

The next morning, dragging her feet to school, Mitzi had one thing on her mind. Retrieving that dollar. That is, if Miss Ness hadn't already found it. As she neared the school, only the sound of the whistling wind fell upon her ears. No one was playing outside. Entering the cloakroom, seeing wraps hung on every coat hook except hers, she assumed she was late. With a heavy heart, she shed her wraps and hung them on her assigned hook.

Rather hesitantly she pushed her way through the cloakroom doors. Her classmates could hear her coming and she could hear them twisting around in their seats. They all saw the downcast look on her face, and she saw a sea of stoic faces directing judgmental stares her way. Embarrassed, she cast her eyes to the floor and hung back. No one said a word. They didn't have to. She knew they knew that she, *the lowly White trash girl* standing forlornly before them in a shabby dress, had committed the cardinal sin, *stealing*. And not just once.

Hearing footsteps, she lifted her head to see Miss Ness making her way to the reading table at the back of the room. "Mitzi, I found the dollar you stole yesterday and stuffed under the card box in my office. Now, come. Come over here and sit down on this chair."

Mitzi's wobbly knees slowly carried her to the sentencing table. Turning sideways to sit down, she glimpsed her classmates. All, turned around in their seats, were breathlessly waiting for the drama to unfold.

"Give me your hand," Miss Ness ordered. Twenty-nine students looked on as their teacher pressed ten little fingers of a fourth-grade thief—one by one—onto a black ink pad. No one so much as sneezed as she sequentially, rolled each digit onto a white sheet of paper. Right hand fingers left to right. Left hand fingers right to left. "See this envelope. When that ink dries, I'm going to mail your fingerprints to the police department, and then, . . ."

And then, the elfins kept staring and time marched on.

Four years later, the summer after eighth grade, Mitzi ran. Ran the morning after her stepbrother Willy cornered her in an upstairs bedroom when no one else was at home. Mustering more energy than she knew she had, she struggled free from his exploring hands and ran down the stairs and out the backdoor. His attack was the last straw. If she stayed, she knew he would pursue her until he managed to overpower her. Of course, the hammer would fall on her head, not his. The redhead would accuse her of seducing her firstborn. She would label her a slut and that would give Willy license to pursue her again and again.

The family she ran to—they had five kids—said she could stay one week. "Who else will take me in? Perhaps my dad's cousin, Martha, in Sleigh Valley. Will she and her husband Earl open their home to me?"

Remembering past visits to their reindeer farm—Martha heaping generous portions of meat and vegetables onto her plate, Earl filling her glass again and again with fresh milk, playing hours on end in the hayloft, feeding the reindeer, going for sleigh rides—recalling all that, plus Martha's sweet smile and Earl's playful teasing, she reasoned, "Since they never had any children, maybe, just maybe, . . ."

Six days into her week's stay, on a Friday, she called Martha and blurted into the receiver, "Hi, this is Mitzi McCully, Pete's daughter. Can I come live with you?"

"Well, I don't know. I have to ask Earl and he's out tending the reindeer."

"But I have to know right now!"

Martha must have sensed her desperation because not more than a minute later she capitulated without first asking Earl. "We'll make a run up to get you on Sunday, after church, between two and three o'clock."

Mitzi knew she was going to a good home. What she didn't know was Martha and Earl went to see her father the day after she called them. During their visit, Earl managed to pull him away from the redhead long enough to ask permission to *unofficially* adopt his daughter.

Two days after she had begged them for a home, Martha and Earl escorted Mitzi into their farmhouse kitchen. As she stared at Martha's welcoming feast—her first meal as their *unofficial* daughter—she heard Earl saying, "You may stay as long as you're *good*." When Martha followed his words with, "Eat all you want," she, drooling over the spread on the table, decided instantly, "I will stay. And I will be good. Super good."

Mitzi, popping out of her daydream, said, "*Good.* I tried being good all my life for my stepmother. So, when Earl said that, I decided I'd aim for perfection, I'd be good beyond redemption."

Santa's boots, clopping on the floorboards overhead, momentarily distracted Mitzi. "Still going strong, eh? Yes. I know, sweetheart. You'll be daydreaming up there another couple of hours. Hmm. Guess I'll get back to where I left off in mine."

Leaning back in her chair, she closed her eyes and focused on the word *good*. "Whew! Did I ever work hard to be the *good-girl* I surmised Earl expecting me to be. Trouble was, I thought pleasing others was what being *good* was all about. So, I went out of my way to please Marth and Earl, all their friends and relatives, and even my teachers. Did I vent any anger? No. In my quest to be perfectly good, I always squelched it. Not only that, I truly believed I was responsible for making and keeping everyone happy. Did I know my bowing to everyone's beck and call was turning me into a people-pleasing robot? No. Did I realize I was putting others' needs before my own? No. Did I see that everything I did fed into my faulty perception of *good*? No. Did I see that my faulty thinking was short-changing me? No."

"My, my," Mitzi mumbled as Santa's boot-clopping distracted her. "This sunshine sure has a hold on you. Yeah, I know. You're hooked into a long daydream up there. Well, guess what, sweetheart? I'm doing the same down here.

As the word *good* dredged up an eight-year-old memory, she readily succumbed to replaying all its facets. First, she saw herself rocking back and forth, angrily jabbing her darning needle into one of Santa's holey socks. Stressed to the hilt, depressed about life passing her by, she was yelling, "I'm done with always trying to be *good*. I'm fed up with enslaving myself to others. And holy walrus turds, I'm more than ready to give up believing I've got to prove my worthiness to everyone. And perfection? I'm booting you out of my life, too. Yeah. It's time I stopped being afraid to try new things. Sooty bricks. What've I got to show for my life? Nothing. Fiddlin' nutcrackers. I've lived my married life in this cottage getting good at doing what? Darning socks and baking pies? Pugh. Aren't those great accomplishments!"

Mitzi's ho-hum, humdrum lifestyle hadn't bothered her much until she started watching *The Oprah Show*. On it, she saw so much of herself in Oprah's guests. But they, unlike she, had made great strides in their lives. Through Oprah, they were telling their stories to the world. Stories of how they were breaking old patterns, treading new waters, taking charge of their lives and viewing themselves as worthwhile in their own right.

Seeing similarities in her life and many of Oprah's guests, she suddenly realized she didn't know much of anything beyond baking pies and darning socks. All her life, she, at the expense of *not* meeting her own needs, had directed all her energy into pleasing others. Rarely did she take her own needs into account.

Thinking about how she readily succumbed to *you should* statements in her efforts *to be good*, anger, a lifetime of fermenting anger churned her whole being as she wove, . . . No. It was more like as she *jabbed* her darning needle between and betwixt the threads of Santa's holey sock. Looking up, she spotted Santa coming through the front door. The next thing she knew she was shoving her darning ball, his sock, her darning needle—the whole kit 'n caboodle—under his Soweto nose, shouting, "Do you see this sock?" Through a sliver of a needle anchored haphazardly in his half-mended sock, she funneled— No. she *aimed* a lifetime of suppressed anger and frustration at him. "See this sock? It's the last one I'm ever going to darn. Do you hear me! The last one. I swear to the four winds on Saucer Plateau, I'll never, ever darn another one. Never!"

Mitzi couldn't remember what else she said as she chased Santa around the cottage that day. She did remember, after he suggested she take a vacation—*alone*—

her anger spiraled downward faster than a punctured, hot-air balloon. The idea intrigued her. Not the vacation part. Rather, the doing it *alone* part.

"Taffy tarnation. I haven't taken a trip *alone* for what? Thirty-two years? And why not? Because when I married Santa, cousin Martha told me my place was by my husband's side. 'Always put him first,' she said, 'and he'll take good care of you. And don't be fretful. A man has enough problems at work without having to come home to a nasty tongue.' Dumb me. I took her advice literally. I let it feed right into my faulty belief that *I had to always be good.*"

Above Mitzi and the control panel, Santa, having reached the point in his daydream where he suggested Mitzi take a vacation *alone*, remembered thinking, "Whew, I must've said what she needed to hear." Breathing a sigh of relief, he watched her hand, still clutching his sock with her darning needle anchored in it, drop limply to her side. He rubbed his nose, inspected his fingertips. "Good. No blood. Just perspiration. Guess I can thank my snowy-white whiskers for that small miracle."

Mitzi, sighting Santa squinting his eyes, directing a stare her way, knew he was daring her to play *who's gonna out stare who*. Rather than biting the bait, she threw her head back and stomped down the hall, muttering, "A vacation. A vacation by myself. Just me alone. Not a bad idea. I think I'll start packing right now."

Santa, having second thoughts, groaned. "Oh, no. Why did I add that *getting-away-from-me* part? How will I get along without her? Sooty bricks. I don't know how to cook, or sew, or wash clothes, or shop, or anything. All I know is toy making and, . . . and managing money. Money! She'll need money. But what should I give her? How can I set a limit when I told her to go wherever she wants, for as long as she wants? Oh, well. Guess if I have to, I have to."

Yanking his debit card from his wallet, he made his way to their bedroom. "Here," he said, throwing it on the bed. "Take this. It's good at any North Pole National Bank and the code is 7268 or SANT on the machine's keypad. So, go ahead. Take it. I'll get another." Stalling, he reiterated, "Like I said. Go wherever you want. Do whatever you want. Take as long as you want. But please, remember one thing."

"What's that?" she asked, her tone sarcastic.

"Just remember that I love you. Okay?"

Mitzi, having nothing better to do while waiting for the ruckus above her and below her to stop, stayed with her daydream.

Emptying one hanger after another, she hurriedly packed before losing her nerve. Suddenly, Santa was in the room, throwing his debit card on the bed. He started wooing her to stay. Yes. His words were giving her permission to go, but his eyes were pleading, "Please, dear, please. Please stay." A cold stare let him know she wasn't about to be swayed by sweet talk.

Now, thinking about how cruel she must have appeared—dashing about, collecting essentials for her alone journey, treating him like he was nothing more than a rickety old clothes rack standing in her way—she felt a pang of guilt.

Santa, still marching around the platform, remembered the agony he felt while watching Mitzi pack. With her lips zipped, he, like a whipped pup, hung his head low and dragged his feet back into the living room. Plopping into his recliner, his fingers wandered to his soot jars. He loved comparing new samples from his latest world-wide Christmas Eve run to those gleamed previously from chimneys all over the world. Sometimes, he would even figure out the kind of wood people burned in different parts of the world. Now, toying with the jars brought him no joy. Despair pulled his head to his chest. His body went limp, but his mind kept reeling.

"Never in my wildest dreams did I see this coming. If only I hadn't suggested she take off by herself. Dancin' Prancer. Now what am I to do? I can't take care of this place. I can hardly take care of myself."

Carpet-muffled footsteps interrupted his thoughts. He looked up. Sighting Mitzi gripping a suitcase in each hand, stepping briskly, he sighed heavily. He wanted to say something. But what? What words had the power to stop a determined woman? He didn't know. He longed to reach out, to grab her, to pull her close, to calm her. She whisked by. His eyes filled with tears. Her shunning was more than he could bear. Still, he watched her every move: hesitating; bending a knee; setting a suitcase down. He longed for her to turn around. "Come on. Can't you see my pain? My heart is breaking. Please, change your mind. Please, please, run back to me."

She reached for the doorknob. He cringed inwardly. "Please, please, turn around. Look at me." She didn't. His heart sank. She stooped slightly to pick up her suitcase. He held his breath. With not so much as a glance back at him, she stepped across the threshold.

WHAM!

He jumped. Her slamming the door on their lives— happy lives as far as he was concerned—left him feeling desolate. Tears streamed down his cheeks. "She didn't even say goodbye. Oh, what did I do to upset her? Wasn't I a good husband? Didn't I give her everything she wanted? I thought she was happy. She always seemed to be happy. So, where did I go wrong?"

While Santa and Mitzi were reliving old memories up on Saucer Plateau, the crowds below were egging each other on by upping their shouts each time they sighted Santa. As group after group spotted him rounding the platform, deafening cheers erupted—again, and again, and again.

By now, all the teen elves had hooked up with their friends. All, except Hunter. "Pietro. Where are you?" Repeatedly, he scanned the crowds, and paced. That is, when Shelly wasn't by his side. "It's not like him to stand me up. Maybe he's purposely staying away because Shelly is with me." Despite such reasoning, he kept vigilant. At long last, sighting him off in the distance, running toward the Victory Trees, he noticeably expelled a sigh of relief. "Hey, Pietro," he called out, waving frantically. "Hey, man, where've ya been? I've been looking all over for ya. How come you're so late?"

Pietro, tripping over his own feet, fell toward Hunter. Too out of breath to say anything, he playfully punched his arm. Hunter found this annoying. The way he handled it depended on his mood. Today, with Shelly looking on, he raised his dukes, inviting playful sparring. The two, facing off, looked like an odd Mutt-and-Jeff pair. One short and squatty. The other tall and slender.

Pietro envied Hunter's rock-hard physic. He longed to be his mirror image. Often wished he could be his twin. "He's lucky. Nobody teases him like they do me. Look at him. He's slim as an eel. And me? I got stuck with this fat gut. And my dad, he calls me *butterball* right in front of my friends. Does that ever hurt."

Each time it happened, Pietro would downplay his father's insensitivity, and his hurt feelings, by laughingly saying to his friends, "Hey, what can I say. It's in the genes."

Afterward, knowing he could eat whatever he wanted in his family's restaurant, he'd gravitate to the pastry counter. Sinking his teeth into a sweet Danish role or a piece of scrumptious pie seemed to deaden his emotional pain. At least, for a little while. And if one pastry didn't do the trick, he could always eat another, and another. And he would, until he felt totally numbed.

"Hey, man, come on. Tell me. Where've ya been? And how come you're so dang out of breath?"

"I uh, I got stopped [gasp] by uh, . . . See uh, my ol' man, he, [gasp] he waylaid me just as I was about to, to uh, skip out. And I had to, I had to, [gasp] to stay and help him."

"Today! What was so important that it had to be done today? I mean, what'd he make you do?"

"Uh, the Candy Man . . . Oh, hi Shelly. I uh, . . . I mean, Mr. Jasselton."

Shelly laughed. "It's okay, Pietro. I know everybody calls my dad *the Candy Man*."

"Yeah. Well, anyway, ya see, the Candy Man, he uh, he set up a meeting this morning at our house with some of the Village restaurant owners."

"For what?"

"Hey, bozo. Whadaya think? To get some food over here. Ya know, in an organized fashion."

"Wow. That's some insight."

"Yeah, well, the Candy Man said with this warm weather and the beautiful view from up there on top, he figured Santa would probably spend at least a couple hours, maybe even the whole day, up there daydreamin' about some new toy project or somethin' fun before givin' his speech and . . ." Pietro stopped midstream. Cupping a hand over his eyes, scanning Saucer Plateau, he grinned. "Yep. Just as I figured. That's just what he's doin', huh?"

"Uh-huh." Hunter grinned knowingly. He, Shelly, and those within hearing distance nodded their heads in agreement.

Pietro, smiling, went on with his story. "Yeah. Everyone knows how easy it is for Santa to get caught up in a daydream. So, gettin' back to Vic Jasselton and my dad. They, and a bunch of other restaurant owners, met this mornin' at our house to figure out where each would set up their food wagons over here. Ya know. To make it handy for everyone to get some chow. And I uh, I just finished helpin' my ol' man set up his."

"So, where's he set up at?" Shelly asked, sweeping her eyes over the meadow.

"Way over on the other side of the mountain."

She looked at him as if to say, "Why?"

Pietro, reading puzzlement in her eyes, didn't hold back. "Hey, I don't want my ol' man anywhere near us." Turning to Hunter, he said, "And you, bozo. You owe me big time."

"Whadaya mean, 'I owe you?'"

"Because I told my ol' man if he wanted my help, then Hanna's Hamburger Wagon had to get the spot next to the Victory Trees. See. Over there. They're settin' up right now.

Just outside *your* so-called tribe's tree."

"You're kidding me. Right?" Hunter's eyes lit up like neon signs. "Wow. That means I get my wish. A hamburger and French fries on Christmas Season Blessing Day." Doubling his fists, jerking his elbows back, he shouted, "Yes! Yes! This is my lucky day. And hey, man, I could kiss you. But trust me. I won't. Hey. What the . . ."

Glimpsing Shelly talking with her brother, giving him a side hug, he hesitated. "Hmm. Jordan doesn't look like he's afraid of her. They look like they're having fun. Sure doesn't fit what everyone's told me about them." Facing Pietro, seeing a dumbfounded look on his face, he surmised he, too, was baffled by the friendly interaction going on between the two.

"Hey, amigo, know what?" Grabbing Pietro's arm, he blurted out what he had intended to say before getting distracted. "For making it possible for me to get a hamburger today, I'll eat that five spot you owe me. That okay with you?"

"Yeah, man. Thanks." Pietro, thrusting his chin to where Shelly stood with her brother, expressed his disbelief. "Hey, would ya dig that. I ain't never seen them gettin' along. Shelly's never been nice to her bro. Never. Hey, man, wha'd ya do to that chick anyway?"

Hunter, smirking, answered nonchalantly, "Just kissed her. That's all."

CHAPTER 6

This old gal's no quitter.

Santa, moving around the platform like a car set on cruise control—and still daydreaming—had no idea Mitzi, sitting below, was reliving her own version of what they had both dubbed as *Mitzi's Charade*.

After slamming the cottage door, the ramifications of what she was about to do hit Mitzi. "Am I really going off by myself? Oh my gosh. What have I done?" Staring out at the world she was about to step into *alone*, doubt, overshadowing her initial determination, played havoc with her thinking. "Dare I? Or, should I say, 'How dare I?' Taffy tarnation. I don't think I can do this."

Knees going rubbery, heart pounding a mile a minute, plus guilt riddling her thoughts, cued her to the fact that panic was fast setting in.

Keep it together, girl. Keep it together.

"Yeah, right. You keep it together, you *nattering Tomacita.*"

Listen, girl, you better start breathing in slower than you're breathing out. And get rid of that should *rubbish in your head.*

137

Mitzi, balling her fists, scrunched her eyelids together as she tried squeezing the life out of the *should* stuff invading her head. Her efforts proved futile. Rather than letting up, the blathering blitz intensified. *"You should* not have done that. *You should* be ashamed of yourself. *You should* go back in there. *You should* beg Santa for forgiveness. Then again, maybe *you should . . ."*

With a head fogged with indecision, Mitzi found it hard to defend her actions. "But I uh, I, I, . . ." Eyes focused on the door, envisioning herself straddling its threshold, she vacillated from wanting to run back to *her* Santa to itching to explore the world. The possibility that she could have both familiarity and an adventure into the unknown didn't occur to her. She felt she had to choose. Indecisiveness tore at her. Part of her wanted to slip back inside and melt into the comfort of Santa's arms. She pictured herself doing just that. Crying, asking for forgiveness. But another part of her wanted . . .

Hey, girl, it's either now or never. Make up your mind.

"Now or never, huh? Okay. I'm going." Her gumption restored, she tightened her grip on her suitcases and marched herself down to Dearborn Bus Station. Once there, she purchased a ticket to Kringleland.

"By tomorrow I'll be on a plane, heading to . . . Sooty bricks. I haven't thought that far ahead, and I'm still not sure about all this." Closing her eyes, she envisioned herself plucking petals off a daisy, like she'd done when longing for her birth mother as a child. Only this time, instead of chanting *Does she love me? Yes. She loves me*, her lips spewed forth *Shall I go, or shall I not go? Shall I go, or shall I not go?*

Fret over making a major decision took the stage. "Maybe I should tear this ticket up and go pour my heart out to Shooting Star. Get her opinion on all this. She's a consultant. She'll take the time to listen to me. But is it fair for me to bother her, especially now, with her recovering from that nasty snowmobile accident and all? Poor girl. She doesn't even know if she'll ever walk again, and . . ."

The loudspeaker blasting—*Now boarding at gate three for Kringleland*—forced Mitzi to decide. "I'm going," she said crisply. Rising to her feet, she headed for gate three.

Boarding the bus, sliding into a window seat, she continued to mull over her dilemma. "So, where do I go after I get to Kringleland? I certainly don't feel like going on a tourist binge. Hmm. Maybe I'll stay in a hotel for a few days, do some shopping and then go home. No. I want to do something different. But what?" Hoping to spot something that might trigger an idea, she stared out the window. To her chagrin, only pitch-blackness greeted her probing eyes. "No help there." Tilting her head back, she studied the ads plastered above the windows.

"Snowmobile parts. Sorry. Machinery is not my thing. The best shampoo. I'll stick with mine, thank you. Sable's Department Store. Ah, those are spiffy looking shoes. Computer software. Sooty Bricks, what I know about computers wouldn't even fill a thimble. Trade school. Hmm, trade school." Reading on, Mitzi's eyes sparked with interest. "Want to make some changes in your life? Courses at Vixen Vocational Center will change your course of life forever." As the ad's meaning sank in, she nearly jumped out of her skin. "School. That's it! That's what I'll do." A bubbly feeling filled her chest. Bouncing up and down, she grinned from ear to ear. "Yes. School, it is. Hmm. Elfins take vacations *from* school. But me? I'm going to spend my vacation *at* school. Now that's a switch."

Is that what you want, girl?

"Sure is."

Mitzi felt like broadcasting her decision to the whole bus, but rather than making a fool of herself, she sat quietly, engrossed in thought. "Wow. What a way to escape my humdrum life. Instead of flying off somewhere and spending Santa's money on stupid stuff, I'll invest in myself. I'll take some classes. Yeah. I can brush up on those office skills I learned way back in high school but never used. Yes! Yes! Yes! School, it's gonna be."

A smile lit her lips. "Santa, you wouldn't expect me, or even want me to do this. But come to think of it, you did say, 'Go anywhere you want. Do whatever you want. Take as long as you want.' So, in a way, I already have your blessing. Yes. For a change, I'm going to invest in myself."

Mitzi, still floating on cloud nine, not only pictured herself as a happy, energetic student, she started thinking beyond school. "So, what will I do afterward? Get a job? Become a nine-to-five professional woman? Hmm. I wonder what Santa would say if I did. Guess I'll cross that iceberg when I come to it. But this is something. In one day, I've made two major decisions. Now that's progress."

Well, kudos to you, girl. You're finally taking charge of your life.

Mitzi, exhausted, ignored her *nattering Tomacita's* dig. To no avail, she fought sleep's invasion. The drone of the bus motor, plus a musical ditty coming from a passenger's transistor radio—*Let your fingers do the walking*—began pulling her into la-la-land. She drifted off mumbling, "First, I must change my identity, change my ident-i-ty, change my . . ."

◇•◇•◇

As sleep's hold took effect, Mitzi's subconscious whisked her off to the theatre. From her balcony seat, the stage seemed miles away. Through binoculars, she panned over it. Dipping the ocular lenses to the floor, names—column after column of names—met her eyes. "How odd. That stage looks like a page from a telephone book."

The musical ditty, *Let your fingers do the walking*, filled her ears. "But where's the orchestra pit?" Tilting her binoculars, she scanned the front of the stage, but found no sign of one there. Next, running the ocular lens up a side curtain, she spied a baton dipping to and fro. A closer look had her saying, "It's not a baton. It's a radio antenna conducting an orchestra that isn't there. Now, that's weird."

Cued to enter when the radio's antennae dipped toward the on-stage entrance, two ballet dancers pirouetted

141

onto the telephone-page stage. Up, down and across it they cavorted in sync with the advertising ditty, *Let your fingers do the walking*. Mitzi, enthralled, watched as they contorted their limbs and heads, mimicking thumb-finger movements. "How poetic and expressive. And what a novel idea. I've never seen dancers pretending to be hands in a ballet before."

When the music ended, the male dancer bowed low. To his left, his partner gracefully lowered herself to the floor in a perfect split. Down, down, down she went, rhythmically swaying her arms like two cobras being charmed by the movements of a flute. Mitzi, lifting her binoculars for a better view, caught sight of the young dancer touching the toe tip of her right slipper, signaling the finale of her bow. As she zeroed in on the gal's fingertips, the lens also captured part of the telephone-page stage. This drew her eyes to the list of names raying out from under the dancer's foot. Drawing her binoculars down the row, she mouthed one name after another until she came to one that appealed to her. For some reason, she felt compelled to memorize it. Why, she didn't know.

"Last stop, Kringleland. We'll be pulling into Snowcap Hotel in a few minutes, folks."

The bus driver's announcement roused Mitzi. Like many of the other passengers, she stretched and yawned herself to wakefulness. She checked her watch. "Hmm.

Almost ten-thirty. Glad we're finally here. These old bones of mine are aching for a comfortable bed." Sluggish and cold, she stood in the aisle, waiting her turn to exit the bus.

Stepping off, she pulled her parka's fur collar up around her face to appear less conspicuous. "No way do I want any elf recognizing me and messing up my plans." Lugging a suitcase in each hand, she approached the lobby.

"Name, please," the perky desk clerk greeted, giving her his most professional smile.

Mitzi didn't hesitate. The name the dancer's fingers had pointed to in her dream was still fresh in her mind. "Ponseta," she said, tensing her vocal cords in an effort to disguise her voice. "Elf Laura Ponseta." Knowingly avoiding the clerk's eyes, she picked up a pen and scribbled Elf Laura Ponseta on the hotel's registry.

"No way do I want any elf finding out I'm here on a self-improvement journey. So, until I complete it, I'm going to think, eat, sleep and be Elf Laura Ponseta. It'll be my own private secret. But I probably should let Santa know I'm okay." Scoping out the lobby, she spied a postcard rack at the far end of the reception counter. Wasting no time, she selected one and quickly penned a short note.

> My dearest Santa,
> Just want you to know I'm taking a different kind of
> vacation. I'll be home when it's done. When that will be,
> I don't know. Yes, I'll remember that you love me, and I
> love you, too. Mitzi

Spying a Penguin Courier mailbox near the revolving

doors, she deposited it before running to catch the elevator, held open by another late-night traveler.

"Well, here goes." Feeling somewhat lightheaded, she reminded herself to breathe. "I can't believe I'm doing this. To think, I'm going to sleep in a strange room tonight, alone for the first time in thirty-two years." Briefly glimpsing the other woman in the elevator, she wondered if she, too, was seeking reprieve from a humdrum life.

Upon awakening the next morning, Mitzi blinked to get her bearings. As she took in her surroundings, she pulled herself up and swung her legs over the side of the bed. Stretching and yawning lead to questioning the merits of her actions. "Oh, what in taffy tarnation have I done?" Santa, in his frantic state, flashed before her eyes. "I can't believe I nearly shoved my darning needle up his nose and not just once, but . . . Oh my God, how many times did I do it!" She shook her head, hoping to rid herself of the haunting image. "That was a ghastly thing I did last night. And this school idea. It's probably stupid. Fiddlin' nutcrackers. Whatever possessed me to run off like that? Am I losing my mind?"

Your mind? Girl, you're insane. Oh, go ahead. Hightail your fanny back home. Beg Santa's forgiveness. Go on. Go. Let your passive side reign.

While her nattering Tomacita played havoc with her doubt, Mitzi scoped out the room. A full-length mirror

144

hung on the opposite wall. Her clothes, thrown helter-skelter the night before, lay strewn on the floor and across a leather chair. A wall-mounted TV, she noted, could easily be viewed from the bed. "All typical hotel stuff," she said, setting her eyes on the telephone beside her.

Yes. Go ahead, you yellow-bellied snow goose. Call the desk clerk. Find out when the next bus leaves for North Pole Village. Go back to the same old, same old. Go on, girl. Get it over with.

Mitzi's shoulders sagged. Indecisiveness, like a yoke around her neck, weighed her down and triggered guilt. "Dumb me. What I did last night was stupid. Really stupid. And poor Santa. I shouldn't have . . ." Reaching for the phone, sighting her aged body in the full-length mirror across the room, she drew a hand to her mouth and cringed. "Is that what I really look like? Holy walrus turds. It's been . . . It's been forever since I've taken a good look at myself." The aged reflection greeting her eyes was enough to quell her *nattering Tomacita.* She did not like what she was seeing.

"Yuck. You're a mess, Elf Mitzi Claus. You look worse than a 99-year-old mistletoe berry. And your hair? Land of Icebergs. It's so dull and witchy looking. Sister, you look worse than old. You look ancient."

Mitzi wrinkled her nose in disgust. Scrutinizing the whole of herself in the mirror, she couldn't believe . . . No. It was more like she didn't want to believe what she was seeing. "I look so dowdy. And my hair. It has no luster." Pulling her fingers through it ignited a desire to recapture its vibrant luster, its bounciness, and her youth. She grabbed a clump of hair and turned it upward. Split end after split end met her eyes. "My wedding-day pact with Santa . . . Why did I ever agree to never, ever cut my hair?" Reluctantly, she set her eyes back on the mirror.

"Fiddlin' nutcrackers. What's, . . . what's happening!" Like mist being usurped by the sun, her old-lady image was fading. In its place, the image of a beautiful young bride filled the frame. Immediately, she zeroed in the woman's cascading curls.

"What gorgeous hair. Wow. The way it flows down the back of her gown . . . Why, it couldn't be more beautiful."

In the mirror, the bride turned, exposing her face. Mitzi's heart skipped a beat. "Why, . . . why, that's me. In my wedding gown. But, . . . but how can that be?"

Before her startled eyes, Earl, cousin Martha's husband, materialized in the mirror. His weather-beaten face tugged at her heart. "Oh, Earl, you were the best father ever and even though you weren't my bio dad, I loved you dearly."

As his image receded into the background, her face saddened. A second later, she brightened as Santa's young face, framed by his signature-white hair and well-trimmed beard, came into sharp focus. She stared at his gallant figure. "Oh, you were so young, so handsome in your red tuxedo. Red. It reminds me of his favorite saying. *I like red, no matter what color it is.*" She giggled.

In the blink of an eye, the scene changed to Santa stepping up and slipping an arm around the young bride's waist. Mitzi, gasping loudly, drew a hand to her lips. "Oh, that long-ago day. Santa, you knew my nerves were a jumble mess, didn't you? That's why you put your arm around me. To steady me. And me? I was so taken by how handsome you looked in your red tuxedo, I never heard a word the minister said." Mitzi didn't know why she was being gifted this glimpse back in time. She did know though, that she was transfixed by it. She was also aware of the gratitude she felt in her heart.

In the next scene, she couldn't help smiling as the minister turned and said to Santa, "You may kiss the bride now." A bit giddy, she wiggled on the bed. "I know what you're going to do. You're going to zero in on my ear instead of my lips." As he fulfilled her expectation, the mirror panned over the attending guests. Their giggles delighted her.

Unexpectedly, an elderly gent seated in the front row blurted out, "Oh, my, I think Santa needs some lessons in love." Again, the whole sanctuary burst forth with laughter.

Drawn into that long-ago moment, Mitzi chuckled. "Holy walrus turds. I'd forgotten all about that."

Looking on, she anticipated Santa would . . . No, she knew precisely what her gallant sweetheart was about to do. True to form, the mirror showed him pushing aside her beautiful curls. Holding her breath, she watched him whispering into the bride's ear.

"My love, your hair is more beautiful than Northern Lights dancing across a midnight sky."

"You're such a romantic," she said, "and I like it."

"Promise you'll never, ever cut your gorgeous hair?"

Mitzi nodded agreement along with the young bride. "Yes. I promised that all right. I wanted to please him so much I willingly agreed to it. Actually, back then, I was so insecure, I feared if I didn't watch my Ps and Qs, if I didn't do everything he asked, he'd reject me."

As quickly as it had appeared, the bride image faded from the mirror. Watching it wane, seeing it being overtaken by her old-lady image, Mitzi's smile faded.

"That was a dumb pact I made with Santa. And so long ago. Funny, back then it didn't seem dumb. Yeah. I willingly agreed to it. Guess it just proves how submissive I was back then, and still am. Oh, how I wanted to please him. Holy walrus turds. Not only did I want to please him, I wanted to please everybody else, too. How sad. I guess I was just too scared to risk being real. Too afraid if I did, others would reject me. Especially if I screwed up."

Mitzi flung her head back. Glaring at her mirrored reflection, she jokingly said, "Well, now, you drab old hag, are you going to spend your morning crying over those gray hairs, or, are you going to do something about them?" Taking charge of her life for the first time *in her life*, she turned away from the mirror, picked up the phone and pressed zero. To the operator, she spoke in a voice echoing her new-found spunk. "Operator, connect me with the hotel's beauty shop, please."

An hour later, strolling into Crystal's Hair Styling Salon, Mitzi felt like a teenager primping for her high school prom. This was especially true since she had never experienced the magical touch of a trained beautician's fingers. While waiting, she flipped through a hairstyle magazine. Just as a confident young elf approached to take her under his wing, a short hairdo with curly ringlets caught her eye. "This is what I want," she said crisply. "And I want that auburn hair color, too."

As the beautician snipped off her dull, gray tresses, Mitzi let out one gasp after another. By the time the hair on her head—what was left of it—matched the picture she had chosen, excitement had her heart beating wildly. Staring at her *new 'do* in the mirror, impressed by the way the color accented her eyes, she coolly remarked, "Looks great. And, and my eyes. They look like . . . Why, they look like they're full of life now."

Bolstered by her *new 'do*, she trotted off to sign up for classes at Vixen Vocational Center. Under the fictitious name of Elf Laura Ponseta, she enrolled in a business refresher course, a displaced homemaker's class, a computer class and an assertiveness training class. When the counselor urged her to take the latter, she thought, "I better not question him. I probably need that one more than the others."

As Mitzi moved through her self-improvement journey, she not only conquered her fear of trying new things, she started seeing many old incidents in a new light. One day, arriving early for her assertiveness training class, her mind drifted back to what her high school classmates had coined about her for their graduation memory book. At the time, their conceived ditty, *Elf Mitzi McCully, she thought she couldn't, but she could*, seemed odd to her.

"I thought what my classmates penned about me was stupid. But oh, how right they were. All these years, I not only thought I couldn't do many things, I held back from trying many things. I was afraid others would judge me as *not okay* if I didn't achieve perfection at whatever I did. Dancin' Prancer. I've been a prisoner of my own worries. All that time wasted. Well, not anymore. I'm not wasting one more minute. I'm done trying to meet others' expectations. I'm done being afraid to take risks."

To fill her evening hours, Mitzi joined a fitness club. Working out faithfully, she felt more vibrant, slept better and lost thirty pounds. To outfit her *slimmer* figure, she sought the advice of a wardrobe consultant. Learning spring colors complimented her skin tone, she went on a shopping spree that would've sent Santa spinning like a top.

"Elf Laura Ponseta, you look dazzling," she said, taking stock of her slim figure in the department store mirror. "Wow. You look twenty-to-thirty years younger. Santa will never recognize you."

Even though taken aback by her mirrored reflection, Mitzi felt something was not quite kosher. Scrutinizing her face from every angle, she finally figured it out. "It's these kinky, wire-rimmed glasses." Planting her hands firmly on her hips, flinging her shoulders back, she lectured away.

"Say, spectacles, you might've gone well with my dull, gray tresses, but you sure play havoc with my *new 'do*. Sorry, spectacles, but you'll soon be out of my life."

Not wanting her new look to *look* off kilter, Mitzi made an appointment with an optometrist. At her office a few days later, she chose blue-tinted contact lenses. "Might as well go mod all the way. Be a little different." Catching the doctor's dry smile, she felt like she was being sized up. "Hmm. Does this doctor think I'm a crazy old lady?"

Her *nattering Tomacita* quickly brought her to her senses. *Hey, girl, you gave up being perfect. Remember? So, stop thinking you have to act a certain way to please this doctor.*

"Perfect I'm not. But this is the perfect time to practice what I learned in my Assertiveness Class." To counter any signs of uncertainty in her body, Mitzi held her head high, squared her shoulders and smiled. In her remolded stance, she studied the optometrist's eyes. To her, they were projecting, "My, you're sure an assertive woman."

Three days later when she picked up her new contacts, the optometrist surprised her by asking, "Would you mind if I kept your old wire frames?"

"Mind! Be my guest."

"Thanks. You know, most people won't part with these things when they're this old."

"Really. Well, I'll have to say, they are old. I got them from my second cousin Martha. See. Whenever I had my eyes checked, I had new lenses put in them. I'm a little sentimental about them, but change is in the wind. It's time

I let them go."

◇•◇•◇

Mitzi, cognizant of Santa's boots thumping overhead, remembered leaving the optometrist's office and heading for the nearest North Pole National Bank to make a cash withdrawal. Staring at his debit card, she felt a pang of homesickness. She missed Santa. Missed him terribly. Still, she would not let herself think about him, except, when using his debit card. Self-preservation she called it. Her way of coping without him.

Call him. Call him, her *nattering Tomacita* badgered as she slipped the card into the bank machine.

"No. If I were to do that, I'd never finish what I've started. Besides, I know him. If I call, he'll pressure me to come home and this old gal's no quitter." Quickly, before her *nattering Tomacita* could rattle her cage with any more homesick thoughts, she tucked the card back into her wallet. Even though she said, "Out of sight, out of mind," her thoughts lingered on Santa and his debit card.

"Why didn't I ever get a debit card of my own? Stupid me. I just relied on him to give me cash for everything. Well, if I ever get a job, I'm going to open an account and get one. And hey, even if I don't get a job, I can still do that. I'll just tell Santa I want a monthly stipend to spend as I see fit. After all, homemaking is a real job."

CHAPTER 7

Enough is enough!

Santa, set on milking every second of the unusually gorgeous day, kept circling the platform like a robot programmed for automation. Approaching each suburban post, he'd raise his hands and wave to the crowds below. Moving on, he'd pick up where he left off in his daydream. He had just reached the part where Mitzi's postcard puzzled him. Especially the words, *different kind of vacation.*

"Mitzi, what in taffy tarnation are you up to? Are you hiking across Siberia? Or, maybe riding an elephant on some African safari? Did you join a commune somewhere in the States? And what do you mean by, *I'll be home when I'm done*? Done? Done with what?"

At first, the passing days didn't bother Santa much. Figuring a week or two of resort pampering would subdue his wife's needle-jabbing, ornery attitude, he went about his business as usual, a little lonely, yet tolerating her absence. At the end of two weeks, he assumed a suntanned Mitzi would come running home, fully cured of her ornery attitude and ever so happy to resume her wifely duties.

Sadly, by the time another week had passed, he was pacing the floor every night. When the crossed-off days on his calendar leaped over a second month and into a third, he was more than beside himself. He jumped every time the phone rang and ran to check the mailbox each evening. The days dragged. Worry consumed him. His stubborn nature, plus believing Mitzi's leaving was his fault, prompted him to keep her disappearance to himself. On the seventy-fourth day though, as he circled the date on his office calendar, his tightly wound nerves snapped.

"Enough is enough!" BAM! Down went his fist, rattling everything on his desk. The aftermath of that forceful blow pulsated through his arm. He winced. However, the pain in his arm was nothing compared to the anger singeing his nerves. It, pushing for release, was coursing through his veins like a herd of elk running amok. He wanted to scream at the top of his lungs. He felt like fist-pounding the walls. Knowing Malka was sitting on the other side of his office door, he held back. "No. I can't blow my stack now. Not at my toy factory. I've got to keep myself in check."

Feebly attempting to halt that which he couldn't, he sucked in and spewed out what seemed like every air molecule in the room. It didn't work. His mind, racing out of control, and his gut, blasting his breakfast with acidic juices, were sabotaging his efforts.

"Mitzi, where in taffy tarnation are you? Disappearing for two and a half months is not okay!" The heat of those words set his eyes ablaze and triggered more wrath. "Taffy tarnation. If you were planning to stay away for good, why didn't you tell me? What are you anyway? A yellow-bellied snow goose?" Pausing, he sipped his latte, which he'd taken to drinking each morning to calm his nerves.

"Okay, Lady Snow Goose, just what kind of moose malarkey are you up to? If you think you're coming back here and making me believe resort hopping is all you've been doing, you're crazy. Icebergs would have to turn into gushing geysers before I'd believe that story. I'm not stupid. I know you too well. You're up to something." As he stopped to gulp down more coffee, his frustration escalated.

"Mitzi, are you dying or something? Oh, don't tell me you've got some kind of life-threatening disease. Fiddlin' nutcrackers. I'm your husband. You're supposed to share things like that with me. And if it's not that, then what can it be?" Pausing, staring into his empty cup, he grumbled, "Sure downed that fast and twenty ounces of caffeine on an empty stomach isn't good. Should've known better. Now I've got the jitters." Boy, did he ever. He couldn't stand still. Nor could he keep his mouth shut.

"Mitzi, have you got yourself hooked up with some weirdos? Holy walrus turds. Much as I hate to think it, that could happen to you. Especially since you're so gullible. Yeah, with your willingness to do anything to please anybody, I could see that happening. Oh, what if some weirdo has finagled my Mitzi into drinking or using drugs?" He shuddered. "Or, maybe she's found herself a new lover." As those pitiful words left his lips, his thoughts, along with his anger, spiraled into the unthinkable. "Taffy tarnation, Mitzi. You better not be supporting some gigolo with my money!"

An unexpected knock at the door startled him.

"Yes?" he said in a civil tone.

"Santa, are you all right in there?"

It was Malka, his office manager. The lady who had applied as a fill-in eleven years ago. The lady who agreed back then to stay until he found someone permanent.

"I have lots of experience," she stated confidently during the interview. "I taught school for twenty years in a Midwestern state down in the USA under the name of Marlene, so nobody would know I was Jewish. But I'm not hiding it anymore. I am who I am. Besides, I'll only be here for a few more months. That is, until my husband completes his research on glaciers at Blitzen University. When his grant runs out, we'll be retiring to my home state of New York. Uh, New York City to be exact."

Six months later when her husband's grant ran out, he got it renewed, year after year. And she stayed on, year after year.

"Are you all right in there?" Malka asked again, this time with a little more concern in her voice.

"Yes. I'm fine, Malka. Believe me. I'm fine."

"But all that racket. What were you yelling about?"

"Oh, uh, I just stubbed my big toe soldier. That's all."

"Not quite the truth," he mumbled, moving away from the intercom. "But how can I tell her or anyone else my wife is on a *different* kind of vacation. That she'll be home when she's *done*. If I tell anyone that, they'll think I'm crazy. Holy walrus turds. They might even think I did away with her."

"Okay. What are you mumbling about now? Is it something I need to hear?"

Malka's voice, startling him, drew his eyes to the intercom. "Fiddlin' nutcrackers. I forgot to hit the off switch." Caught off guard, he groped for an acceptable answer. "Oh, I'm, uh, . . . uh, I'm just thinking out loud about, about how to uh, . . . about how to change the design of one of my toy scooters."

"Really?"

Santa knew by the schoolteacher tone in Malka's one-word reply that he hadn't fooled her one bit. Still, refusing to leak a word about Mitzi's disappearance to her or anyone else, he held fast to his little white lie.

"Are you sure it's just your *big toe soldier* that hurts?"

"Yes, Malka. But it only hurts a little bit. Believe me. It'll be fine. Sorry for the racket. Guess it brought out the worst in me, huh?"

"Yeah, well, it sounded pretty bad. Now, how about if I get an icepack for it?"

"No. No. That won't be necessary. It'll be okay."

After that little episode, Santa made sure he didn't raise his voice until after he left his toy factory at quitting time. Like every evening since Mitzi's departure, he'd cut loose with lonely-man sorrows as he half ran, and half walked the distance to his cottage. Huffing and puffing as he neared his lane, he'd spill words of wishful anticipation. "Please, God. Please let there be light. Just a little light in the kitchen window or, at the least, a postcard in the mailbox." His praying pleas went unanswered. He'd find no postcard in the mailbox. Neither would his eyes be greeted by light pouring from any of his cottage windows.

Night after night, disappointment sliced his hopes into shreds. With stress weighing heavily on his shoulders, he'd drag his tired feet up the porch steps and into his hauntingly quiet cottage. Knowing he had to eat, he'd force down a TV dinner. The rest of the evening he'd sit, teary-eyed, staring at their faded wedding picture on the fireplace mantel.

Sadly, he'd lament, "Mitzi, my beautiful Mitzi, what did I do to make you leave me? Did you get tired of my long whiskers? I told you before we married, 'Don't ever buy me a razor.' Is it my weight? You know I have to store up lots of calories for my Christmas Eve trek. Ah. Maybe you're sick of living with a guy who looks different every year. Yeah. That's it. Isn't it? That's got to be it. Why else would you stay away so long?"

Often, he'd yell defensively, "Sooty bricks, girl. I can't help it if sometimes I'm Caucasian White. And sometimes I'm Indian Red. And sometimes I'm Asian Yellow. And sometimes I'm Chicano Brown. And then again, sometimes I'm African Black. It's not my fault my momma came from Black, White and Brown lineage and my poppa was a combination of Red and Yellow. Then, when they married and made me, Mother Nature mixed all their colors into some weird DNA concoction that produced me. Me! A frickin' freak of nature. It's all her fault. She put this curse on me for life."

Many nights, he'd stare at his Soweto nose in the mirror and growl like a grizzly bear. "Nose, why do you have to change every year? Why can't you be like everyone else's nose? Why can't you just stay the same?"

Night after night, he'd wallow in self-pity.

"Tell me, Mother Nature. Why me? Why'd you have to make me different from every other living soul on the face of this earth? You know you could've given me an Indian nose, Asian eyes, Hispanic skin, and Nordic blond hair. Whacky walruses. I would've been the happiest elf alive if you would've just mixed some of this and some of that together in one stay-the-same package. But no! You had to conjure up these weirdo genes that, in one dip of your magic wand, changes my whole appearance every year. Tell me. Why on my birthday do you have to rearrange my face and turn my skin into an entirely different color? Why did you do this to me? Huh? Why did you curse me? Why did you make me into a frickin' freak of nature?"

At this juncture, he'd stomp his feet and yell, "It's not fair. It's just not fair." Then, he'd follow his whining with demanding arrogance and a full-blown pity party.

"Yeah, I know. Everybody loves me. Nobody makes fun of me ever, huh? Hey, if that were true, why's my Mitzi gone? Tell me. What happened to that undying love and loyalty she vowed to give me *forever and ever* on our wedding day? Hey, Lady Nature, why don't you tell me that, huh? You won't, will you? That's because you haven't got the guts to show your face."

As if half expecting to glimpse a little, old lady clutching a wand, climbing his porch steps, he'd peer out the window. "There's no such person," he'd remind himself. "She's just an illusory figment that most folks blame bad weather on. And a figment my poppa used when I was a little elfin to explain why I woke up looking different every year on my birthday."

Despite this logical reasoning, he would go on and on with his guilt-laying trip.

"Listen, Mother Nature. Do you know how much I've wondered what the elves and Mitzi *really think* of my yearly racial changes? They don't say it, but I bet you a gazillion snow crystals that they're all thinking I'm a frickin' freak of nature and it's *all* your fault."

As always, his ranting would bring on more and more tears until exhaustion drew him into a fitful slumber.

Now, lying in bed on the seventy-fourth night since Mitzi's departure—totally convinced his wife could no longer handle his racial changes—he moaned pitifully into his pillow. "Hon, did you get tired of living with a freak of nature? Is that why you're staying away? Oh, please. Don't let it be that. Please don't think of me as a frickin' freak of nature. Mitzi, please come back. Don't you know how much I miss you and love you? Don't you understand? I love you more than anything. You're the most precious gift I've ever had. Oh, Mitzi, I don't think I can go on without you. I'm so miserable. Please, Mitzi. Please, please come home."

Mitzi, sitting next to the control panel, clicking her fingernails on the arm of her chair, was unaware that both she and Santa were reliving the same events, each from their own perspective.

"Shimmering icicles. He's sure into a long daydream. Well, if he can keep it up, so can I. Let's see. Where was I? Ah, yes. I had just completed my classes at Vixen Vocational Center, and I was packing to go home."

Closing her eyes, she envisioned herself standing in her hotel room, beaming with pride for not only doing well in all her classes, but for also getting through the whole ten weeks without a single elf in Kringleland recognizing her.

"Am I ever anxious to get back home and just be Mitzi Claus again," she said, tucking her certificates of completion into a side pocket on her suitcase. She had planned to take the evening bus home. That, however, went by the wayside when Luba Zemlic and Molly Pollard, friends from her displaced homemakers' class, pressed her to attend their graduation ceremony and dinner celebration. Oh, how she longed to, but couldn't find the courage to tell them she wanted to skip the hoopla to go home to a husband they didn't even know she had. Reluctantly, she agreed to join them, even though it meant postponing her departure until morning. "How could I tell those two I'm Santa Claus's wife when I told them, and everybody else in that class, that I'm a widow?"

As she stuffed her running shoes into a large Ziploc bag, she thought back to the first day of her assertiveness training class, when her instructor asked, "And why are you here, Elf Laura?" Instantly she blurted out the lie she had rehearsed. "I'm here because my husband died in a mining accident last year and uh, I need to figure out how to move on with my life."

Mitzi had felt pleased at pulling that off. Now, she felt frustrated and trapped. "I've lived a lie for ten weeks. Oh, why in taffy tarnation did I start this charade anyway?" Annoyed at questioning her own motive, she threw her hands into the air. The bag of shoes she was holding swung about, almost bopping her on the head. Glancing from her shoes to the bed, she carelessly heaved them toward her open suitcase. Overshooting her target, she watched as they rolled off the other side of the bed.

"Why'd I lie? Why did I lie? Oh, why *did* I lie?" Stomping around the bed to retrieve her shoes, two *lying* incidents vied for her attention. In one, she had gotten away with lying. In the other, she had been helplessly drawn into her stepmother's scapegoating web. A web in which telling the truth would have cost her dearly.

The first incident, the one in which she had gotten away with lying, happened when she was eight years old. Awakened by hunger in the middle of the night, she was heading for the kitchen to raid the breadbox when the flick of a light switch startled her.

In reaction to the sudden infusion of bright light filling the hallway, plus the harshness of her stepmother's voice— *Bohunk, what the hell are you doing out of bed?*—she pulled her elbows to her sides, crossed her hands over her bare chest and stared down at her feet. Fear, intermingling with the chill in the house, set her to shivering. Her skimpy underwear, permeated with the stench of squalid living, afforded her no warmth. Feeling trapped, she could do nothing but stand, shivering in the submissive position expected of her. She dared not move a muscle. Her mind though was racing like crazy.

Setting her eyes on the hemline of her stepmother's *warm* flannel nightgown, she quickly made up a lie. "I, . . . I must've been sleepwalking, Mommy." Stiffening, steeling herself for a cuffing that would send her flying, she closed her eyes and waited. At the least, she expected a hard slap across her face along with some harsh reminders of her unworthiness while being dragged by the ear back to the bedroom she shared with her five blended siblings. When that didn't happen, she cautiously raised her eyelids. Her stepmother, she could see, had caught sight of her father stirring in bed. As his sleepy eyes shifted back and forth from his wife to her, Mitzi's heart thumped wildly.

Hoping to prevent explosive fireworks between them, she haltingly repeated her lie. "I, . . . I guess, . . . I guess I must, . . . must've been sleepwalking, Mommy."

In the silence that followed, she prayed her father wouldn't get up. If he did, they would fight, and that would set her fate for the following afternoon.

Just like Pavlov's dogs salivated every time they heard a bell; she trembled every time her father and stepmother argued. It was a given. After they fought, after he'd leave for work, the redhead would go ballistic. She'd come at her like a screaming, hair-yanking, face-slapping tornado.

While envisioning this hellish scenario, Mitzi heard, "Get back to bed." The redhead's directive, like music to her ears, sent her feet scampering. She had gotten away with lying. The year before though, back in Harlan, Kentucky, at age seven . . . Well, that was a different story.

"I did not start that fire," she yelled adamantly, telling the truth. Again, and again, she pleaded her case. "Mommy, please. Please, please believe me. I did not start that fire. I'm not lying. Honest. I didn't start it." Despite her persistent claims of innocence, the redhead refused to believe her.

The fire happened in the middle of August on a hot, muggy day. Weeds, dry and brittle, crackled underfoot. Why her stepmother picked such an energy-draining day for yard cleanup she did not know. Mid-morning heat and high humidity had already zapped the energy produced from her slice-of-bread breakfast. Her stomach screamed for nourishment and her mouth felt drier than a dust-throbbing desert.

Water. She guzzled it whenever she could get it. And to get it, she had to buck her fear of the dark, plus her fear of getting caught. Often, her dehydrated body would push her to rise in the middle of the night. On such occasions, she'd sneak downstairs to the hand pump over the pantry sink. Once there, she'd pump and drink until her stomach could hold no more. During the day, when the redhead wasn't looking, she'd drink from cups left unattended by her younger half-siblings. When outside, she'd often scour the weeds for tin cans holding rainwater.

Mitzi, her mouth drier than a sun-bleached clamshell, drooped like a wilted flower. She couldn't clench her thirst until the opportunity arose to sneak some water. As for her hunger, weeds she would normally eat were growing abundantly at her feet. But under her stepmother's watchful eye, she didn't dare stoop down to pick any.

Of the four kids directed to collect and throw rubbish into the loose-stone fire pit—which lay a mere stone's throw from the house—she was the only one not whining. She didn't dare. She could tell the other kids' bellyaching was getting on the redhead's nerves. As Mitzi expected, it wasn't long before she caved. "Oh, go on. Get in the house. I'll be in as soon as I light this fire. Not you, bohunk. You're not finished yet. You get around to the other side of the house and pick up all the trash over there. All of it, hear! Go on. Get. And be quick about it."

Dutifully, Mitzi did as she was told. A short time later, rounding the eastern-front corner of the house—intending to deliver her armload of trash to her stepmother—she stopped short. Flames, bright red flames raying out from the loose-stone fire pit, tongue-licking dry weeds, met her eyes. Immediately assessing the situation as bad—really bad—she sprang into action.

Dropping her armload of trash, she ran up the porch steps and burst through the screen door, screaming, "Fire, Mommy, fire!" Frantically she tugged at the redhead's arm with one hand while pointing toward the door with her other. Again, and again, she screamed, "Fire, Mommy. Fire!" The redhead, tending her baby of one year, repeatedly shoved her away. Mitzi, astute enough to know at the tender age of seven that disaster was looming, refused to give up. Repeatedly, she screamed, "Fire, Mommy, fire! Fire, Mommy, fire!"

Annoyed by her persistence, the redhead, who had thrown a lit match in the fireplace, said to Willy, "Go outside and see what the bohunk is yapping about."

Seconds later, Willy came flying through the screen door, screaming, "Ma! Ma! The whole field is on fire."

After Willy peddled his bike five miles to the nearest neighbor to call the fire department, after Karen, Mitzi and Janice worked the child bucket brigade all afternoon from the hand pump over the pantry sink to the burning field, after the coal shed burned to the ground, after the fire came within ten yards of the tinder-dry farmhouse, after the firetruck *finally* arrived, . . . Well, the morning after all that, the redhead forced her to stand in front of the man called Daddy and confess to him that *she* had started the fire.

That morning, with her stepmother's cruel threats

looming over her head, a bedraggled little girl—eyes aimed at her bare feet—slowly approached the man called Daddy. Mitzi didn't want to lie. But it was either lie or endure the cruelty threatened by her sinister stepmother.

Don't tell me you didn't start that fire, you lying bastard. You did. And you will tell your daddy that you started it. Do you hear me? And if you don't, I'll give you such a beating you'll be sorry you were ever born.

As she stood before the man called Daddy—who slept and ate at the house, but never acknowledged her existence with so much as a *Hi*—she heard her stepmother saying sweetly, *for his benefit,* "Now, tell the truth. Tell daddy who started that fire. Tell daddy the truth. Come on. Tell daddy the truth."

The truth? She didn't dare tell the truth. It would bring wrath upon her head. After *Tell daddy the truth* registered in her mind for the fourth time, she, visualizing the fate that awaited if she failed to meet her stepmother's expectation, reluctantly forced the expected lie up her throat.

"I started the fire."

The lie, traveling up her dry throat, was barely audible. Even so, she knew her father had heard it because no other sound in the room competed with it.

After the lie left her lips, she glanced up at him. Despair, outlining his haggard coalmine face, seemed to be sucking the will to stand erect out of his shoulders. Reading sadness in his eyes, she knew the lie she *did not* dare *not* tell—for fear of being beaten unmercifully—had pierced his heart.

Sneakily glimpsing her stepmother's face, she immediately grasped the meaning of the gloating satisfaction she saw blooming there. The hatefulness in her stepmother's eyes, highlighted by a cruel, victorious smile, told her she was enjoying the emotional pain her husband was experiencing. At that moment, Mitzi knew her intent had not only been to scapegoat her, but to also pierce her father's heart, to convince him his firstborn child had committed this horrific deed. And he bought it.

The next thing Mitzi caught sight of was her stepmother's hand motioning her to get out. Thankful for the dismissal, she hurriedly pushed her way through the kitchen screen door. As she burst forth into the stifling summer heat, she believed in the eyes of the man called Daddy, that she would, from that day forth, be viewed as a very, very bad girl, never, ever to be trusted.

Sitting alone on a porch step with the pain of entrapment enveloping her spirit, she dropped her head to her knees and cried her heart out.

"Back then, I lied to survive," Mitzi reminded herself as she shook off the feelings associated with that memory. "But why did I have to lie in my classes for ten weeks?"

Placing the bag of shoes in her suitcase, she rationalized, "But I wasn't lying. I was pretending. And it must've been okay for me to do so because Santa does it every Christmas Season when he goes out into the world as a Santa Claus helper. Does he tell anyone he's the *real* Santa Claus? No. He even lets the whole world believe his symbolic color is *always* White when it's not. So, if he can pretend for a whole lifetime to be something he's not, surely no harm can come from me pretending to be someone else for a measly ten weeks."

Done with that spiel, she opened the closet. All but two hangers were empty. One held her navy blue suit for her morning bus trip home. The other held her casual black slacks for the evening's farewell dinner. She pulled her slacks off the hanger and laid them neatly across the bed.

"I wonder what Luba and Molly would think if they found out I was playing this charade." On her way to the bathroom to shower, she resolved, "I'll tell them who I am after I get back with Santa. That is, if he'll take me back. It's been ten weeks. Stupid me. I should've called or at least sent him another postcard or two. But if I'd called, most likely I'd have caved to his pleas to come home."

Later, at the farewell dinner, when she announced she'd be leaving for North Pole Village in the morning, a startled Molly Pollard blurted out, "What! Elf Laura, you're leaving us? Why? Why are you going up there?"

"Well, I have some family up there," she answered, deliberately keeping her response vague.

"Are you coming back?" Luba Zemlic pressed.

"I'm not sure." And she really wasn't. For days, she had been plagued with vacillating visions. On the one hand, Santa greeting her with open arms. On the other, him exploding with anger and rejecting her. So, to everyone's probing questions, she kept her responses vague. "I'm just going up there to visit some family. I might look for a job. Maybe I'll stay. I don't know. Right now, I'm just keeping my options open."

Around midnight, back in her hotel room, looking northward out the window, she said, "Santa, tomorrow I'm gonna give you the biggest surprise of your life."

Pulling back the bed covers, she prayed this would be her last night sleeping alone. "Oh, please let him greet me with open arms in the morning. Please, God. Please."

As she slid under the covers, she felt her body trembling. Whether her trembles stemmed from the night's chilly air or from fear, she did not know. She suspected it was more from fear. Fear that tomorrow she'd be rejected by the person she loved most dearly.

The night passed slowly. She tossed and turned. Sleep eluded her. Far into the night, she fretted. "Will Santa like the new me? What should I say to him? How can I explain what I've done to myself? How will he react? How will he handle all my changes? Will he be pleased? Will he be proud of the new me? Or, will he bellow angrily, 'Get out! I never, ever want to see the likes of you again.'?"

Mitzi's anguish kept her nerves in a frenzied state. Sleep came fitfully. As dawn approached, tension from worrying all night pressed her to leap out of bed. She dressed quickly. Stuffing her PJs into her suitcase, she said, "Oh, I can hardly wait. I'm going home."

Unable to go any place until the bus came, she paced the floor, chewed her nails and checked and rechecked to make sure she'd packed everything. "Shimmering icicles. I can't stay in this room another second." Still, she lingered, sweeping her eyes across the room one last time before heading for the elevator.

To the desk clerk, who suggested she take advantage of their free, continental breakfast, she said, "Thank you. But I think I'll skip breakfast. My stomach is way too queasy to handle food. Especially this early."

With too much time on her hands and nothing to fill it, she found herself pacing the lobby. After a few back-and-forth trots, she lifted her eyes to the clock in the reception area. "Dancin' Prancer. That bus won't arrive for another hour yet. Maybe if I read, time will go faster." Sinking into a plush leather chair, she picked up a travel magazine. Flipping through its pages, she scanned the words, but the ability to comprehend their meaning just wasn't there. All she could think about was getting on that bus and going home to *her* Santa.

CHAPTER 8

Do it! Would I dare?

"Last stop, Dearborn Station," came the driver's voice loud and clear over the bus intercom. As he intended, it roused those who were snoozing. "And hey, folks, looks like we're going to have us a decent day."

"Yes, it does," Mitzi said, spotting a small fleet of wispy-white clouds in an otherwise clear sky. "Hmm. I'd say it's going to be a great day to come home to my sweetheart." Her words rang true even though her eyes pulsed with concern about her upcoming face-to-face encounter with Santa. "Fiddlin' nutcrackers. The sight of me will probably knock the ghost of winter out of him."

Mitzi paid no mind to the sound of Santa's boots clip-clopping overhead. At this point, she hoped he'd keep daydreaming a little while longer. At least, until she finished reliving the best part of hers, which, never in her wildest dreams did she expect or plan to do. "This, I'm really going to enjoy." Chuckling, she leaned back in her chair, closed her eyes and surrendered to fate's twist.

Making her way through the bus terminal, Mitzi felt like an unwelcomed prophet in her own village. Again, and again, she waved at familiar faces. Many, in turn, nodded politely, but none smiled recognition. Some reticent glances she construed as, "Lady, I don't know you. So, why are you waving at me?"

"Hmm, nobody seems to recognize me. Or, maybe I should say, 'Nobody recognizes Elf Laura Ponseta.' That being the case, I think I'll stroll down to Santa's toy factory and see if I can fool him before going home. Yeah. That oughta be fun. Except, no way do I want to lug these heavy suitcases around with me. Let's see. What can I do with them? Ah, I know. I'll stash them here in a locker."

Minutes later, a locker key pinned to her inside purse lining, Mitzi started hiking to Santa's toy factory. Upon arrival, butting a shoulder against its heavy door, she heaved with all her might. Creak, creak, . . . Slowly its old hinges gave way to her efforts.

Stepping across the threshold, her eyes went straight to the elevator at the far end of the lobby. It's cage-like interior—facing a rider-operated, accordion-action door—screamed antiquity. Even so, the old, paint-peeling monstrosity still worked. Today, that was all that mattered. "Run. Run. Catch it," she demanded of her legs. Run, run, her legs did run, but catch it, they did not. "Prancing Dancer. I missed it and this thing takes forever to come back down."

She glanced through the accordion-action door at the

two cables traveling in opposite directions. One pulled the elevator up, the other acted as a counterweight. As soon as they stopped moving, she pushed the up button and cocked an ear. Only faint *I'm-not-going-anywhere* clicks responded to her finger tapping.

"Bushwhacked walruses. Some toymaker must be loading the dang thing up with cargo. Oh, why doesn't he install more elevators. Like modern ones?"

Running her eyes around the room, the *new Mitzi*, disgusted with the drabness of the lobby, started pacing and venting. "This place is a mess. Shimmering icicles. There's only one bulletin board to break the monotony of these walls. Why, there's nothing esthetic or calming in this whole lobby. Hmm. Some plants and a few pieces of artwork should brighten it some. Yeah. I can make that happen."

Bored, she stopped in front of the bulletin board to take stock of its postings. "Might as well see what's going on around here." Her eyes flew over the coming month's production quota, a worker of the month picture, schedules of bowling leagues—all stuff of interest to Santa and his toy makers, but not to her.

As she muttered, "Boring," through a long yawn, Mitzi caught sight of a notice in big red letters, she brightened. "Ah, what's this? Hmm. It says, 'Wanted, regional production coordinator for Santa's toy factories. Applicants must apply in person. Schedule an appointment with Malka, Santa's office manager.' Well, blow me down an iceberg slide. It's the job Santa was talking about creating before I left. Betcha I could do it." As her mind played with that *unlikely* possibility, her fingers flew to her lips and her eyes popped wide. "Do it? I wouldn't dare."

That's right, Mitzi Claus. You wouldn't dare. But if you, as Elf Laura Ponseta applied . . .

"Yes. If I were to go in as Elf Laura Ponseta, why that would put a whole different spin on things. I bet I could pull it off, but . . ."

Into Mitzi's pause, her *nattering Tomacita* interjected: *You really want that position, don't you? Admit it. Hey, you've got the skills, so, why not go for it?*

"Nah. I better not. I *should* just be a *good* wife and go home."

Should? What gives with that, girl? And good? That word enslaved you for the better part of your life. Girl, you need to stop playing those old tapes. You don't have to prove you're good to anyone. Neither do you have to live by should. But if you want to be a so-called good wife, then, so be it. Go home. Forget what you've learned these past ten weeks. But don't do it simply because you think you should. On the other hand, if you want to take a risk, for taffy tarnation, take it.

Mitzi, overwhelmed with the pros and cons of her mental tug-a-war, hopscotched her eyes from the bulletin board to the elevator to the factory door then back to the bulletin board again. "Dancin' Prancer. This is hard. I'd like to apply for that job, but I miss Santa and I feel badly about staying away so long."

Girl, wake up. Stop piggybacking guilt with familiarity and all its comforts. Stop letting them influence your thinking.

Resolutely curling her fingers into tight fists, Mitzi shot back, "I've got to go home and clean my cottage. Maybe make Santa an apple pie. Yes. That'll please him."

Please him! Is that what you want? Girl, you're hopeless.

"What do I want? What do I want?" Mitzi stared at the clunky door she had pushed so hard against to open a few minutes earlier. "Shimmering icicles. That sure took a lot of muscle power. Now, I've got to drum up some brainpower, . . . think, make a decision."

Yes, you do, girl. So, what's it gonna be? Are you going to launch your life in a new direction or are you going to go back to the way you were?

At this juncture of her mental tug-a-war, a question posed by her assertiveness training instructor—one that caught her off guard—popped into her head.

"Laura, what do you do to take care of yourself?"

Automatically, "I do things to please others," flew off her tongue.

Her instructor's comeback, "But that's not taking care of yourself, now is it?", forced her to look hard at the way she habitually ignored her own needs. Thinking on it now, she set her eyes on the old elevator bidding entrance. "Let's go for it, Elf Laura." Running with zest, she caught it. Ignoring her stomach's queasiness, she pulled the accordion door back and stepped inside the old box.

As the elevator rose, a mixture of fear, anxiety and

excitement set her heart palpitating. Quickly, she gave herself the once-over. "No runs in my panty hose. No lint on my pantsuit. Hope my hair looks good enough."

Hey, girl, you need to rethink that last remark. Replace it with, "My 'do is good enough." And add, "I'm good enough, too."

"Yeah, yeah. I know. I've got to stop worrying about every little thing. But this is risky and . . ."

The elevator's arrival on Santa's floor, prompted her to zip her lip. Pulling back the old box's accordion-like door, she stepped out onto worn, red carpet. Heading toward Malka, she mumbled, "Okay, Mitzi girl, remember, you've got to think, talk and literally be Elf Laura Ponseta."

Malka lifted her eyes from her proofreading task to size up the woman approaching. Tucking a strand of silver-gray hair behind an ear, she greeted her cheerily. "Good morning. May I help you?"

Mitzi cleared her throat. Despite feeling a flush creeping up her neck, she managed to disguise her voice and respond calmly. "Hi. I'm Elf Laura Ponseta and I'm here to apply for the Production Coordinator position posted in the lobby. Are you still scheduling interviews?"

"Actually, interviews were supposed to end yesterday. But no need to worry, dear. Santa hasn't taken down that notice yet, so I can schedule a time for you."

"That's kind of you. So, uh, when may I see him?"

"Let's see." Malka flipped through his appointment book. "Hmm. Looks like he has an hour free this morning. At nine o'clock, to be exact. So, you could see him then. Or, I see he has some time on Friday, in the late afternoon at three-thirty. So, what would work for you? This morning or Friday afternoon?"

"I'll take this morning. I'm from Kringleland and . . ."

"Oh, you live in Kringleland. My husband teaches there. At Blitzen University. He heads up the department that's doing some kind of research on glacier ice."

"Really," Mitzi said, feigning surprise.

"Yes. He was supposed to retire ten years ago, but every year the U.S. government renews his grant." Malka blew a strand of hair off her forehead as she let out an exasperated sigh. Frostily, with emphasis, she added, "I daresay, I think it's just an excuse to keep us from moving to New York City where all my family lives."

"Yes. I know how that goes. Uh, has Santa come in yet?"

"Yes, he has. And even though it's a bit early, I suppose I could buzz him. What's your name again?"

"Elf Laura Ponseta."

Mitzi, realizing she had passed her first test, breathed a sigh of relief. Malka, whom she had known for years, had showed no sign of recognizing her.

During the interview, Mitzi couldn't believe how totally oblivious Santa was to her facade. With him accepting her as Elf Laura Ponseta, she didn't have the courage to say, "Hey, sweetheart, can't you see? It's me. Mitzi. Your wife."

"Elf Laura, how did you acquire all these skills?" he asked with great respect.

"Oh, I've been organizing my husband's business affairs for years."

"You have?"

"Yes. My husband always bounces new ideas off me."

"I'm amazed at how much you know about toy production. You seem to know more than any other elf I've interviewed."

"Oh, toy production has always fascinated me."

"Really." Santa's eyes lit up. "Fascinated you, huh?"

"Yes. For years."

Mitzi watched Santa leaning back in his chair, drawing a hand down his beard. "Uh-huh. He's checking me out from head to toe." She held her breath. "Surely, he knows it's me. He must know." Clutching the arms of her chair, she braced herself for the inevitable.

"My eyes. They'll give me away. At every masquerade party, he's always been able to pick me out. No matter what, I've never been able to fool him. He's always said, 'Hon, your eyes give you away every time.' And today? Oh, I feel so vulnerable. I have no mask. I have nothing to hide behind, except my new contacts and my new short 'do. Watch. He'll realize I'm playing him and then, he'll explode." As she said this, Mitzi released her hold on the chair's arms and started folding and refolding her tissue.

180

"I've made up my mind," Santa announced, rising to his feet. Volleying his arms forward, grabbing both sides of his desk, he stared pointedly into her eyes.

She, stiffening, looked away. The way he was looking at her, she expected him to say, "Mitzi, is that you?" He didn't. Instead, he shocked her by saying, "The job is yours. When can you start?"

Uncomfortable with his stare, she leaned back in her chair and lifted her eyes to the ceiling. She parked them there partly out of fright and partly because she didn't know what else to do with them. "I can't hide them. I need them to see. But he keeps seeking them."

Mitzi knew her eyes could give her away. She also knew it wasn't just hers but his eyes, too. All through the interview, she had sneak-peeked his when he wasn't studying hers. She could tell he was trying to take in the whole of her without being obvious. Clearly, he was being obvious. She knew her husband. She sensed his loneliness. She also sensed he suspected she was his wife. At one point, believing he knew for sure, she had clutched the arms of her chair and steeled herself, preparing for his rage. However, when he offered her the job, she realized he hadn't recognized her at all. Perplexed as to what to do next, she lowered her eyes to the tissue she had been kneading in her hands. Her nervous fingers had beaten it to shreds. Despite her desire to yell, "Santa, sweetheart, it's me. I'm so sorry. I know I've put you through a lot," she just sat tightlipped, wrestling with her thoughts. "I can't believe he offered me the job. Dare I take him up on it?"

"You do want the job, don't you?" Santa asked, his eyes telling her he was eager to hear her answer. "Or, do you need some time to think about it?"

"Job?" The word echoed in her head like a yodeler's voice in the Swiss Alps. *Job. Job. Job.* She struggled to regain her wit. Initially, she intended to say no. Surprisingly, when her lips parted, out came the words, "Oh, yes. Yes, sir. I do want the job."

"Well then, tell me. When can you start?"

"Is tomorrow morning okay?" Dazed, actually shocked that she'd agreed to take the position, she rose from her chair and extended a hand to seal the deal.

Santa grasped her hand, not tenderly as her husband, but firmly as a businessman. "Yes, tomorrow morning is fine." Seeking her eyes, he added, "Oh, there's one more thing. I forgot to mention you'll need to check in here every day for the next two weeks so I can train you. After that, we'll set you up in the Mistletoe Office Building. Uh, it's just a few blocks from here. Does that sound okay to you?"

"Sounds fine to me," she said, nodding agreement. Heading for the door, she added, "See you in the morn."

"At eight-thirty sharp," he returned.

"On the dot," she shot back swiftly.

Minutes later, as she playfully bounced her feet down Santa's toy factory steps, excitement poured from Mitzi's lips. "He hired me. I got the job. Yes, yes, yes. He hired me. But, but . . ." In the blink of an eye, somberness, like a menacing black cloud, overshadowed her elation.

"Hmm. I guess I didn't realize how much I've changed. To think, my own husband didn't recognize me. But what if I can't pull this off? Wait a minute. Elf Laura, *you* told him *I* wanted the job. So, you have to do this for me. You have no other choice but to help me swim through this pickle stew. And you've got to do this without messing up. No way can you let Santa see the *me* in *you*. You got that?"

CHAPTER 9

Why didn't you stop her?

Santa, still daydreaming, glanced down at his watch. "Shimmering icicles. I've been hiking around this platform for more than two hours. Oh, well, if the elves have the energy to keep cheering, . . . Hey, that's great. Hopefully, they'll keep going until I finish my daydream."

Stopping at the Sleigh Valley post, resting longer than usual, he looked down at the crowds. "Yeah, I can keep up with you, but luckily for me, I get to take four breathers every time I go around this thing." Once re-energized, he moved on. As he did, he visualized himself sitting in his office, reflecting on his interview with Elf Laura Ponseta.

"What a relief. No more interviewing and I know that elf will be a cracker-jack worker. She really knows her toy stuff. But where'd she come from? I know every elf in this Region, or at least, I thought I did until she walked in. I've always had an excellent memory for names. So, why can't I recall ever hearing hers? Who is she? And where in taffy tarnation has she been hiding all these years? How could a smart elf like that live in my homeland without me at least meeting her? Fiddlin' nutcrackers. If I had, I would've put her to work years ago. Maybe she's an immigrant. Nah. She can't be. She knows too much about our toy production. Wait. Maybe she is Mitzi in disguise. I must say, she looks like Mitzi did thirty years ago, except, except for that short hairdo and those surreal blue eyes. If it weren't for them, I'd have sworn she was my Mitzi."

Santa, perplexed about the sudden appearance of this strange woman who in many ways reminded him of his wife, thought about the two times during the interview when he had looked deep into her eyes.

"Her eyes are so like Mitzi's, but she can't be Mitzi. Mitzi's eyes are hazel, and that applicant's eyes are blue. The deepest sky blue I've ever seen. And she sorta walks like Mitzi. Maybe . . . Could she be? Nah. She can't be. Mitzi's too shy and accommodating and that woman is anything but. Besides, my Mitzi's a homebody in the truest sense and that gal has a springy, go-get-'em personality. Why, my Mitzi would never pretend to be somebody else. She's too honest. Still, if it weren't for that gal's blue eyes and short hairdo, I would've sworn she was my Mitzi. But then, Mitzi hasn't looked that good in what? Twenty, thirty years? And she'd never break a promise. She'd never cut her hair. No. She'd never break our wedding-day pact. Not my Mitzi."

Santa slide forward in his chair and propped his chin on his upturned palms. For the longest time, he sat, wracking his brain for a memory of Elf Laura Ponseta. Try as he might, he couldn't pull forth one smidgen of information on her.

◇•◇•◇

Nearing the next platform post, Santa thought back to how his pulse had quickened every morning when the time clock clanged 8:30 a.m. He knew Elf Laura was punching in. Always on time, she brought certain magic, making life worth living again.

Before hiring her, his work interest had plummeted. Often feeling blue, he'd spend hours staring into space. Other times, he'd switch back and forth from the good times he and Mitzi had shared to worrying about her present welfare. At day's end—his gut wrenched—he'd go home grumbling, "Sock darning and home-cooked meals I can do without. It's sitting in that empty cottage night after night without my Mitzi's laughter that's the pits."

Her happy spirit was what he missed most. It, and the many other things he had taken for granted. Now, he was enjoying another woman's wit and laughter. Not in his cottage each evening, but in his office every day. And he loved it. Still, loving it scared him. At times, he even felt guilty. He often wondered what Mitzi would think if she knew how much he loved Laura's company.

Love! Thinking about love and all its complications— especially if he were to slip up with Elf Laura—scared the ghost of winter out of him. Often, he'd say, "That woman, whom I've yet to find any information on, is an employee and nothing more. But why, why does my heart tug every

187

time I look at her? There's something extraordinary about her. Almost familiar. But what it is, I do not know except, she sure reminds me of Mitzi. If it weren't for those deep blue eyes, I'd swear she was my Mitzi. Hmm. Might Laura be related to my Mitzi? Now, how funny would that be? Yeah. Ha, ha. A distant relative of Mitzi's working right under my nose and me not knowing it. Fiddlin' nutcrackers. I should've never hired her. But I had to. I knew the moment she walked in she was right for the job. On the other hand, if I hadn't, maybe that stupid moose dream wouldn't be haunting me every night."

Santa wasn't stupid. He knew there was a connection between his fondness for Elf Laura and the dream that was plaguing him since the day he hired her. Night after night, an adult moose, standing sixteen hands tall, not including its antlers, appeared in his dream. Everything about him spelled moose, except his snorting snout. That frightened him. Not that the beast was ugly. He wasn't. But his twinkling eyes, Soweto nose and snowy-white whiskers—mirroring his own—startled him. So uncanny was the resemblance, he referred to him as Santa Moose.

Once a roaming-free creature—before being shackled to a cart—Santa Moose would stubbornly weld his shanks to the ground whenever his peddler owner needed to make an important delivery. It made no difference how much his owner prodded him to move, he refused to budge. Sometimes he'd stand rigid for the entire day.

His behavior frustrated one peddler after another.

Fourteen peddlers in less than three years bartered him away; each, in succession, settling for less money than the previous one.

Even though he was strong and could pull quite a load, Santa Moose's reputation plummeted. Word about his stubborn streak traveled fast. One day, an old woman peddler, the spitting image of Mitzi, purchased him for three cents. Three cents! What a comedown. A good working moose was worth at least seventy dollars. Santa Moose, believing a value of nothing was a sure-fire ticket to independence, chuckled. "Freedom is just around the corner. I'll soon be living a carefree life. Yahoo!"

Each night, after falling asleep, the same scenario unfolded. Santa Moose, assuming Mitzi Peddler would get frustrated with his stubbornness and set him free, boasted to a moose friend passing by, "Hey, Homer, pretty soon I'll be roaming free, doin' whatever I please."

His friend, slowing a little, yelled back. "Yeah. Right. And how ya gonna eat? How ya gonna defend yourself?"

"Eat!" His friend's comeback not only squashed his zeal, it put the kibosh on his plan. "Yikes! I don't know the first thing about foraging. How can I make it in the wild tundra? For years I've been pampered with fresh moss and all the fodder I could eat. If I screw up and she sets me free, I might starve to death. Or, worse yet, some hunter might shoot me. Yikes! I'd be a goner."

Haunted by these fears, Santa Moose didn't mind Mitzi Peddler tricking him into doing her bidding by dangling a clump of fresh moss over his head. He loved fresh moss and he willingly did anything to get it. Day after day, eyeing that moss, he'd trot on and on. From morning until nightfall, he'd concentrate on catching and sinking his teeth into it. So fierce was his determination to get it, he never realized crafty Mitzi Peddler was guiding him right to where she wanted him to go.

Santa, upon awakening each morning, could not unravel the meaning of this dream. "Does it have something to do with my feelings for Elf Laura? Is my conscience reminding me I'm a married man? Is it trying to tell me I'd better not fool around with another woman?"

Ever since hiring Elf Laura, he found himself wrestling not only with this dream, but with a gamut of lovesick emotions as well. Sometimes he'd catch himself dreaming what it would be like to be married to Elf Laura instead of Mitzi. That was scary. Still, he couldn't bring himself to admit his feelings for Elf Laura were much like those of a man falling in love.

Repeatedly, he fought to keep his lovesick feelings in check. Often, he'd scold himself. "Listen, Mr. Soweto Claus. Even though you go home to an empty cottage every night, you're still a married man and don't you forget it." Forgetting would've been easy if he didn't have to contend with that darn moose dream every night.

The last day of Elf Laura's training Santa entered his office grousing up a storm, "Mitzi, where in taffy tarnation are you? When I suggested you take a vacation for as long as you liked, I didn't expect you to be gone forever." Halting abruptly, he stared at his desk calendar—the one he was using to mark off the days since her disappearance. "Holy walrus turds," he said, setting his Latte on the corner of his desk. "As of today, it's been three whole months since my Mitzi flew the coop." Plopping onto his swivel chair, he elbow-propped his chin and stared straight ahead. His glazed eyes, along with his pouty lips, clearly broadcasted his foul mood.

"What if something's happened to her? What if she never comes back? What if she divorces me?" Fear of being served divorce papers loomed over him like a storm cloud weighted down with a ton of hailstones. Lately, whenever some briefcase-toting guy walked toward him on the street, he'd freeze. On such occasions, his fear of being served rose from the slightest to the highest possibility. "Surely that couldn't happen. Or could it?"

The sound of footsteps drew him away from his worries. Grabbing his Latte, taking a sip, he stared longingly at Elf Laura strutting into his office. "She's so fit and trim." Setting his Latte down, he cracked a smile. "She must've forgot to punch in, or was I so deep in thought, I missed hearing the time clock? Oh, Laura, what I wouldn't give to spend some time with you, away from the office." Knowing his last thought could lead him down a path he'd later regret, he pushed it out of his mind. But his melancholy? It pulled his chin to his chest and morphed his eyes, his lips, his whole face, into a pout.

Mitzi, nearing his desk, commented on his haggard look. "Is something bothering you? You look so down in the cranberry bog."

"Oh, it's nothing." Dropping his eyes, he picked up his Latte and gulped down a few sips.

"Hey. That cranberry-bog look tells me something's troubling you. Come on. Fess up. What's wrong?"

Mitzi, pert and alert Mitzi—alias Elf Laura Ponseta—skidded to a halt in front of his desk. Looking expectantly to Santa, she waited for his response.

"Shows that bad, huh?"

"Sure does. And I know you won't be teaching me much today if you don't get it off your chest."

"Well," he timidly admitted, "it's my wife."

Mitzi's brow shot up three notches. Deciding to play along as though she knew nothing, she kept her tone subtle. "Your wife? Is she sick or something?"

"I don't know. I mean, she could be. Then again, maybe she's really happy. Happier than she's ever been."

"Santa, you're not making any sense. Can't you tell whether your wife is sick or happy?"

That did it. After three months of bottled up frustration running amok in his head, frazzling his nerves, he blew his stack. At the top of his lungs, he yelled, "I can't when she's not around and I haven't heard a word from her in three months!"

His words, bouncing off the walls, pulled Mitzi's hands to her ears. Fighting a pang of guilt, she drew in enough air to effectively fire back an exaggerated, yet believable response. "Three months! What a long time to be without your wife."

"Yeah. For all I know, she could be dead or dying. Or, maybe she's lying unconscious in a hospital somewhere."

Santa stood up and threw his hands into the air. Realizing he was swinging them around sort of out of control, he quickly shoved them into his pants pockets. Still antsy, he started pacing behind his desk.

"I know she's using my debit card to get cash, but . . ."

As he stalled, Mitzi reasoned, "He's too frazzled to say another word. His anger has his tongue tied in knots and something deep inside is pushing for release." Saying nothing, just watching, she noticed him retracting tight fists from his pant pockets. That cinched her prediction. "Yes. My prophecy is right on. He's going to explode."

Santa's eyes not only pulsed with anger, but with awareness. Awareness that his anger was getting the best of him. "I've got to hit something. Something right now." BAM! He let his fist fly. BAM! BAM! BAM! BAM! BAM! After repeatedly hammering the corner of his desk, setting everything on it rattling, he glared at Elf Laura and yelled, "But, as to *where* she is or *what* she's doing with *my money*, I haven't the slightest clue."

Taken aback by his angry outburst, although expecting it, Mitzi jumped. "Should I give up this crazy charade? No.

Such a revelation now, especially in his state of mind, wouldn't be good. I'd better not say anything. At least, not yet. Best to keep up this act a little while longer." Faking surprise, she exclaimed, "You haven't heard from your wife in three months! What happened? Did you two have a big fight or something?"

"No," he answered, his voice much lower since getting some physical release. "We didn't fight. I mean, she hardly ever got mad at me in all the years we've been married. Sometimes I'd get mad at her. Especially when she'd put herself down. But her getting mad at me? No. Never. Maybe that was the problem. She was always sweet and lovable and, and agreeable, until one evening when I came home from my toy factory."

"Until you came home from your toy factory? What on earth did you do to make her leave?"

"I don't know. I mean, I uh, . . . uh, I don't remember doing anything. All I know is she started complaining about never doing anything but darning my socks. Then, when she almost jabbed that stupid darning needle of hers up my nose . . . Well, I just blurted out the first thing that popped into my head."

"What did you say?"

"I told her to go take a vacation. By herself." Santa said this with reluctance, as if he were ashamed to admit it. "Grant it. I didn't expect her to leave so willingly. Just like that. POOF! She was packed and out the door."

"Why didn't you stop her?"

194

"Why didn't I stop her? How could I? I was the one who suggested she leave. I even gave her my debit card. Dumb me. She's free. She's got her plum pudding and can eat it, too. *Alone!* Or, . . . or she could have a new lover. No, no. I don't want to think that. But who knows? She could turn into a floozy dame or . . ."

"Or, she could be afraid to come home," Mitzi interjected meekly, shrinking back slightly.

Santa's voice rose. "Afraid to come home? Why would she be afraid to come home? She knows I love her. That was the last thing I told her before she walked out." Plopping down in his chair, seeking something to busy his hands, he picked up a paperclip and started uncurling it.

Mitzi, although startled by his outrage, managed to say, "What if she's changed? Maybe your wife's afraid you'll not like what you'll see when she comes back."

Santa's nostrils flared. "Listen here. I don't care if she's turned into a monster. I don't care if she yells and screams at me every day. I don't care if she never, ever darns another one of my holey socks. I just want her home because, . . . because I love her, and I miss her. Terribly."

"You do, huh?"

Like a locomotive running low on steam, Santa responded through a labored breath, "Yes. I do."

Sighing, he looked down at the mutilated paperclip in his hand. "Stupid me. Why did I blurt out the story of my wife's disappearance to this elf, of all elves?" Feeling a little embarrassed, he glanced up to check Elf Laura's reaction but couldn't see her face. She had turned away.

"Listen, Santa," Mitzi said as she moved across the room to her desk. "Women's intuition tells me your wife knows you love her, and she loves you, too. Just wait. She'll pop in one of these days. Probably when you least expect it. You just have to have faith."

"Faith! My faith is running out."

Laura jumped. Santa, noticing, said with sensitivity, "I'm sorry. So, sorry. I kinda lost it, huh? Please. Please, forgive me. I mean . . . Fiddlin nutcrackers. I don't know what came over me."

"That's okay. Better to get it out than to sit on it."

As she spoke, Santa took note of her posture—back toward him, bent over, hands clutching her desk. He also detected sadness in her voice. Sadness that tugged at his heart and prompted him to make his move, despite knowing he shouldn't.

"Look, Laura, I probably won't be very good company, but how about dinner tonight to celebrate your graduation from this training? I could make reservations at Snow Goose Restaurant. How about it? Hmm? I promise I won't load you down with any more of my troubles. I'll be a perfect gentleman."

Mitzi answered in a voice hinting nervousness. "Santa, I'm sorry. I can't."

"Why not?"

"Why not?" she repeated, biting her lower lip. "Because, . . . because I have a special celebration planned for tonight and to do it, I need to ask you for something."

"What's that?"

"Well, I know I might be pushing it a bit, but I was wondering if I could leave a couple hours early today. Maybe have the whole afternoon off. See. I'd like to go home early to prepare one of my husband's favorite meal. It's gonna be *private*. Just him and me. Actually, he doesn't know anything about it. Uh, I uh, I plan to surprise him."

"I can understand that. Besides, you've been such a fast learner, we'll probably wrap up early today." He said this with zest, but secretly longed to be included. Also, her word *private* tore at his heart. "Yeah. Private time with a woman. How long has it been?" Pushing that thought out of his mind, he eyed Elf Laura. "Guess I should be pleased for them. Her asking for time off to cook *him* a special dinner. Now that's special. Wow. He's sure a lucky guy."

Opting to weigh his misery against her and her husband's happiness, he proceeded to bury himself in self-pity. "What moose-pucky luck. While she's pampering him, I'll be forcing down a tasteless TV dinner. Then, I'll sit there staring at the TV, trying not to worry about my Mitzi. Yeah. I'll try not to worry, but I'll worry long into the night. And she and her husband? Bet all night long they'll cuddle and keep each other warm. And me? Yippy! I get to sleep in a cold bed all by myself. And when I fall asleep, that stupid moose dream is gonna haunt me until my alarm goes off in the morning. Fritterin' fiddlesticks. Why do I always get the short end of the icicle?"

As the morning wore on, Santa noticed Elf Laura seemed unusually high spirited, like a high-strung horse anxious to get on with a race. "Bet she's glad the training is ending. Not me though." Sadly, for him, the prospect of her leaving triggered flashbacks of Mitzi walking out three months earlier, something so painful he visibly shuddered.

For the rest of the morning, despite feeling down, he forced himself to concentrate on finishing her training. A few minutes before noon—masking his melancholy with a smile—he stood at the door bidding her goodbye. "You've learned well, Laura, and I'll miss your cheery smile. But I suppose we'll see each other now and then."

"Oh, we'll probably see a lot of each other. And I want you to know I'm ever so grateful for all you've taught me. Thanks so much."

As he gripped her extended hand, he pressed a key into it. Watching her look quizzically from it to his face, he forced another smile. "It's for your own suite on the fifth floor of the new Mistletoe Office Building. Right now, it's just a bunch of empty rooms. So, your first assignment is to order your own furniture and office supplies. Decorate it to your heart's content. Oh, and also hire your own office manager."

"Nice." Spontaneously, she threw her arms around his neck.

Her hug caught Santa off guard. Closing his eyes, he, in turn, lifted his arms to embrace her. Her closeness, her tenderness awakened emotions that had been lying dormant since Mitzi's departure. Emotions that seemed to be screaming, "Come on. Get with it. Caress her cheek with your soft whiskers. Run your fingers through her curly ringlets. Kiss her, you old codger. Kiss her!"

Such thoughts set off an internal alarm. Like knights dueling, his logical side began sparring with his emotions. "I have to keep myself in check. My reputation is at stake." Still, with her nearness awakening his passion, he felt his self-control waning. Opening his eyes, connecting with hers, he said without thinking, "Oh, Laura, you're so beautiful."

For a moment, Mitzi studied his eyes. She had willingly succumbed to his tender touch. She didn't want to, but she felt she had to pull away. "Thanks, Santa," she said, lowering her eyes as if embarrassed. "That was a sweet compliment. But I'm sorry. I have to go. Remember. I've special plans with my husband tonight."

Santa reluctantly broke the connection. Still dreamy eyed, he continued to drink in her loveliness. "Oh, her eyes are so soft, so tender, so penetrating. Penetrating! Mitzi's eyes are penetrating, too." As he took in her loveliness, he let himself believe Elf Laura was Mitzi. That is, until his need for self-preservation kicked in. "Stop that. Pretending isn't going to make it real. And even if Laura's eyes are penetrating like Mitzi's, it doesn't mean they are Mitzi's. Besides, the eyes you're gazing into are blue. A deep-sea blue. And Mitzi's eyes are hazel. Always have been, and always will be."

Santa loosened his grip. Although overwhelmed with emotional pain, he held back his tears until Elf Laura walked away. Then they, along with his head chatter, flowed freely. "Oh, I'm so miserable and she seems so happy. Fiddlin' nutcrackers. Will I ever find happiness again? If Mitzi doesn't come home soon, what . . ." He hated to admit it, but his hopes for her return were waning.

Slump shouldered, feeling as low as he had felt high a few seconds earlier, he closed the door and said wistfully, "Sure wish that moment didn't have to end. But then, it's best that it did." Longingness drew him to the window across the room. As he waited to catch a glimpse of Elf Laura, he tried stopping his flow of tears. He couldn't. A minute or so later, sighting her bouncing down his factory steps, his eyes brightened. Thoughts of their embrace kept him staring at her until she disappeared around the corner.

"Oh, that hug felt so good." Trembling at the thought of what could have happened, he scolded himself. "Listen here, you old bloke, you're a married man. So, you better get all thoughts of courting that woman out of your mind. You're not going to be unfaithful to your wife no matter how long she stays away. Hear! Besides Elf Laura is married. OMG, she's married!" That fact, sinking in for the first time, raised his brow. "So, why, in the past two weeks, didn't she say a word about her husband? Not a word since the interview. Not until today. He must be an important person. Dancin' Prancer! Why don't I know a thing about the Ponseta family?" He scratched his head, hoping that would bring something forth, but it didn't.

"Might as well complete her training report even though right now I've less energy than a polar bear in hibernation." Dragging his feet over to his desk, he searched through his computer for the right form. "Shouldn't take me more than five minutes to complete it. Then what? Humph. Guess I could hop an iceberg and head south. Meet up with a polar bear for lunch. Yeah. Wouldn't that be fun?"

Ripe with self-pity—much like a cranberry left behind in a vast bog after all the others had been harvested—he felt lonely, abandoned and angry. "You cheated me, Elf Laura Ponseta. You cheated me out of an afternoon of your wit and laughter. Now I have no one to spin tales with for the rest of the day. Anyway, who wants to keep company with an old, roly-poly Santa Claus? For sure, Mitzi doesn't and probably no one else does either. Yeah. Everybody wants my toys, but does anybody want me? No. That's because I'm a frickin' freak of nature. And another thing, Elf Laura Ponseta, if you hadn't asked to leave early today, I wouldn't be doing this report until after five." Momentarily stopping his chatter, he looked down at his clenched fists. They seemed to be saying, "Go ahead. Pound your desk again."

"No," he resolved. "Ain't any use pining for someone I can't have. Got to let it go."

Setting his fingers to flying over his keyboard, he boasted, "I can type as fast as I can chimney hop on Christmas Eve. Not a person alive can type as fast as me."

That remark drew him back to when he signed up for typing in high school, when he had reasoned, "It'll be an easy credit and a sure-fire way to get attention from girls."

School had only been in session one week when his teacher, Mrs. Gardner, became concerned about him being a distraction to the other students, and her teaching efforts. Her concern pushed her to say to principal Fields, "I've never seen anyone pick up the skill so fast. He's good, but also a showoff. Can we give him full credit and move him to another class? One he knows nothing about?"

"Full credit? Absolutely not, Mrs. Gardner. He's not getting full credit if he doesn't put in his time."

Later, after school that day, Mr. Fields, upon hearing a commotion coming from the typing room, ran to investigate. At the door, he stopped cold, stared, rubbed his eyes, and stared some more. What he saw struck him not only as odd, but also as unbelievable.

In the first seat of the third row sat Santa, hunched over a manual typewriter, pecking away like crazy with only one hand. A young girl, he noticed, was holding his left hand behind his back while another was running her fingers through his snowy-white hair. And of all things, he was blindfolded. A dozen or so kids were prancing around, trying their best to distract him. Their attempts, he could see, weren't fazing him at all.

Mr. Fields, asserting his authority, marched over and yanked Santa's paper out of the typewriter. As he did, a hush fell over the room.

Santa, knowing full well who had walked in, slumped down in his chair. The others, taking advantage of their principal focusing his attention on Santa's paper, slithered away. Reaching the door, they ran.

Santa, realizing the gig was up, removed his blindfold. Not knowing what else to do, he stared at the floor and waited.

Mr. Fields' forehead cut into deep valleys as he scrutinized Santa's errorless typing. Clearing his throat, he thrust an arm out, pointed to the door and said, "Go."

The next day, when called to the office, Santa assumed he was in serious trouble. To his surprise, he was awarded full credit for his typing skills and assigned to another class, one in which he had to work doubly hard to pass.

"Done," he said, smiling smugly. "What that principal didn't know is, I can run through a whole daydream while I type. Actually, I can think about anything while I type." At that moment, he pictured Elf Laura and her *unknown* husband clinking wine glasses, toasting their happiness and enjoying a blissful evening together. The image spoiled the moment.

"Whacky walruses. Some men get all the breaks. Bet she'll serve him roasted turkey bird with all the trimmings, including cranberries. Or maybe a nice ham or prime rib. And I bet she'll spoil him with a homemade apple pie, too. And what do I get? Nothing. Nothing but a tasteless TV dinner. Fiddlin' nutcrackers. I'd go home in a minute if my Mitzi was there making me an apple pie."

Like a soldier defeated in battle, weariness showed in his sagging shoulders. Having long given up hope of finding his wife there when he'd arrive home, he decided to lollygag around his office until six. Going home any earlier to a wife-less cottage was just too painful.

CHAPTER 10

What kind of joke is this?

Like the Energizer Bunny, the elves' enthusiasm kept going and going. Somehow, the shouting mania evolved into a game nobody had planned. The unspoken rules were simple. When you see Santa, shout like crazy. When he walks away, hush up. Rest your lungs for the next go-round. It was a grand game for all, especially for the little elfins.

Santa broke out of his daydream and peered down at the crowds. "Still cheering me on, huh?" At the next post, he expressed his gratitude. "Glad, you're still hyped up because that means I can stay with my daydream. I sure didn't expect this, but it's nice. With luck, I'll finish before all of you wind down."

Marching soldier-like across the platform, hoping to get through his daydream before the crowds ran out of steam, he shouted, "Yes. Do keep it up so I can play out *Mitzi's Charade* to the end." Picking up where he left off, he saw himself slumped over his desk, fast asleep, snoring.

◇•◇•◇

Jethro, the night janitor, finding Santa slumped across his

desk, snoring loudly, nudged his shoulder and yelled, "Santa! Come on, Santa! Wake up!" Hearing a moan, he stood back, crossed his arms and waited for sleep's hold to break. It didn't. Instead, one groggy *Huh?* followed by Santa's rhythmic snoring, signaled he needed to try again. "Come on, Santa. Ya gotta wake up."

Lifting his weighty head, half opening one eye, Santa let out a moan. "H-u-u-uh." Plop! Down went his head.

Frustrated, Jethro upped his voice even more. "Santa! Come on! You've gotta get out of here. It's lockup time."

That did it. Bolting upright, Santa yelled, "Lockup time!" Wide-eyed now, he zeroed in on his big wall clock. "Twenty after six. It can't be that late. Can it?"

"Afraid it tis. Had you a nice little snooze, huh?" A smile crossed Jethro's face as he watched Santa funneling his next words through a stretched-out yawn.

"O-o-oh, I wasn't suppo-o-osed to fa-a-all asleep."

"Yeah, well, ya did."

"But I've never fallen asleep on the job before."

Jethro, heading for the door, yelled over his shoulder. "Happens to the best of us, Santa. Betcha you've been wearing yourself out working and worrying lately."

"Working? I don't know about that. But worrying? Yeah, I've been worrying all right. Worrying about where in taffy tarnation my Mitzi is." As thoughts of Mitzi brought him to full wakefulness, Santa sucked in his lower lip and rose from his chair. Thoughts of Mitzi, especially in the evening, easily prompted tears. Navigating around his desk, sniffling a bit, he filled his briefcase with stuff to keep his mind occupied after dinner. *Stuff* to distract him from worrying about the *no good* he feared his wife was up to. "Glad that's done. Now, to get some fresh air. Pronto." Grabbing his parka, he flipped off the light switch and headed for the elevator.

A few minutes later, stepping into the night's Arctic air, he started venting his sorrow. "If only I was as lucky as Elf Laura's husband. He has her. And tonight, he'll get something like prime rib. And what do I get? Chicken? Turkey? Meatloaf? Ham? Yeah, I wish. Taffy tarnation. A working guy should have more to look forward to than a tasteless TV dinner and cranberry-bog loneliness every night. It's not fair." As usual, he nursed his poor-me feelings all the way home until . . .

"Fritterin' Fiddlesticks! Dancin' Prancer! Shimmering icicles! Holy walrus turds! Fiddlin' nutcrackers!" Off in the distance, down his cottage lane, he saw it. "Light!" Several windows pushing brightness into the inky night met his startled eyes. His excitement spiraled. His feet skidded to a stop. His jaw dropped. His eyes nearly popped their sockets. Caught off guard by the unexpected, he blinked and blinked. "Can it be?" Reluctant to accept what his eyes were seeing, he pleaded, "Please, God. Please don't let me be dreaming. Please, please, no tricks."

Suddenly, everything seemed surreal, as if he were an actor in a play about to step onto a stage that had just popped up before him. Again, he blinked and blinked, rubbed his eyes and blinked some more. Fearing disappointment—that his Mitzi might not be there—he held back from accepting what his eyes were shouting. "It's real, man. It's real!" For a moment, his mind teetered between disbelief and *Wow. This is wonderful*. He felt, and heard, something giving. An explosion. His own voice screaming, "Mitzi. My Mitzi. She's home at last."

Trembling like the earth does in the throes of an earthquake, he pressed his wobbly knees into action. He took a few steps. Then doubt set in. Slackening his pace, he resolved, "No. This old moose ain't gonna get all lathered up over nothing. I probably left those lights on this morning." Still, he couldn't stop himself. He had to find out. With the get-up-and-go of a twenty-year-old, he sprinted up the porch steps. Bursting through the front door, his sniffer, assaulted by the aroma of hot, apple pie, gave him reason to pause and catch his breath. Smiling, pulling a hand to his chest, he drew in another good whiff of the sweet smell. "Ah, my favorite pie. She's here. My Mitzi. She's home at last."

Into the nearest chair he dumped his briefcase. That act, plus his excitement, nearly sent him tumbling over his feet. After he steadied himself, he raced to the kitchen, shouting, "Mitzi, Mitzi. Hello, hon. Am I ever glad you're . . . What? What the . . ." The sight before him not only pushed his eyelids to their outer limits, it busted his happy bubble and sent him reeling. Frazzled, trying to catch his breath, he lacked the wherewithal to know he was on the verge of hyperventilating. His face turned white. Gasping for air, he looked aghast at the woman standing in front of him, a woman he knew as Elf Laura Ponseta, *not* his wife. The sight of her—in his cottage, cooking, using everything dear to *his Mitzi*—was beyond his comprehension.

"What kind of joke is this?" Unable to make sense of it, he flinched inwardly. The woman before him, whom he had grown fond of the last two weeks, whom he had taken care not to overstep his bounds, whom had made his heart flutter every time he looked at her, was standing not more than ten feet away from him—in his kitchen—holding a fresh-baked pie between two potholders.

"What? What is Elf Laura doing here in *my* kitchen?"

His trembling lips, intent on speaking, couldn't. He kept his head level while his eyes, like yo-yos, shot up and down the length of her figure. He took in her every move, from her hands setting the hot pie on a cooling rack to the flirty smile she was directing his way. Eyeing her stepping forward with outstretched arms, winking at him no less, he stiffened. Then, he exploded.

"Elf Laura Ponseta!" His booming voice brought her feet to a halt. It also wiped the smile from her face. "What are you doing here in *my* kitchen, wearing *my* wife's apron?" At that moment, the inflection in his voice matched Papa Bear's in *Goldilocks and The Three Bears*. However, there was a big difference between that fairytale and what he was experiencing. That story was fiction. What was happening in his kitchen was real. Too real.

Elf Laura, still beckoning to him with outstretched arms, stepped forward. He, scared silly, pulled back. Squinting, sending a distrustful scowl her way, he momentarily forgot to breathe. This caused his face to flip from ghostly white to beet red. Gasping for air, he drew a hand to his chest and clutched his coat collar. A shiver coursed through his body and chills, sweaty chills, turned his skin clammy. Physically, he was a mess.

As he exhaled his long-held-in breath, he sought plausible answers to the jumbled mess in his brain, but his probe only stirred up more questions. ""This elf refused my dinner invitation and then asked to leave early to fix a special dinner for her husband. So, why is she here in *my* kitchen, using everything *my* wife owns? And where's *her* husband? Sooty bricks. What would he think if he knew his wife was standing here flirting with me? Why, he'd probably want my neck. And Mitzi, what if she were to walk in now? God, please help me out of this pickle stew. Give me some answers. Tell me what to do, and fast."

Sweat beaded up on Santa's brow. Feeling crazed, as crazed as a dolphin caught in a fisherman's net, he began doubting his own sanity. "Oh, what in taffy tarnation did I do after falling asleep? Shimmering icicles. I don't remember doing anything. This has got to be a crazy dream. Oh, God, please, please let me be dreaming."

Clamping his eyes shut, gripping his head, he yelled, "No! No! No! This can't be real." Wanting Elf Laura gone, he willed her to vanish like a bad dream does upon awakening. Seconds later, opening his eyes, casting them over to where she stood, he was forced to accept—albeit unwillingly—that she, still beckoning to him with outstretched arms, was no dream. "Shimmering icicles. Does this woman ever have gull! Standing here in my kitchen like she owns the place. But why?" As much as he struggled to come up with an answer, he couldn't. His gut, sensing that, seemed to be shouting, "Run, Santa. Run!" But he couldn't run. He could only move backward, one step at a time. And as he did, Elf Laura, sexily sashaying toward him, matched each of his steps with one of her own.

Rounding the coffee table, a light popped on in Santa's head. "Ah, I've got it. Since learning my wife's gone, this dame schemed all day to take her place. That's it. She didn't want a dinner invitation. No. That wasn't good enough. She decided to move in. Holy Walrus Turds! She thinks she can take over *my* cottage, and *me*, too."

In an effort to dodge her clutches, he stepped behind his recliner. Feeling safeguarded by the chair, he, fear still modulating his voice, tried reasoning. "For, . . . for fiddlin' nutcrackers, Elf Laura. You, . . . you know as well as I do that, . . . that, we're both married. And, . . . and just because my wife isn't here, doesn't give you the right to, . . . to barge in here and, . . . and take over like this."

"Are you surprised, Mr. Soweto Claus?" As Mitzi spoke in her natural voice, she watched the color draining from his face.

"What did you say?" Stepping forward, looking at her

instead of paying attention to where he was going, Santa tripped. Thrusting his hands forward, he managed to grab the edge of the coffee table to break his fall. Holding on, allowing time for his wobbly knees to stabilize, he stared at the flower arrangement sitting in its center. "These are Mitzi's favorite flowers. And that's Mitzi's voice coming from *Elf Laura's* mouth. But how? How can that be?"

Thrusting his upper torso backward, he bolted upright. Planting his hands on his hips, he, too confused to say anything, just stared at the woman standing before him.

"I said, 'Are you surprised, Mr. Soweto Claus?'"

Santa's jaw dropped and the hairs on the back of his neck stood up straighter than upside-down icicles. "Am I going mad? I swear this woman sounds just like my Mitzi. And she called me mister and Soweto. Only Mitzi calls me mister and my ethnic nicknames."

Mitzi, her eyebrows arched like two mountain peaks, repeated, "Are you surprised, Mr. Soweto Claus?" His reaction, his baffled, bug-eyed look tickled her funny bone. She couldn't keep it together. Doubling over, laughing fitfully, she managed to say, "Oh, the look on your face. If only I had a camera."

A scowl cut deep furrows across Santa's brow. "Huh? For sure, that's Mitzi's voice." Rattled, he shook his head. The possibility of Elf Laura and Mitzi being one and the same person was hard to swallow. "Is it possible? Might Elf Laura be my Mitzi?" As if needing proof, he scanned her slender figure from head to toe. As he did, he felt transported back in time, to when they were both thirty years younger. Putting two and two together, it took but a moment for him to realize he'd been duped. Fury exploded from every cell in his body. His mad side, rising in crescendos, showed in his rapidly pumping chest. His fingers, like angry snakes, curled into tight fists. With his eyes flaring like twin volcanos in the throes of an eruption, and his jaw clenched tight enough to break his teeth, he yelled, "I've been tricked. How could you, Mitzi? How could you do this to me? You, . . . you . . ."

"Do what?" Despite feeling vulnerable, and nervous, Mitzi decided to use her most reliable tactic: flirting. "It will calm him. I'm sure," she reasoned. Sensuously, she fluttered her eyelashes, inviting eye contact with him. Then, spreading a coquettish grin across her face, she, slowly like a cat on the prowl, moved in closer.

"O-o-oh, o-o-oh," Santa moaned. The softness of her touch, her skin meeting his and the warmth of her breath seeping deep into his whiskers, quickened his heartbeat, and also pulled the plug on his anger. "Ah, closeness." Yes. He wanted nothing more than to succumb to what he'd missed for the last three months; but craving answers more than tenderness, he checked himself.

Drawing on his determination to find out why she had stayed away so long, why she didn't write or call, and especially why she had tricked him into believing she was someone else, he pulled her hands down from around his neck. Stepping back, he squared his jaw and nailed his eyes to her startled face. Slowly, in a dead-serious voice, he formed his words. "Why, Mitzi? Why? Night after night I've sat in this cottage worrying about you. Why did you stay away so long? Why didn't you write or call? And, lady snow goose, I think you had some nerve playing this imposter game right under *my* Soweto nose. So, tell me. Why, Mitzi. Why? Why did you pull this charade on me?"

"Pretty good acting, doncha think?" she said, deliberately skirting his questions. Inching in a little closer, looking faintly apologetic, she smiled nervously. "Come on. Admit it. You didn't know it was me. Did you?"

Santa, his ego bruised, threw her an icy stare. "Women," he said frostily.

"I do love you, you know," she said, unease cracking her voice. "And I didn't mean for it to go this far. But when I saw that announcement posted in your lobby . . ."

As she spoke, Santa studied her eyes. "Oh, they're so penetrating, so deep sky blue. No! No! No! This can't be."

What he saw twisted his heart into twenty million loops of agony. Anguish immediately constricted his airway. As the two stared into each other's eyes, only the sound of his labored breathing filled the air. To her approach, he threw out his arms, sending her flying backward onto the sofa. His reaction startled him but didn't lessen his rage. Hovering over her, he bellowed angrily, "Lady, you're not my wife. I don't know how you found out Mitzi calls me Mr. Soweto Claus. That's our private secret. And yes, you do a magnificent job imitating her voice. But I'd swear to the

Four Winds on top of Saucer Plateau that, . . . that . . . you're *not* my wife!"

"I am too," she retorted, tears welling up in her eyes.

"Oh, no you're not!"

"Yes, I am. What more do I have to do to prove it?" she demanded, turning on him with her own temper. "Do I have to tell you all our private secrets? Like the one on our wedding day when you *made* me promise to never, ever cut my hair. Do I have to tell you what you whispered in my ear then?"

Thrusting an arm out, waving an accusing finger in her face, Santa, still on a sizzling tirade, countered with, "Lady, I don't know who you are, you, . . . you conniving snow goose. And, I don't know how you found out so much about Mitzi and me, but you can tell me every secret pact I've ever made with my Mitzi and I still won't believe you're my wife." Dropping his head, swinging it from side to side, showing apparent disgust, he turned and walked over to the picture window.

"Hey, sweetheart, that old sun has traveled some distance since you went up there. So, what's it gonna be? Midnight before you come down?" After voicing that rhetoric, Mitzi, knowing she had no choice but to accept the situation for what it was, picked up where she left off in her reminiscing. She recalled how excited she had felt that first night back home, lovingly preparing a surprise dinner for her sweetheart. However, when the ticking of the kitchen clock started eating up the dinner hour, her worry about Santa being a *no show* set her nerves on edge.

"The apple pie is just about done and he's still not home. Where is he?" Standing on tiptoe, leaning over the sink, she stared out the kitchen window. Her squinting eyes struggled to penetrate the night's darkness. "He's always home by five-thirty when it isn't the Christmas Season. I sure hope he didn't decide to stop by Pietro's Diner or Hanna's Hamburger Joint for a quick bite. Or, for a leisurely dinner at Snow Goose Restaurant."

Ding, ding, ding . . . Click.

Mitzi's shaky fingers grabbed two hot pads. Hurriedly she pulled the sweet-smelling pie from the oven. Hands full, she nudged the door up with the toe of her shoe. Its loud bang was followed by a muted sound coming from the living room. She froze. Her eyes rayed wide. Her lips trembled. Her heart fluttered. The moment she had both dreaded and longed for was finally upon her. She hadn't anticipated how she would feel, how Santa would feel, or how they would play it out. Her lungs, demanding air, triggered a gasp. On the tail end of it, she whispered, "Someone's in the house. My sweetheart's home."

"Mitzi, Mitzi."

Her name. Her real name. She hadn't heard it spoken in three months. No sooner had it enter her ears than there he was, standing under the archway in all his Soweto glory. She stared at him and he stared back. She tried deciphering the look in his eyes. "He's shocked. No. He's confused. No. I think he's frightened. Or, . . . or is he mad?" Somehow in the midst of her fluster, she managed to set the pie on a cooling rack.

Longing to hold him close, to soothe him, she stepped forward. Noticing his look of utter terror—him recoiling— she stopped short. In an attempt to calm him, she asked, "Are you surprised, Mr. Soweto Claus?" It didn't work. Rather, the sound of her *true* voice widened his eyes and dropped his jaw. Why she found his discombobulated look so funny was beyond her. She tried but couldn't squelch the laughter exploding from her lips. Seconds later, one glimpse of his fast-reddening face—a sure sign he was about to explode—was enough to snuff out her giggles. His cutting words, "How could you? How could you do this to me?", pierced her heart like a bevy of dead-on arrows. Thinking a huge hug after three months of missing her would calm him, she wrapped her arms around his neck and said sweetly, "Do what?"

She remembered him loosely putting his arms around her and looking tenderly into her eyes. She expected him to draw her in close, to kiss her. His hesitation alarmed her. When he shoved her onto the couch and yelled, "Lady, you're not my wife!", her eyes welled up with tears, but she, determined not to crumble, held them back.

She remembered yelling and him yelling back. The image of him clamming up, planting his feet over by the window was indelibly printed on her mind. His standing there, smoldering like a hot ember, left her feeling chilled to the bone.

Now, as she stared at him, she mulled over the possibility that her changes had shocked him beyond acceptance. She felt like running but squelched the urge.

With him standing over by the window—back toward her, too stubborn to voice what he was thinking—she wondered what was keeping him from seeing she was his wife, his Mitzi. "Have I changed that much? Maybe too much?" She worried about him rejecting her and visualized living alone in an apartment. "I could make it alone. But moose malarkey, I don't want to live alone. I want closeness again with the man I love." Unable to stand his silence any longer, she asked crisply, "Okay, *Mr. Soweto Claus*, just what in taffy tarnation do I have to do to prove to you that I am Mitzi Claus. Your wife?"

Seconds ticked by. Ill at ease with the tension mounting between them, she grabbed a couch pillow and crushed it to her bosom. "Is he going to answer me or is he going to walk out? I hate this. Taffy tarnation. I guess there's nothing I can do but wait."

As she contemplated his rejection, Santa, usually quick to express his feelings, maintained a stiff stance. Little did he suspect his prolonged silence, like a lead-heavy lull before a storm, was unnerving his wife.

Santa's shuffle around the platform was starting to drag.

Even so, he pressed on. "I'm so close to the end, I have to keep going." Spiking the air with a thrust of his fist, he yelled, "It's on to the finish." Leaning over the railing, he directed his next comments to all below, even though no one could hear him. "And you down there. Keep up the good work." He loved that the whole Region was cheering him on. But he had no idea everyone, from the youngest on up, was partying. Yes. Thanks to the insight of Vic Jasselton, they were fueling and refueling themselves with all the food brought in by the village restaurant owners.

Dialing into where he left off in his daydream, Santa recalled how shocked he had felt holding the woman he thought was his wife in his arms and then suddenly realizing her eyes were definitely not Mitzi's. He remembered staring out the window for the longest time, pondering her question: *Just what do I have to do to prove to you that I am Mitzi Claus, your wife?*

Sinking into his stubborn nature, he resolved not to give this imposter, whoever she was, an answer. "I don't even want to look at her. So, why should I tell her what I know?" Time pulsing into silence, seemed to calm him some. Rethinking his pigheaded stance, he realized he had to tell her. If he didn't, he had no just cause to kick her out and he wanted her out, like right now. He could no longer stand her playing with his emotions. Whirling around, beaming his bugged-out eyes at her, he sneered, "You'd have to change the color of your eyes, Elf Laura Ponseta. You thought of everything but that, didn't you? And, Elf, . . . Elf, whoever you are, you know as well as I do, you can't change what you've been born with. Nobody can."

Anticipating a shocked look and a quick skedaddle from his cottage, he stood tall, folded his arms across his chest and compressed his face into an angry grimace. Eyeing Elf Laura, he expected her to crumble. But she didn't crumble. Neither did she look shocked. Nor did she look surprised. On the contrary, she looked rather amused.

Mitzi, rising from the couch, walked slowly toward him. Halting two feet from him, matching his stiff stance, she stared into his wary eyes. Purposely tipping her lips into a sly, smug smile, she said sweetly, "You're absolutely right, Mr. Soweto Claus. I can't change what I've been born with. I wasn't blessed with racial and facial-feature changes like you were. Yes. I know I can't change the color of my eyes. But who says I can't cover them up, eh? Maybe tweak them with a little color." Leaning forward, she cupped a hand under one eye. A moment later, straightening her back, she thrust her hand under his Soweto nose for his inspection.

"Contacts!" His own naivety slapped him in the face as he stared at the tiny saucer in her outstretched hand. Feeling stupid, he hit his forehead with the palm of his hand. Then, as the words, "Blue contacts," slid reflexively off his lips, he lifted his eyes to inspect hers. One blue and one hazel eye peered back at him.

"Had you royally fooled, didn't I?" she said, grinning shamelessly.

"Royally? Yes, I guess you did," he answered, casting a penitent glance her way.

"My dear Mr. Soweto Claus, you might have been born uniquely different than anyone else in the world. And yes, your ethnic color magically changes every year on your birthday. But hey, you don't have the market on all the magic in the world."

Raising an eyebrow, taking in his reaction, she noticed he seemed too stunned to speak. As she leaned back to slip the contact into her eye, she heard him clearing his throat. "Good. He's found his tongue again."

"I never claimed I could corner the market on anything. But there's one thing I'd like to know."

"What's that?" she asked, putting her arms around his neck. This time he didn't pull away or push her away.

"I want to know who else was in on this little caper?"

"Who else? My dearest sweetheart, I didn't seek the help of one little ol' elf in this whole North Pole Region." Pausing, she worked her fingers into his beard. After fluffing it a little here and a little there, she raised her brow and said playfully, "Actually, sweetheart, you were the one who put me up to it."

"Me!" Clasping her arms, holding her at bay, he yelled, "Bog wash! I didn't tell you to lose weight. I didn't tell you to use all that make-up. I didn't tell you to buy a whole new wardrobe. I didn't tell you to stay away for three months. I, . . . I didn't tell you to apply for that job. And, . . . and I certainly didn't tell you to get those stupid contacts. Now, did I?"

Slipping out of his grip, triggering a finger at him, Mitzi promptly switched the blame to him. "You're absolutely right about all that. But it was *you* who gave me permission. Did you *magically* forget that?"

"What! Me? I gave you permission?"

"Yes. You gave me permission by telling me I could take a vacation for as long as I wanted. Remember?" Mitzi hesitated. Tilting her head, orienting her nose to his, she sent him an indignant stare. Then, stepping back, she said in an even tone. "I think, my dearest, your exact words were, 'Go any place you want. Do whatever you want. You don't have to tell me where you go, or what you do, or anything.' And to make it all possible, you handed me your debit card. And yes. I did do something different. Really different."

"But fiddlin' nutcrackers, did you have to become a completely different person? You know, I loved you just the way you were."

"Really," she said, her tone clearly indignant. "Well, Mr. Soweto Claus, I might've been A-OK the way I was for you, but I was not A-OK the way I was for me. You see I didn't like 'the me' I had become, or, actually 'the me' I had always been. So, I went on a self-improvement journey. And I learned a whole lot about taking care of myself. Like holding my own and speaking my mind. And now, Mr. Soweto Claus, I like myself a whole lot more, but . . ."

Hesitating, standing on tiptoe, she pushed her nose up

to his. Fluttering her eyelashes just short of his spectacles, she honey-coated her next words. "But more than anything else, sweetie, I like that you hired me as production coordinator under the name of Elf Laura Ponseta. Because if I, Elf Mitzi Claus, had applied for that job, you and I both know you would've found every excuse in the book *not* to hire me."

Santa, quick to protest, yelled, "What! You're still going to keep that job? Mitzi, you've got to be kidding. All my toy makers will have moose-malarkey conniption fits. Why, I can hear them now. They'll say, 'What? You hired your own wife for that position!' And they'll all be thinking, 'Why not me?' For sure, they'll accuse me of using favoritism."

"So," she said, directing an indignant stare his way. "They can say whatever they like. And, listen." Pausing, she pulled her shoulders back and propped her hands firmly on her hips. In this stance, exuding the confident of a high-powered attorney, she retorted firmly, "Let me remind you, Mr. Soweto Claus, you hired me because I have the skills and if you try firing me just because I happen to be *your* wife, I'll file a lawsuit with the North Pole Discrimination Board. And you can bet those flapping-red snow britches of yours that I'll win it, too."

As he mulled over her huffy comments, Santa scowled. Thirty seconds later, after letting the reality of her words sink in, he shook his head and smiled ruefully. "I can't believe you did this, Mitzi. To tell you the truth, I can hardly believe it's you, standing there. How could you change so much? And so fast? Like, . . . like, you look like, and even act like, a completely different person."

"Sweetheart, I worked really hard, and really fast. And believe me, never, ever again do I want to be the dowdy person that I sadly let myself become. Not ever."

Grinning with a hint of boyish pleasure, Santa stared at his newly *reconditioned* wife. "Well, I know when I've been had. Guess I'll just have to learn to live with the new you, huh?"

Mitzi, meeting his eyes, said, "Guess so, Mr. Soweto Claus. Yes. You'll just have to learn to live with the new me because no way am I letting you out of my life. So, face it. You're hitched to me for eternity and then some."

Her words sent a flutter through Santa's heart. Smiling, reaching out, he gently tugged on her hand. She willingly fell into his arms. Planting a kiss on her forehead, he teasingly inquired, "What's for dinner, my love, besides that luscious-smelling pie? I am invited to dinner, aren't I? After all, I remember a gal named Elf Laura Ponseta asking her boss for some time off, so she could prepare one of her husband's favorite meals tonight. Would she accept a dinner invitation at a nice restaurant from her boss? No. Imagine. Even after he spent two weeks slaving away, teaching her everything he knows, she refused. Can you beat that? Guess she thinks more of her husband, Mr. Ponseta, than she does of her boss, Saint Nicholas Claus, huh?"

Santa remembered Mitzi snuggling in close, laughing.

Laughter. He loved hearing the laughter he hadn't heard for three months. At least, not as hers. Playfully he tickled her, saying, "Hey, I can feel your ribs. Let's go put some meat on those bones."

Quick to respond to that comment, she narrowed her eyes and shot him a look that clearly said, "Hey, buster, don't try making me into what I used to be."

He knew what her eyes were saying, and he liked it. Locking his eyes with hers, he wrapped his arms around her and drew her toward him. Her closeness set his heart throbbing. He needed no coaxing to kiss her, which he did passionately. Afterward, still feeling amorous, he slid his lips to her ear and whispered tenderly, "I'll always love you, my dear, no matter what you do to change yourself."

Jerking her head up, she asked, "Then, you don't mind that I cut my hair?"

"Looks pretty good to me and feels nice, too. And I must say, it sure makes you look younger."

"That was my biggest fear, you know. I was afraid you'd hate me for breaking our wedding-day pact."

"Mitzi, if there's one thing you've taught me, it's, 'I've got no right to run your life.'"

"And all the time I worked with you as Elf Laura Ponseta, you never suspected who I was?"

"Hon, as hard as it is on my *male ego,* I have to admit you did pull the moss over my eyes. And speaking of moss, I had this weird dream night after night after that woman, *Elf Laura Ponseta,* began working for me. You were in it, too.

I mean, the old you. And now, I think I've got it all figured out." With a snap of his fingers, he smiled the same way anyone does after solving a difficult riddle. "Yes. That clump of moss you were dangling over my head, *Elf Mitzi Peddler*, represented this little charade you were playing, didn't it? And I was stupid enough to stomp after it."

"Reindeer moss? Elf Mitzi Peddler? What are you talking about?"

"Ah. That's my secret. But maybe I'll share it with you while Elf Laura Ponseta has a *private* celebration with her husband tonight."

Mitzi laughed. "I bet you'll never let me live this down, will you?"

"Listen, I'll tell you one thing," he said, pausing to kiss the tip of her nose. "No one, not one of my toy makers has ever pulled anything like this on me. Tell me. What did you do? Plan this caper for months?"

"No. It just happened as I sat there on the bus."

"The bus? What bus?"

"Come on," she said, pulling him toward the kitchen. "I'll tell you all about it while we eat. You are hungry, aren't you?"

"Am I hungry? Shimmering icicles. You're asking a man who's barely survived on TV dinners for the last three months if he's hungry? Oh, Lady Snow Goose, let me tell you. My mouth is watering for some of that hot apple pie and whatever else you cooked up out there."

◇•◇•◇

CHAPTER 11

Am I dead or alive?

Santa's feet felt pretty good considering he hadn't sat down for quite some time. When he started his daydream, little did he know Jingle-Jangle mountain would quiver, on average, two to five times each hour. Its effect on his feet . . . Well, he ranked it up there with the kneading fingers of a professional masseuse.

His stomach, though, was a different story. Desperate for nourishment, it was howling worse than a tornado descending on Kansas City. Knowing he wouldn't be eating until late evening, he tried appeasing it with a little pep talk. "Yeah, I'm aware you're hungrier than a polar bear coming out of hibernation, but you're just gonna have to wait until tonight's feast. Then, I'll fill you up good."

Weary at this point, he approached the Kringleland post with a drag in his feet. Leaning over the railing, he took stock of the commotion below. "Still going strong, eh? It sure tickles me to see how much fun you're having. Oh, what a day this has been. Absolutely perfect for daydreaming. Just wish I had time to run through another. Nope. Can't let myself do that. Wouldn't be fair. Not after spending what? A little over two hours . . ." Pausing,

227

glancing at his watch, his eyes flared wide. "Well, throw me down an iceberg slide. I've spent over four hours daydreaming up here. Okay, Mr. Hum-Bow Claus, you've got to get on with your speech. So, just one more go-round to motion everyone to hush and that's it. And don't you dare start another one. Hear?"

On the lower platform, Mitzi's thoughts lingered on the blissful dinner she and Santa had shared on that long-ago night. When he winked at her and said, "Mm, yum, yum. This is so delicious and so much better than TV dinners," she knew he was overjoyed at having her home. And, too, she felt confident he'd soon forget about the worry she caused him. "He's so happy to see me, he'll . . ."

Cre-e-e-e-eak. The sound of wood stressing startled her. She lifted her eyes to the interlocking beams above her. Spotting nothing amiss, she merely shrugged her shoulders.

Thud-thud, thud-thud, thud-thud, . . .

Overhead, the familiar sound of Santa's boots lessened her concern. "It must've been him stepping on a loose board. Or, maybe he was tweaking something up there." Hoping he'd hear her above the din of the cheering crowds, she yelled, "Hum-Bow, you better stop your daydreaming and get on with your speech."

She cocked an ear. Listened. His footsteps, getting fainter and fainter—never breaking their methodical pace—

let her know he hadn't heard a word she said. "Dancin' Prancer. He's still going strong. For all I know, he'll likely spend a couple more hours up there daydreaming before getting on with his speech. And me? What can I do? Twiddle my thumbs? Yegads. I should've brought a book. Why I didn't is beyond me. Not good planning on my part. Should've known with this warm weather, he'd spend half the day up there daydreaming."

Wilting back into her chair, she stared at the underside of the platform. To this point, she hadn't paid much attention to the mountain's little quivers. She just chalked them up to all the racket pelting its sides. Now, realizing they were getting stronger, and seeing a crossbeam shift slightly, she *shifted* to hyper vigilance. Bolting upright, gripping the sidearms of her chair, she heard a voice cracking—her own. "Holy walrus turds. Did that thing just move? Yes, it did. I know it did. I saw it."

Rat-a-tat-tat. Rat-a-tat-tat. Rat-a-tat-tat.

"What's that noise?" Startled, she jumped. Catching sight of something rolling on the table beside her, she grabbed it before it hit the ground. "A pencil. Just a pencil." Relieved, she breathed a little easier. "Guess I shouldn't get worked up over nothing." Still, a feeling of doom swept through her, indicating otherwise.

Super hyper alert at this point, she hopscotched her gaze from post to post, checking for movement. "Those things are planted in deep wells of cement and couldn't possibly topple. Or could they?" Despite such reasoning, queasiness—much like seasickness—drew her hands to her stomach. She felt her chair shifting. "Yikes. This platform is swaying and, . . . and a whole lot, too."

Survival mode kicked in. Her back stiffened, her limbs splayed wide, her hands grabbed the chair's side arms and her legs anchored her feet to the ground. Despite fearing for her life—and Santa's—she worked to keep panic at bay. "Got to think rationally. Can't stay in this chair. Got to do something to secure myself. Maybe tie my body to something. But where? And with what?"

A quick scan of the area landed her eyes on a box overflowing with extension cords. Knowing what she had to do, she dropped to all fours and crawled over to it.

Minutes later, with a tangled cord hoisted over her right shoulder, she crawled to the backside of the fireplace. Once there, she braced herself against it and looped the bulky thing through a few ladder rungs. Doing that was fairly easy. However, wrapping it around her waist and knotting it with trembling hands, proved to be a challenge. She pulled the knot as tight as the cord would allow. Then, lifting her eyes to the swaying platform, she yelled, "Santa, I sure hope you have enough sense to secure yourself up there. If you ask me, you'd better get on with your speech, so we can get down from here before this thing comes crash . . ."

◇•◇•◇

CR-RACK, CR-R-A-ACK, RUMBLE, RUMBLE. CA-POW!

All around the mountain, unexpected, ear-splitting rumbles drew eyes to the sky. All, partying, looked up for signs of an impending storm; but from hither and tither, the sky appeared exceptionally clear.

CR-R-R-R-R-A-A-ACK, CR-R-R-A-ACK, CR-R-R-A-A-A-ACK, RUMBLE, RUMBLE. BOOM! BAM!

Hunter, his face showing concern, shaded his eyes and double-checked for signs of thunder-threatening clouds. Within the sky's blue-dome rim, all he could see was a tight-knit group of cottony clouds far to the south.

CR-R-R-A-ACK, CRACK, RUMBLE, RUMBLE, . . .

A slight jolt coming from the ground set the elves on edge. Earthquake! Most, in the throes of panic, ran in circles, looking for friends and loved ones. All feared not only for their own lives, but for Mitzi's and Santa's as well. Around the mountain, many—popping up on their toes—tried sighting the two. Within seconds, a young woman on the south side of the mountain thrust a hand into the air and yelled frantically, "I see red up there. It's, . . . it's Santa's legs. Yikes. They're dangling off the platform."

"Are they moving," came a voice from the far left.

"I don't know. I can't tell from here."

"And Mitzi? What about her?"

"Sorry. Haven't spotted her yet."

The news, *Santa's down; don't know if he's dead or alive,* traveled around the mountain faster than an e-mail zipping over the Internet. As this troublesome news registered, many a worrisome word tumbled off tongues.

"What should we do? What should we do?"

Fear set everyone on edge. Bickering erupted. It, in turn, played havoc with reaching a consensus on how to respond. It also ate up precious minutes.

"Doncha think we should send up a rescue party?"

"I don't know. Do we want to risk losing our lives?"

"I know it's dangerous, but what about *their* lives?"

"Hey. If that mountain blows, we'll all be goners."

"Well, if it does blow, I'd rather die attempting to rescue them than waste precious time arguing with you."

"I say we wait a little while. At least, until the rumbling stops."

"No. Come on. We need to rescue them. Like right now!"

"No. It's too dangerous. This whole mountain could blow."

"Listen. Santa and Mitzi, they're helpless up there. Let's go."

"No. It's too risky. Many lives could be lost."

"We can't just abandon them. After all, they're . . ."

"You're not thinking rationally. We need to wait until . . ."

While voices escalated, and tempers flared, the mountain's inner caldron worked another belch up its throat. CR-R-R-A-A-A-A-ACK. CRACK, CRA-A-ACK. CRACK, CRA-A-CK. BOOM! BAM! CA-POW! PI-SHOO!

These rumbles—much more ear piercing than the previous ones—were followed by fissures breaking through the upper crust of snow on the south side of the mountain, quite close to the Blessing Day platform.

CR-R-R-A-A-ACK. CRA-A-ACK, CRACK, CRACK. BOOM! BAM! POW! PI-SHOO, CLATTER, CLATTER, CLATTER. CR-R-R-A-A-ACK, BOOM! BAM! POW! CLATTER, CLATTER, CLATTER, PI-SHOO-O-O!

Like unrestrained popcorn, boulders and ice chunks spewed haphazardly into the air. The heavier pieces dropped to the ground with a thud close to the platform. PLOP, PLOP, PLOP, PLOP, PLOP. The smaller ones, looking like competitors in a marathon, vied for positions as they tumbled helter-skelter down the mountainside. Fortunately, crevices, lying in wait, gobbled them up before they could make it to the bottom and hurt someone.

Mere seconds after the mountain stopped rumbling, the elves turned their attention to the platform again. Word through the grapevine was, "Santa is still flat on his back with his legs dangling over the platform, and there's no sign of Mitzi yet."

Exercising its mighty jaws, the mountain fired another round of CR-R-R-A-A-ACK, BOOM! BAM! CA-POW! CLATTER, CLATTER, CLATTER, PI-SHOO-O-O into the air. When the rumbling subsided, someone shouted, "Jumpin' seal pups! Look. Look up there at the platform." Eyes oriented upward. Jaws dropped. Phrases like "What! How can this be?" slipped through many an elf's lips as the Krisville post, like a mere twig, snapped in two, flinging Santa high into the air.

The masses, hardly able to comprehend the gravity of the situation, screamed, "NO! NO, NO!" as Santa's body sailed through the air like a limp, red sock before coming down with a thump.

Suddenly airborne, Santa's lungs exploded. "YEE-OW-E-E-E-E-E! HE-E-ELP! HELP! HELP ME!" His desperate screams splayed out no further than the mountainside he was flying toward. And his weighty body? It, landing with a thud on a narrow ledge, sent snow flying twenty feet or more into the air. That snow, riding the air currents at the weightless speed of fluffed-up goose down, settled, flake by flake, on top of his hushed body. Seconds later, covered with three-to-four-inch of snow, he could've easily been mistaken for a bowled-over snowman.

Shocked, baffled senseless, the elves below, stumbled about, frantically crying out, "Santa. What's happening to our Santa? Has anyone sighted him yet? And Mitzi? Any news about her? Oh, what can we do?" In the ensuing chaos, everyone kept asking questions; questions no one could answer.

Santa, thankful for the soft, snowy landing, and glad to still be alive, lifted his head. Shaking off the wet stuff, his eyes met unfamiliar territory. His heart sank. "Where in taffy tarnation am I?" He turned sideways to get a better view. Pressing a hand into the snow to gain leverage, his palm, rather than meeting a firm surface, went straight down, clear up to his shoulder. His fingers, grasping for something, latched onto nothing. Thinking this odd, he withdrew his hand and peered down the hole his arm had just created. Color drained from his face. Seeing nothing but a snowy landscape fifty feet or more below, he cringed. "Holy walrus turds. I'm on a narrow ledge and, . . . and I'm too far up to jump. Oh, I hope this ledge is strong enough to hold my weight." Turning to explore the possibility of hiking out, his eyes met a sheer cliff. "Mercy me. There's no way to get off this thing. I'm doomed."

Fright pumped a loud scream up his throat. "Help! Help! Somebody, help me!" Desperately hoping for a response, he cocked an ear and listened. Nothing but silence befell his ears. The sobering truth hit hard. Almost crying, he dropped his chin to his chest. "I'm too far up. Might as well save my breath because nobody's gonna hear me. Sooty bricks. I'm gonna freeze to death in this wet suit. Yeah. By morning, I'll be stiffer than . . ." Suddenly, an aftershock threw Santa forward, almost spilling him over the edge. "Oh, no. No! Please, please stop. Please, no more vibrations."

Unlike the slight quivers he had welcomed earlier, these aftershocks weren't wanted, and they weren't relaxing him either. Coming one after another, each exceeding the previous ones in intensity, they terrified him.

When they finally stopped, he hardly had time to think about securing himself when the mountain's next jolt came with a vengeance. Far more tumultuous than the others, it shot him straight up with what seemed like the thrust of a missile. Flying haphazardly through the air—mimicking an airplane with a clipped wing—his lungs exploded with frantic screams. "O-o-oh. O-o-o-o-oh. Help! Help! I'm fa-a-alling. Ye-e-e-ow-e-e-e-e-e!"

Ker-plunk. Thud. His descent into a deep snowdrift created a stir of snow that mimicked a raging blizzard. As a weighty force crimped his legs toward his chest, his forearms reflexively flew up to protect his face. He couldn't move, but he felt himself moving, slowly at first, then with immense speed. "Dancin' Prancer. Am I falling into a deep crevice? If I am, I'll never be found. No. I'm bouncing."

BOING, BOING, BOING, BOING, BOING, . . .

"Oh, God, help me." Encapsulated in total darkness, Santa had no idea how much time had lapsed since he flew off the ledge. When the mountain shook, he had reflexively shut his eyes. Now open, he desperately sought, but could not see, a speck of light. Light, elusive light—seemingly nonexistent—sent his thoughts running rampant in the direction of doom.

"What happened? Did I pass out? Did I just come to? Am I dead or alive? Am I in purgatory? Am I stuck between Heaven and hell? Does earth still exist? Is my spirit being sucked into a *dark hole* somewhere in outer space? Oh, God, help; please help me."

With Santa's where-with-all usurped by total darkness, his anxiety quadrupled. "What's happening? I know I'm bouncing around in something, but what? *[gasp]* Oh, my God, I can't move. I can't . . . Air, air. *[gasp, gasp]* There's no air. *[gasp, gasp, gasp]* I can hardly breathe . . . *[gasp, gasp]*."

Unbeknown to Santa, his body, now the core of a growing snowball, was racing helter-skelter down the south side of Jingle-Jangle Mountain. And as it rolled, that snowball, licking up every snow crystal in its path, was not only growing exponentially on each revolution, it was fast becoming a death trap. Fear set him to shaking. He couldn't see anything. He couldn't move a muscle. He didn't know where he was going. And worst of all, he couldn't catch his breath.

"What's happening? Why am I being tossed about like a loose football?" Seconds before his airless tomb robbed him of consciousness, a meek "Help! Help!" slipped through his lips.

As the mountain belched yet again, the elves, looking up, caught sight of Santa flying through the air. From whence he came, they did not know. Many knowing, or at least hoping he was still alive, sighed with relief. His landing sent a geyser of snow gushing high into the air. While it was fluttering back to earth, a small avalanche of ice and snow, coming from behind, flipped him over backward. Thinking this funny, the elves looking on, chuckled. However, when one flip turned into another, and then another and another, causing more and more snow to be drawn to its orb, their jaws dropped. All were thinking, "How can this be happening? How can our beloved toy maker survive this peril?"

Before their startled eyes, a snowball-in-the-making, with Santa entombed in its belly, was bouncing down the mountainside. Starting slowly, jogging from one ice boulder to another, it quickly picked up more and more speed, and snow, on each revolution. Below, those looking on—their anxiety rising tenfold—started voicing pitiful comments.

"It's growing too big. Coming too fast."

"Isn't there anything we can do to stop it?"

"I don't think so."

"It's apt to roll right through Krisville."

"Yeah. And it's gonna destroy everything in its path, too."

"Poor Santa. He's doomed."

The whole ordeal was too much. Shocked, scared, stunned, dazed, numbed, bewildered—overloaded with all these emotions and then some—the elves, eyes glued to that humongous snowball, failed to realize they were standing in harm's way. Wholly mesmerized by its growing girth and its ever-increasing speed, they stood rigid as fence posts, staring at it barreling straight at them like a truck with no brakes. It was like they were standing on death's doorstep; unaware they were playing Russian roulette with a loaded snowball.

"Taffy tarnation! It's coming right at us! Yee-ow-e-e-e-e-e!"

Thank goodness someone had the sense to scream. Just in the nick of time, too. Fortunately, that scream broke shock's hold on the masses. Elf after elf snapped to. Their own fear-of-death screams fueled their quick getaway from the path of that gigantic snowball.

"Yee-ow-e-e-e-e-e! It's going to . . . It's . . ."

"Run! Run!"

"Go! Go! Go!"

"Hurry! Hurry! Faster! Faster!"

"Move it. Move, move. Come on. Don't stop."

"That way. Go that way. No, no, turn this way."

For a mere thirty seconds, pandemonium reigned. Elves pushed, shoved, yanked coat sleeves, swooped up little elfins, then scattered like mercury spattering from a broken thermometer. Whew! Miraculously all came through the human stampede with very few scrapes. That's not to dismiss, some barely escaped the path of that speeding orb.

SWI-S-S-S-S-SH, THUD.

The ground, undulating like a gigantic tsunami wave, played havoc with everyone's equilibrium. Swaying this way and that, one elf after another toppled over like game pieces on a wobbly table. PLOP, PLOP, PLOP, PLOP, PLOP. By the volume of their screams, it was evident everyone feared for their lives. Panic now superseded concern about

Santa and Mitzi's welfare. Terrified, many yelled, "The world's coming to an end. The world's coming to an end. We're all going to die. This is the end. We're doomed."

In less than a second—faster than a TV screen blanking out after hitting the OFF button—the inner earth applied its brakes and the screaming stopped. For a few moments, an eerie stillness hung in the air.

One by one, the elves, cautiously, bravely, rose to their feet. As they worked to regain their bearings, a few could be heard yelling, "That snowball. That giant snowball. What happened to it? Did anyone see where it went?"

Questioning eyes met questioning eyes. Shoulder shrugging and palm-up gestures indicated no one knew. *Hark!* One lone voice, like a ripple of hope, broke through the deafening silence. "Hey, look. I found it. It's over here. Inside the Victory Trees."

Sure enough, the massive snowball, with Santa still entombed inside it, had glided dead center into the Victory Tree formation. As it did, it tore down the crepe paper streamers woven across the entrance. It now lay wedged up against the Mediator Tree. The mighty Mediator Tree had done what all the elves had feared couldn't be done. It had stopped that gigantic snowball.

Fortunately, the sudden impact caused some of the outer layers of snow to loosen and drop off. Even so, a tangled mess of crepe-paper streamers, crisscrossing over and around the whole sphere, like crazy zigzag stitching on a darned sock, held the rest intact. And Santa? Poor Santa.

Everyone knew he lay trapped within its core.

Precious seconds ticked by as the elves stumbled about, trying to orient themselves to what had just happened. In reaction to a shrill whistle, thousands lifted their eyes upward to where Mitzi stood clutching a microphone on Saucer Plateau. Seeing she was safe, many sighed with relief.

"You down there," she belted into the microphone. "About twelve of you strong elves get into those Victory Trees and dig Santa out of that snowball. Hurry. Be quick about it."

No longer did any elf worry about breaking Santa's edict, *No one is to ever enter the Victory Tree formation for any reason.* They had just cause and just cause was better than any reason. Santa had to be rescued. Those closest to the Victory Trees rushed to his aid, tromping right into his off-limits, sacred V formation.

One elf, known simply as Spice, had the foresight to grab Hanna's hamburger flippers and hotdog skewers. "Now, remember," he said hurriedly as he passed them around to his buddies, "only use the handle end of these skewers to do your digging. And be careful. We don't want to jab Santa with one of them."

Soggy crepe paper and slushy snow flew helter-skelter as the elves frantically dug into the snowy hull. Within seconds, one shouted, "Look, I've found the toe of Santa's boot." Knowing what that meant, all scooted to the other side and began tunneling like crazy, searching for one thing, and one thing only: Santa's Hum-Bow nose.

Mitzi knew Santa would need medical attention, and fast. Unfortunately, transportation, all means of it other than hoofing it, was two miles or more away. Most locals had arrived on foot and those who came in from the suburbs had left their snowmobiles, sleighs and skis, even their cell phones—as was required—in North Pole Village.

"I'll have to assign a strong elf to go for help. One who can run like lightning. But who?" From so far up, Mitzi couldn't recognize anyone. However, she could see one elf bending over, picking up a pair of skis.

"Skis!" She couldn't believe her eyes. Skis were the answer to an unspoken prayer.

"You, down there," she shouted into her microphone. "You, with the skis. Get them on your feet and ski over to the nearest cottage and telephone for an ambulance. And tell them to use the service road to get in. And, . . . and be quick about it."

Mitzi's frantic voice startled Hunter. He glanced from where she was standing on high to the skis he'd just picked up. "She's asking me to go for help? Sooty bricks, I would never have bombed over here on these things if Shelly hadn't acted so uppity-like this morning. So, I decided . . ."

"Hunter, Mitzi's talking to you. Are you going to go for

help or not?"

Shelly's words jarred Hunter to action. He dropped his skis and stepped into them. Turning to face her, he asked, "Will you snap my bindings, please?"

Stooping down to connect them, she surprised him by saying, "I'm sorry. I guess you were right about your feelings this morning."

"What? She's telling me I was right and she's apologizing. I can't believe this. This girl, who Pietro said was a stuck-up snob, is apologizing? Stuck-ups don't apologize."

"Did you hear me?" she asked, pushing for a response. "You were right about your feelings this morning."

"Yeah, well, my feelings didn't tell me something like this would happen to Santa."

"Will you forgive me?"

"Forgive you?"

Smiling shyly, she reached for his outstretched hand. As he leveraged backward, she rose to his level.

"Yes, of course, I'll forgive you. But only if you'll give me a shove to get started."

Hunter readied his ski poles. Glancing over his shoulder, seeking Shelly's eyes, he nearly lost his balance as she, shoving him off, shouted, "Ready. Set. Here goes. Look out belo-o-ow."

◇•◇•◇

Up on Saucer Plateau, Mitzi spoke into the microphone

again. "If any of you brought blankets, please get them over to the Victory Trees. Santa may need them."

After giving that order, she stared down at the crowds. "Ah. They must be waiting for news about Santa. Taffy tarnation. I've got to get them to leave before the ambulance arrives. Otherwise, they'll be in the way. Oh, what if he doesn't make it? No. I mustn't go there. Better to think positive. And I'd better think up something for those elves to do, too. But what? Ah, I know." Leaning into the microphone, being careful not to sound preachy, she said, "Attention, everyone. If you aren't helping with the rescue, please head over to Dasher Hall and start preparations for tonight's feast. Or, . . . or, . . . or go home."

To her surprise no one budged. "Why aren't they moving? Ah, I know. They're scared. Scared Santa is dead. Oh, what if he is dead?"

A somber funeral procession flashed before Mitzi's eyes. She felt her knees buckling. "No! No! No! You can't die yet. Sweetheart, please. Please be alive when I get down there."

Hey, girl, stop stressing yourself. Think positive. Hold yourself together. Say something that'll give these elves hope.

Heeding that nudge from her *nattering Tomacita*, Mitzi took a deep breath. Leaning into the microphone, she spoke calmly. "Listen, all of you. I know you must be scared. Believe me. I am, too. But we must have faith. Now, by the time Santa gets dug out of that snowball, and examined at the hospital, he's going to be mighty hungry. You all know how he likes to eat. So, please. Go start preparations for tonight's turkey feast. Oh, and whatever you do, don't forget the cranberries."

Casting an expectant glance toward the crowds, she waited for them to disperse, but no one moved.

"Well, that approach didn't work."

Disappointed, she sucked in a deep breath to build momentum for her next command. To her surprise, before she could utter a word, someone heading toward Dasher Hall thrust a fist into the air and started chanting, "Don't forget the cranberries. Don't forget the cranberries. Whatever you do, don't forget the cranberries." The beat caught on. One by one, others fell in line, fist thrusting and chanting, "Don't forget the cranberries. Don't forget the cranberries. Whatever you do, don't forget the cranberries."

A smile lit Mitzi's face as she watched one elf after another joining the line, fist thrusting and chanting, "Don't forget the cranberries. Don't forget the cranberries."

"Well, I'll be. One elf induced the whole crowd to action. Hmm. I wonder who it was. Well, when I find out, I'm gonna do something to express my gratitude."

Having diverted the elves to a useful task, Mitzi had one thing, and one thing only on her mind—finding out if Santa was still alive. Antsy to get off the mountain, she chanted, "I must have faith. I must have faith." Down the snowy path she hurried. Still, with each stride forward, her fears mounted.

The moment she reached the clearing below Jingle-

Jangle Mountain, she glanced over at the Victory Trees. An opening between some lower branches afforded a peek. Catching sight of a figure dressed in red, stumbling about, clearly disoriented, she shouted her relief, "Santa! Thank goodness you're alive." The sight of him on his feet, wobbling about, triggered joyful tears and brought a smile to her lips.

Swiping the tail end of her scarf across her wet cheeks, she pushed her feet forward. "Got to keep moving." With determined gumption, she picked up her pace and ran as fast as her legs would carry her through the deep snow. By the time she neared the grove of Victory Trees, overexertion had slowed her legs to a slow walk. "Oh, do my legs ever ache. But I've got to keep moving." Rising above the pain, she pushed on. As she got closer, the on-coming lights of the ambulance kept her from seeing an elf approaching. She jumped when she heard his voice.

"Mitzi. Oh, Mitzi. Spice here. Sorry if I startled you. But am I ever glad to see you. Come. We need your help."

"Why? What's the matter?"

"What's the matter? I'll tell you what's the matter. It's your husband. He's a stubborn moose. He keeps insisting he's fitter than a brand-new toy fiddle. And look. You can see for yourself, he's not."

"Yes. I can see." Sighting his tight fists, steely eyes and set jaw—what she had long ago dubbed as his *I'm-ready-to-take-on-the-world stance*—her heart sank. Immediately she understood the reason for his raging-bull posturing.

Twenty or so elves, circling him, were ready to stop him if he tried to bolt.

"It's for his own protection," Spice said, reading her questioning stare. "Actually, to be truthful, we did it because he seemed so discombobulated after we dug him out of that snowball. We'd say something to him and a minute or so later he couldn't recall who said what. And he keeps insisting on climbing back up that mountain to give his speech. Whew! You and I both know that would spell disaster. And if you ask me, he really needs to see a doctor. Good thing you sent that young elf to fetch an ambulance."

"Who was *that* young elf?"

"Hunter Swift Bear."

"And the elf who led everyone to Dasher Hall?"

"Oh, that was Shelly. Elf Shelly Jasselton. She has spunk and . . ."

"Thanks," Mitzi said hurriedly. Lifting a hand, signaling him to hush, she strained to hear what Santa was saying.

"All of you. Go on. Get away from me. Hospital? Bog wash. Nobody's going to make me go to the hospital on Christmas Season Blessing Day." Catching a glimpse of his wife approaching, he ordered, "Get rid of them."

"No. Now, you listen to me. You've had a terrible accident and . . ."

"Fiddlesticks. That was nothing but a little joyride."

"Joy ride! You could've been killed."

"But I wasn't now, was I?" Crossing his arms, he glared

defiantly at her.

Mitzi instantly met his stubborn gaze with one of her own. "Hey. Stop being so difficult and listen. Every elf here is trying to help you. We all know you're in pain. So, come on. Cooperate. You've got to go to the hospital."

"Oh, no I don't. What I've got to do is get back up there on that platform and give my speech."

"Mr. Hum-Bow Claus, either you walk into that ambulance, or I'll order you strapped to a gurney and carried in. It's your choice. Now, what'll it be?"

"Oh, all right."

Santa, wanting to avoid such humility in front of his toymakers, reluctantly moved toward the ambulance. Midway, he turned around. Grasping his head, he made a scrunched-up, mistletoe berry face at Mitzi. His behavior alarmed her. Not the face making. That she dismissed as normal. But gripping his head? She knew he only did that when he had a horrific headache.

Upon arrival at Sleigh Valley Hospital, Dr. Swift, Santa's long-time ice-fishing buddy, immediately had him wheeled into an examining room. Grabbing a metal instrument, he ran it from heel to toe on the bottom of his feet. Santa went into a fit of laughter. "Ho, ho, ho. That tickles. What are you doing?"

"Just checking to make sure your wires aren't crossed. Now, lie down here. I need to check you out a little more.

And then, I think I'll have my attendant take you to the next room to do an MRI."

Santa held back. Looking through the glass between the room he was in and the room housing the MRI equipment, he pulled a hand down his whiskers and said, "You're gonna run me through that? Through something that looks like a model railroad tunnel? You've got to be kidding."

"Got to. Got to see if that tumble messed up your head. Or your back. Or, maybe a bone or two." Realizing his answer was not what Santa wanted to hear, he teasingly added, "Okay, you old bloke. If you must know the truth, it's really to see if your head is full of snowballs."

Santa, thinking on that, said nothing; but his failure to match or exceed Dr. Swift's witty sarcasm drew a dumbfounded look to doc's face.

"Hmm. What's with him? Has he lost his quick wit? He usually loves a good round of bantering and he prides himself at being a master at it. So, why not today? Could he be afraid of the MRI machine? Is he claustrophobic? Or has something gone whacko with his head?"

Deciding to try a softer approach—much like he used with children—he said more thoughtfully, "Come on, ol' buddy. There's no need to be afraid. This procedure won't hurt one bit. I promise. All you have to do is close your eyes and lie still while you're in there. Maybe do a little daydreaming. And in no time flat, it'll be over."

"I've done enough daydreaming for one day." Linking his fingers behind his head, Santa oriented his eyes to the ceiling. "Hey, Doc. There's a big cobweb up there. In that corner. Don't they ever clean this place?"

Dr. Swift, knowing Santa wasn't the tidiest man in the world, sensed something more than a bump on his head was bothering him. "He probably thinks the holiday is ruined. Probably feels bad about what happened and doesn't want to talk about it." Leaning toward Santa, he joshed, "Hey, ol' buddy, what's troubling you?"

Santa, tearing up, looked away.

Dr. Swift, placing his hand on his shoulder, said, "Listen, we need to talk about this before I buzz my attendant. Come on now. You know you can trust me."

"Well," Santa said hesitantly, "you'll probably think I'm sentimental, but I'm afraid you'll keep me here overnight. And then, the feast will be called off and, . . . and that'll mean every elf from here to yonder will be disappointed. And, . . . and, me, too! We'll all miss the merry making."

"Is that what's bothering you?" Dr. Swift swallowed hard to check a chuckle. Gripping Santa's shoulders, looking him straight in the eye, he said, "Hey, ol' buddy, you can stop worrying. The feast is still on."

"It is?" Santa brightened.

"Yes, it is."

"How do you know?"

"I happen to know because a young man named Hunter got word from some young gal that orders were given to get that feast ready before you were ever dug out of that snowball."

"Orders! Orders from who?"

"From your wife, of course. Why, I hear tell her fast thinking saved your life."

"Really?"

"Yes. Really. And about attending that feast, you may on one condition."

"Condition! What condition?"

"You must invite me to be your honored guest."

"Honored guest! Why, you, . . . you conniving old fox. You just want to be second in line, behind me, to get the choicest pieces of turkey." To drive home his point, he repeatedly finger-tapped Dr. Swift's chest. "Listen. That's not going to happen. Hear? I've never singled out anyone to be a so-called *honored guest* at any of my celebrations, and I'm not going to start now either. So, you can stop trying to roast your chestnuts over my hot coals."

Usually when Santa refused to listen to reason, Dr. Swift would capitulate. That is, he'd capitulate as Santa's friend, but never as his doctor. As his doctor—despite Santa pulling every trick in the book to disarm him—he'd firmly stand his ground. Today, he'd rely on something Santa couldn't match or refute: sound medical knowledge. It would give him the upper hand. Knowing this, his lips, spreading into a sly smile, foretold the joy he'd experience in the winning.

Steadying his voice, he spoke with authority. "And I, Dr. Swift refuse to be moose whipped by any patient, including you, ol' buddy. So, as I was saying, I insist on being your honored guest if I am to release you. And I do have the authority to keep you here overnight. All I have to do is fill out a little paperwork and it's a done deal."

"So, now, it's blackmail, huh?"

"No. I just want to observe you closely for a few hours. You do have a slight head injury, which probably isn't anything to worry about. But to be on the safe side, I'd like to keep an eye on you tonight. So, what'll it be, a turkey feast or gourmet hospital food? And, Mr. Saint Nickolas Claus, I know you know what I mean when I say *gourmet hospital food*."

The standoff began. Santa drilled Dr. Swift's questioning eyes with an icy stare. Dr. Swift buttoned his lip and sat down in his swivel chair. Eyes still locked with Santa's, he, with an air of flippancy, repeatedly stroked his whiskers. It was his way of saying, "My dear friend, today, I have all the time in the world to wait you out."

Picking up Santa's medical chart, he began doodling in the margins. "Stubborn moose. He thinks he's going to win this one. Well, he's not. Little does he know that I know exactly what I have to do to break through that tight-lipped snow cave of his."

As the minutes ticked by, he eyed Santa several times. "Yeah, I know. You think that stare of yours will unnerve me. Today, that ain't gonna happen. And, you stubborn, old moose, since you won't budge, you leave me with no other choice but to play my next card. Seems you've forgotten all the meals I've eaten at your cottage. So many, I know exactly what you like and dislike in the food department."

One little cough later, Dr. Swift got what he wanted. Santa's attention.

"Say, I hear tell tonight, besides the usual cranberries and turkey, they're serving up fluffy, garlic-flavored, mashed potatoes. And the green-bean casserole? It'll have twice the mushrooms the recipe calls for. I hear tell they shipped in fresh ones for it. Yum, yum. And for dessert, that favorite bakery of yours over there in Sleigh Valley . . . Well, they'll be supplying fresh-baked, hot apple pie, topped off, of course, with French vanilla ice cream. Oh, and there'll be cheesecake with a strawberry topping, too. Mm. Yum, yum. Won't that be finger-lickin' good?

"Now, let's see what's on this hospital menu for tonight's dinner? Hmm. It says here the main course is gonna be liver and onions, with sides of turnip greens and mashed rutabaga. And it looks like everyone gets a nice, tall glass of yummy prune juice to wash it all down. And for dessert? Oh, what can be more soothing on the tummy than some plain old lime Jell-O. Hmm. Sounds like the whole meal is nutritional. Why, it's just the ticket for someone with a head injury. Doncha think?"

Glancing up from his chart, Dr. Swift spied a look on Santa's face only one word could describe. *Yuck!* Spreading his lips into a smirking grin, he almost said, "Good. I've won." Thinking better of it, he held his tongue.

Santa, reading his smug look, begrudging gave in.

"Okay. Okay. You win. You'll be my first and last honored guest ever. Now, let's get on with this picture taking so we can get to that feast. I'm hungrier than a polar bear." To further make his point, he pushed his middle forward, saying, "See this gut? When it's totally empty, I can get pretty nasty. So, watch your back. If I don't get some turkey and cranberries pretty soon, I just might eat you alive. Gr-r-r-r!"

"Threats, threats, threats," Dr. Swift shot back, playing into his game. As he hit the buzzer to summon his medical attendant, he linked his eyes with Santa's and smiled reassuringly. But he, himself, didn't feel reassured. He was too worried about Santa's mental state.

Comments concerning *Five Equals One, Vol 1* can be posted on the site where this book was purchased by the person who purchased it. Doing so would be very much appreciated as it helps generate sales. Thank you.

The following pages are from *Five Equals One*, Vol. 2, chapter 1.

FIVE

EQUALS

ONE

~ ◇ ~

VOLUME

2

CHAPTER 1

He did it that many times?

"Is something wrong? Santa's okay, isn't he?" Mitzi asked, shedding her parka. The panicky look in her eyes betrayed her anxiety, as did the play of her fingers on her purse strap. Taking an office chair, she eyed Dr. Swift warily. The whole previous hour, since receiving his call, she hadn't been able to stay focused on anything work related.

Yesterday she awoke at the crack of dawn consumed with *what ifs* concerning Santa's ethnic secret. Today, a different set of *what ifs* vied for her attention. "What if he has a brain injury? What if he can't work? What if he can't make his Christmas Eve run? What if he . . ." By the time she reached Dr. Swift's office, her worrisome thoughts had whipped her stomach into a spasmodic frenzy.

"Is Santa okay?" she asked, perching birdlike on the edge of a chair across from him.

Leaning back in his chair, eyeing her thoughtfully, Dr. Swift struggled to break the news to her gently. "Well, there is one thing that concerns me, but I don't think it's anything to get alarmed about. Although, if Santa knew, I'd wager

1

he'd really get upset. That's why I decided to call you. And uh, it's important to keep this secret."

"Secret! Of course. What is it?"

Mitzi knew Dr. Swift was a man of integrity. He took his work seriously and he was honest with his patients. Today though, she sensed hesitancy, like he wasn't sure how to put into words what he wanted to say. Or, even if he wanted to tell her the truth.

"Well," he said, patting down the little hair he had left on his balding head, "it's just when I was observing Santa at the feast last night, I noticed he was having trouble remembering present events."

"What do you mean?"

"What I mean is . . . Do you remember him saying, *Please, pass the cranberries,* not more than thirty seconds after spooning a heap of that sauce onto his plate?"

"Yes, I do. But I didn't pay any attention to it. After all, he just laughed it off as a little slip of his memory."

"Mitzi, let me assure you. A little forgetfulness is normal. We all do it now and then. Especially as we get older. But when it happens . . . Uh, just a minute. Let's see. Now, where did I put that list? Ah, yes. Here it is."

Pulling a small pad out from under a stack of medical reports, he began adding up his scratch marks. "As I was saying, when it happens fifteen, sixteen, uh, seventeen times in one evening . . . Well, it sure raised my red flag."

"He did it that many times?"

"Yes, he did. And to be honest, I've never seen anything

2

like it."

As the impact of Dr. Swift's diagnosis sank in, Mitzi lowered her eyes to her shoes. The sight brought forth a long-ago threat. "Bohunk, you'd better keep those eyes on your *shoe station* if you don't want to find out what's good for you."

That threat popped into Mitzi's head whenever she looked down at her shoes. Most of the time she'd dismiss it. However, when under duress, it readily pulled her back to when she was a child of six, doing what was expected of her—sitting stiffly still on a spindle-back chair, hands clasped over her bare thighs, head down, eyes fixed on what her stepmother called her *shoe station*.

Why she chanced a few sneak peeks that day she didn't know. Her defiance, quite normal for a six-year-old, honed the edge of her stepmother's vengeance. Daring another peek, a second warning singed her ears.

"What are you gawking at, bohunk? You'd better stop staring if you know what's good for you." A few minutes later, the Redhead, catching her hated stepchild lifting her eyes from her *shoe station*, made good on her threat. Like a cougar intent on using the element of surprise, she flew across the room, leg-straddled Mitzi, plopped her full weight down on her slim thighs, vice-gripped her head between her hands and pinned her shoulders against the back of the chair with her forearms.

Mitzi, no match for her stepmother's weighted vengeance, could do nothing but scream, kick into empty space and endure.

OMG! They came at her like dual missiles locked on predestined targets. Two thumbs fueled by drunken madness. Mitzi scrunched her eyelids together. It didn't help. The ungodly pressure of those thumbs pushing her eyeballs into space that wasn't there, triggered more screams. Desperate, pleading screams. Screams no one could or would hear. Wait! That wasn't true. Her screams fell on her blended siblings' ears, who, trained to despise her, merely played on in the parlor because to them, nothing unusual was happening in the kitchen.

A minute or so later, her chest still rising and falling with fury, the redhead stood up and shoved her victim to the floor. Then she, in a victorious, vilified voice, yelled, "That'll teach you for not listening to me, you little shit."

Lying in a sobbing heap, Mitzi blinked and blinked. Nothing but midnight blackness edged her vision. Distress pushed a budding scream up her throat. Fighting it, fearing reprisal, she swallowed hard to suppress it. Blink, blink, blink, blink, blink. Finally, the outline of her sentencing chair came into focus. As it did, relief washed over her, laying her worst fear to rest. She rubbed her eyes. They hurt. But *hurt* didn't matter. Seeing did.

"Bohunk, get back up on that chair. NOW!"

She didn't dally. Within seconds, she glued her bottom to the chair's seat, clasped her hands in front of her and dropped her eyes to her *shoe station*.

Her poor eyes? They ached for weeks. No big deal.

4

Pain, she was used to. What mattered was sight. She couldn't imagine enduring her hellish life without it.

Blinking away that horrific scene—and thankful to still have her eyesight—Mitzi directed her gaze to Dr. Swift. Even though her heart was beating wildly, she said calmly, "Now I know why Santa said last night, 'I'm going to get ready for bed,' not more than five minutes after slipping on his pajamas and brushing his teeth."

"You didn't suspect anything? Not then, or at the party?"

"No." Mitzi flinched. Normally she would've considered that behavior odd. Yesterday though, after waking to the *what ifs'* blathering blitz, after hiking up and down Jingle-Jangle Mountain, after coping with Santa's accident, after hosting the long-into-the-night Blessing Day party, . . . Well, after all that, she had been too exhausted to notice anything out of the ordinary.

"Doc," she said, grasping the chair's arms and leaning forward, "what can I do to help him?"

"I don't know. Perhaps you could encourage him to repeat things over and over. Maybe that'll help."

"That's all?" A bit disappointed, she pressed for more information. "Doc, please. Please be honest with me. Will Santa ever be able to remember present events again?"

MARY KORTE

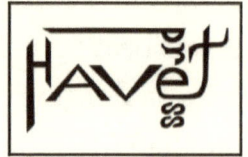

www.HavetPress.com